field notes from an extinction

a novel

field notes from an extinction

a novel

EOGHAN WALLS

SEVEN STORIES PRESS
New York • Oakland

SEVEN STORIES PRESS
140 Watts Street
New York, NY 10013
www.sevenstories.com

LIBRARY OF CONGRESS CATALOGING-IN-PUBLICATION DATA

Names: Walls, Eoghan author
Title: Field notes from an extinction : a novel / Eoghan Walls.
Description: New York : Seven Stories Press, 2026.
Identifiers: LCCN 2025041308 (print) | LCCN 2025041309 (ebook) | ISBN 9781644215340 trade paperback | ISBN 9781644215357 ebook
Subjects: LCGFT: Novels
Classification: LCC PR6123.A455 F54 2026 (print) | LCC PR6123.A455 (ebook) | DDC 823/.92--dc23/eng/20251119
LC record available at https://lccn.loc.gov/2025041308
LC ebook record available at https://lccn.loc.gov/2025041309

College professors and high school and middle school teachers may order free examination copies of Seven Stories Press titles. visit https://www.sevenstories.com/pg/resources-academics or email academic@sevenstories.com.

Printed in the USA.

9 8 7 6 5 4 3 2

For Neasa

from

The Irish Examiner

WEDNESDAY 10TH FEBRUARY, 1847

MURDER AT BALLYFIN

ANOTHER BAILIFF has been slaughtered in the performance of his legal duties this Monday past. Joseph Montgomery arrived at the residence of one Mr O'Leary, in assistance with the sheriff and three other bailiffs, for the purpose of ejectment due to the failure to pay three years rent. Mr O'Leary, we are informed, offered to settle the matter immediately, but the sheriff was not authorised to accept the payment, at which point the sheriff and three bailiffs entered the building for the purposes of rendering it uninhabitable, but when they began removing the roofing an altercation ensued. Mr O'Leary's wife fled the scene with a child, and Mr O'Leary was shot dead, but not without causing a grievous wound to John Montgomery of Strokestown, who was rushed back to town with a bullet in his jaw, and who died later of blood loss on the road. When the sheriff returned the next morning, neither the wife, child nor Mr O'Leary's body were found on the property. Mr Montgomery leaves behind a wife and three children.

For the Deliverer of these Pages . . .

Lest we die here, I implore you, dear reader, however you have procured these documents, please see to it that they find the light of civilization.

I, Ignatius Green, ornithologist & redeemed öologist, do hereby declare *Field Notes on the Garefowl, Volumes i & ii* to be a full & true account of my dealings on Tor Mor Rock. If not every particular of factual minutiae is herein recorded, I have endeavoured to bear witness to all happenings of genuine import to the best of my penmanship. What began as the first & only proper ornithological record of the last surviving colony of *Pinguinus impennis*, commonly known as the Garefowl or Great Auk, as well as the southernmost recorded nesting site of the *Fulmarus glacialis*, has now become a final testimony to the diverse injustices rendered by the native populace of Inishtrahull upon my person & that of the child.

I swear I have committed no harm to the girl, neither by intention nor neglect, but have endeavoured at every turn to keep her alive in unprecedented circumstances. This I declare on the souls of my wife Emily, & of my son William, so help me God.

Kind reader, dear reader, bring these events to light. What the men of Inishtrahull have done amounts to nothing less than marooning & its inevitable outcome, murder.

What they have done to the birds is worse yet.

It is a deliberate act of extinction.

A theft of life.

Deliver these papers to Sir Walpole Phillip of Barrow, Barrow Manor, Furness; or the Marquis Spencer Compton, President of the Royal Society, Gresham College, London; or Cornelia Stubbins of Daly's Manor, Glasson Dock, Lancashire. Any one alone can be relied upon to spread news of my fate. As the major stakeholder of the expedition & sole proprietor of these rocks, Sir Phillip has a direct interest in these matters. Shd remuneration be required in the delivery of these documents, he will gladly pay it. He will also be interested to secure recovery of what scientific materials & documentation may survive us.

If it is you who find this, McGonigle, or one of your hoods, I hope you starve to death. Your children also.

IGNATIUS GREEN FRS ICS FRZ

22ND JUNE, 1847

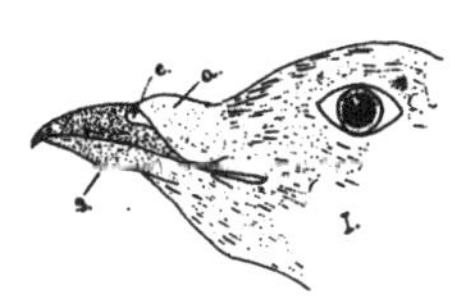

from

Field Notes on the Final Colony of Garefowl

VOL. II

MONDAY 31ST MAY, 1847

The islandmen have smuggled a child onto Tor Mor Rock.

That I did not adequately register the basket in which the child was stowed is likely due to my state of perturbation at the obvious interference with my supplies. I was awaiting the delivery agreed already on October the 17th, 1846, with Hancock of Londonderry (formally of Staffordshire), in addition to supplemental grains to replace what was hitherto lost to rain, spillage & theft from the last delivery; to wit;

pease, one sack;
oatmeal, two sacks;
wheat flour, two sacks;
dried biscuit, one chest;
English cheese, one large wheel;
suet, a five pound slab;
butter, a five pound slab;
coal, five sacks;
whale oil, one bushel;
soured grog, one hogshead;

raisins, ten lbs;
dried apple, five lbs;
personal effects (ink, paper, etc), one chest;
replacement taxidermist's tools, one chest;
brandy, two gallons;
lemon juice, one gallon;
fine tobacco (provenance immaterial), four lbs;
London gin, one gallon;
side of beef, one;
smoked Galician pig, one half-carcass.

Provisions enough for one man alone for one month entire on the rock with no need to journey inland. Missing this time was the beef; both sacks of wheat flour; one flask of brandy; the cheese. As further insult, much of the pig had been roughly cut away & but poorly wrapped thereafter, leaving only a ragged shoulder, the spine & bared ribs protruding from the torn bindings, left to rudely flap in the hail.

Even in the glum half-light of the late hail from Iceland, the theft was obvious, but the men were diffident, blank faced as poachers. Disputed with them at length on the shore. That thin pish Liam McGonigle is the only one of this batch admitting to passing competency in English.

MYSELF: The garefowl have laid, McGonigle. I cannot leave the island currently. It is an act of thievery that has been carried out here. Theft.

McGONIGLE: I can only tell you again what I have told you already, sir, we bring you straightaways what we receive from Hancock. None of my men would dream of touching it, sure don't we depend on the money you bring in.

His tone circumlocutory, his manner obsequious. His fellows scrawny, muttering their guttural tongue. He held the wet manifest to shield his face from the full force of the hail. I snatched it from him.

MYSELF: You are honestly trying to tell me you have not nabbed almost half of my provisions?
McGONIGLE: I would be offended at the suggestion, sir.
MYSELF: Speak up, man.
McGONIGLE: Offended, sir. I would be offended, sir. That is to say, no sir.

The ink wet on the page. The rest of the men, done unloading the goods, were already turning back to their vessel. Two thin boys—couldn't be more than twelve—had already retired from manual labour, having fallen to coughing fits during disembarkation, & wailed loudly from the boat.

Skinny monkey youths, spluttering under a tarpaulin.

MYSELF: Do not turn from me, McGonigle. We are not done here. I must tally the rest of the shipment & keep an exact log of delivery.
McGONIGLE: I must apologise but I am afraid further dalliance will not be possible tonight, sir. The tides as they are, we must get back before dark if we are to not come afoul of the Blind Rocks.

All his bluster & wheedling & still his uneven grin. He comes recommended by Sir Phillip. Worked with him on the tea ships for five years, supposedly one of the decent ones, & my reliance upon these islanders must extend another six to ten weeks yet. Sir Phillip will hang his head when he hears of his oversight in judgment! I shd have seized him, made him open each container before me. But his lank shipmen shook, coatless. It had taken three of them to carry a chest I could have easily managed on my own, & Connie's lamentations of the starving Irish in her broadsheets must have addled my heart.

But not one of them would meet me in the eye, & one of them, I swear, was laughing into his sleeve.

MYSELF: What are they saying, Liam?
McGONIGLE: What, sir?
MYSELF: That one there. What did he say?
McGONIGLE: It is untranslatable, sir.

Half of them wading already into the choppy black sea, trousers still dark from disembarkation. McGonigle would only heed me when I held him.

MYSELF: Do not turn from me!
McGONIGLE: (gesturing to youths on the boat) My nephews, sir. I have to get them out of the squall.
MYSELF: You think I am at your mercy, McGonigle. But it is you & your family who are dependent upon my good graces. Sir Phillip will hear of this.
McGONIGLE: (utterly unabashed) I will inform him myself of the missing supplies, sir. Your unhappiness is my unhappiness. But I can only tell you again, I have delivered exactly what we received this morning.

He squinted into the wind. One of the youths wailed to him from the boat. But before he stepped into the tide, he touched his nose & leaned towards me.

McGONIGLE: I advise you strongly to unbox the goods tonight.

MYSELF: What?

McGONIGLE: Tonight, sir. Unpack the goods tonight. Before the gulls quite eat your pig away, sir.

I looked up the beach. The herring gulls were indeed tugging wildly where the meat hung loose.

MYSELF: In a month, I expect a full half-pig, Liam.

McGONIGLE: I will make sure to pass on your words, sir. But unpack it tonight.

The islanders launched as I headed back up the rock, chasing gulls off the pork with the manifest. I believed I had the size of the matter, by which I mean the theft, but wanted to ensure my tools were intact, & then secure both the oats & the biscuits, as I have missed both sorely, & took my time getting around to the tarpaulins, my sight & hearing much reduced by hail. Odour I detected none; my nose is near bleached by the slant wind & constant exposure to fishy guano. Thus I failed to register the child or even the basket that bore it until the men had nigh passed the Organ Pipes.

But I could smell it indeed when I bent to examine the barrels. Even in the wind, sour as meat, the stench of human waste.

It made no discernible sound as I tugged off the tarpaulin. A wicker basket big enough for a live pig. At first, I thought I had found the side of beef gone rancid; but the weight of the basket shifted as it tilted; then I tugged the lid & knew not what I saw.

Two eyes met mine in the dark.

A face. A child.

A child blinking in the half-light.
Two wet eyes. A nest of hair.

MYSELF: Wait! Wait, you madmen! Wait.
MYSELF: Wait! It will die, you madmen! The child will die!

I ran towards the Organ Pipes, skidding, landing heavily off the lower ledge. Rose uninjured, shouting. The islander skiff was maybe three hundred yards out. Faces of the islandmen distant.

They made as if not to register me.

They saw me though. I know they did.

I was not done. Ran back to the basket, tugged it loose, heaved it to my chest & bore it on the rocks, tho it was heavy, & dropped it into my little rowboat, whereupon it toppled on its side & the lid slipped & the child rolled onto the shale screaming. Lifted it, tho it arched its back, into the darkening sky.

MYSELF: Take it back. I cannot take it. Take it back!

Waded in to my waist. Soaked my good green trousers, my boots wet thru, undergarments too. Shouted, at length, holding the child over the sea, a writhing thing, squealing, its apparel stinking.

The men had their backs to me now, & the boat disappeared behind the waves.

MYSELF: Take it back. It will die here. It will die!

My face & ears stung in the hail & the child's most likely too, tho it gave up kicking & screaming to simply hang, until I stumbled back to the shore & dropped it to the shale.

The islanders were too far out.

In the waves & stormy dusk, with their sails up, I would not catch them in my little rowboat.

They have lumbered me with a thing that mewls on pebbles.

MYSELF: Get back in the basket. Get up. Into your basket.

MYSELF: Get in the basket! You are filthy.

No English in the child. It squealed on approach & on contact. All filth & frail wiriness. For humanity's sake, I might have carried it in my arms, but the bloody thing seized like a board at my touch & writhed, & it proved altogether easier to just drop it back into its basket & carry it like goods.

Its basket now stands at my stove.

Must attend to deliveries. The gulls have picked thru my hasty rewrapping & are worrying my meat once again.

My supplies—or what I have of them—are secured.

The child has not moved.

Initially, it seemed entirely mute.

MYSELF: I must see to the deliveries. I must bind them before the gulls spoil them. (rattling the basket) If I do not go, I will lose the meat. You understand?

The child sobbed, mostly in silence, but yelped at the sight of my hands. So I unpacked my goods, first in hail, then in twilight by lamplight, as the sky cleared to a cosmic chill & Andromeda popped thru the clouds. First carried & hung the meat inside & the various perishables, then the pease & oatmeal, then two chests of tools behind my partition, then bound both dry goods & imperishables in sailcloth in the cabin's lee. Could tell McGonigle had got back to Inishtrahull as his lighthouse began its repetitive scything across the shale & sea beyond Tor Mor. By the time all was secured, the wind had died & a fat full moon chipped the edge of a clear horizon.

The brandy–the single flask I have–is unwatered.

The biscuit coverings are unbroken.

Neither the butter nor the suet have spoiled.

All this time, the child lay silent in its box, by the stove, the fire on full blast, under the bubbling still. It–she, by the pinafore, she–must have been near roasted. The still gives a raging heat at full blast–I have coal enough for weeks, as it appears the Irish cannot eat coal–& the only shelter the child had was its rough & soiled wicker.

I heaved the basket to the door, naturally.

It–she, she–was silent the whole time & but for the heaviness & rapidity of breathing, I might have thought her dead.

MYSELF: You can come out here if you want to.
MYSELF: Come out. I will not hurt you. You can come out.
MYSELF: I am a good man. I am not unkind.
MYSELF: Are you not able to climb out? I will set the basket on its side.

Small yelps as I tilted the box, then nothing. At her continued silence, I peered into the depths, where she was coiled like a beast among her particulars, namely:

Clothing she wore;
a shitten, once white dress;

one blanket (utterly soiled);
one pair of wooden clogs;
one cracked chamber pot, once affixed to the base,
  now unmoored;
one rubber-bunged pewter flask.

The latter despite the age of the girl. Eight? Five? Twelve? I can age a puffin reliably to the season but with a human child could easily be off by four years, give or take. Malnourished, by the look of her, which makes the judgment harder. Just over my waist at full extension I would estimate, closer to four foot than three, skinny & dull of wit, lacking in vigour, filth-cauled & whimperish.

MYSELF: You can come out of the basket. I will not hurt you.
CHILD: *Wishke.*

This it croaked. Its first word: *Wishke.* Gaelic. Obviously there is opportunity for drollery—even Irish children clamour for whiskey etc—but from conversations with Frank, I know the word to mean water.

MYSELF: Water. You mean water, yes? Do you want a drink?

The child flinched as my hand neared. I took its—she, her—her bunged flask, a filthy receptacle possibly for use at sea or in prisons, & there was no strength in her hold on it. Filled it from the cooling tub by the still, returned it to the lip of her basket, & her little talons snatched it back.

Watched her drink. The matting of her hair almost total. Waste visible on the remains of what was clearly once a pretty outfit. What were once ribbons are now twisted & frayed.

MYSELF: *Wishke. Wishke* means water.
MYSELF: Do you want food?
MYSELF: Where is your mother, child?

Might as well have talked to a stone.

Dinner simple but wholesome. Boiled oats & sliced bacon shoulder. Have missed the bacon much. Must ration it carefully now. Oats too. Dregs of old lemon juice softened the meat & a tumbler of grog. Made a little extra. The child can eat with me one night. As I cooked, I tried to engage her. Box on its side. All I could make out from the shadows was greasy hair.

MYSELF: Grog? Do you want some grog?
MYSELF: Are you hungry? Do you want porridge?
CHILD: Wishke.

Refilled her bottle a second time, had it snatched again.

MYSELF: We will have dinner. We will eat. Food? I can feed you tonight.
MYSELF: Can you speak, child?
MYSELF: (chopping bacon finely) You can eat with me tonight. You are very welcome. Then, in the morning, I will take you back to the island. Do you understand? Back to your mother.

Not a flicker of comprehension, even at the word *mother*. But surely their Gaelic word must share some root with *mater, mere, mutter*? I have no idea.

She was entirely fixated on drinking.

Then I noted a puddle seeping from the basket over my boards.

MYSELF: No! No piss in here!

The child screamed as I dropped the knife & leapt to carry her & the dripping basket into the dark to the shale by the outhouse.

MYSELF: You do not piss in the cabin. Hear me? You do not piss in the cabin. Piss here. Piss out here. No piss in the cabin! Piss out here!

The child, distraught, keening. I thought of house-training hunting dogs, & rattled the basket, & shouted some more.

MYSELF: Do not piss in here. Children piss outside. We all piss outside. Everyone pisses outside! Not in the house.

Scrubbed the boards, & once her noise died down, carried the basket inside, dumped it by the stove. Set up table, added brandy to the oats, a sprinkle of sliced apple. Two bowls, two stools, & turned the basket so she would have to face me.

MYSELF: Come out of the basket now. It is time to eat.
MYSELF: Eat. Good food. The porridge is good.
MYSELF: Child! I will not bite you.
MYSELF: Child. Listen to me. I do not know if you can understand me, but it is only fair that I explain to you the situation. I will feed you & put you up for tonight & we will return you to your island in the morning. Whatever nonsense McGonigle is playing will be

> short-lived & I am sorry you are suffering but I am as much a victim in all of this as you. I do not know your full situation but I am here on vital scientific business & while I have all the sympathy in the world for the destitute, I cannot allow you or anyone else to interfere with my studies. I will take you home in the morning. So please, I ask you. Take my food. This is a strong & nourishing porridge. Eat it. It is good.

Not a word in her head. Perhaps she is dumb, or an idiot? When I proffered her a spoon, she sucked on her bottle instead.

MYSELF: Damn you so.

Am tired now from manual labour. Gin is a salve. This whole episode a pointless irritation. I must write to Sir Phillip immediately, outlining the loss of provisions as well as the islanders' tomfoolery, & seal it definitively so as to make sure McGonigle cannot doctor the contents.

The child spoke as I was writing, but merely to ask for *wishke, wishke*! Like a wretch in an alley, she had crawled to the edge of her hutch, blinking in lamplight. For the first time I saw the face under her dank fringe, tear-streaks in mud, a moustache of puckered scabs.

Then, as I handed her the bottle, noted once again a thick stream of piss along the boards.

MYSELF: No! I told you! I told you!

Snatched her up, this time my hands in her hot armpits, regretting the closeness instantly as I bore her high & streaming out the door. She had pissed on my overalls, & where I had touched her, there was grime on my hands.

Bellowed at her, somewhat immodestly.

Then had to touch her again as I carried her wailing & dripping back to her box.

I have scoured the piss now, twice.

I can still smell it. The piss, & the whole child, despite the application of lime.

The situation is ridiculous. I had heard of such things in Barrackpore. Mothers prepared to risk the life of their offspring on the chance generosity of civilised men. More normally a man is protected by the trappings of civil society, his boy or domestic help interceding before the destitute can encroach. But never have I heard of a scientific expedition so disrupted.

It will not be without repercussions. McGonigle's men have not only taken my provisions but now threatened my peace of mind. If Sir Phillip cannot guarantee adequate sustenance & appropriate intellectual solitude, the entire venture is imperilled; if further funds are required for the security of the next delivery, he needs but ask the Royal Society.

Have written him as much.

TUESDAY 1ST JUNE, 1847

A dark day for science & the garefowl.

The child is yet with me.

Last night in the darkness, she was largely silent. Heavy breathing at most. I left one bowl of bacon-porridge & one of water at the mouth of her basket & was awoken in the night by heavy slurping. She had finally dared to eat, albeit by darkness, & I thought myself a kind host.

Woke to a mess of puke about her basket, & soaked my stockings in a fresh puddle of piss.

MYSELF: No! No pissing in here! No!

When I went to rattle the box, thinking to scare her, child was flaccid as shot game. Panting faintly. Smelled strongly of meat & urine. Looked short from death.

I stood, dumbfounded.

Then drank yesterday's cold coffee & washed down a biscuit, wiped the worst of the mess from the floorboards, refilled the dirty bunged bottle—the child could barely hold it—& bore her in her wiry basket to my little rowboat.

It crossed my mind for the first time that I might be committed for murder if she died.

Realistically, I do not believe it would come to that. A man in my position cannot be expected to nurse a stranger's waif. My medical studies in Edinburgh amounted to no more than a few lectures in basic anatomy; I took only what I needed to paint the human body & for the dissection & mounting of game, & headed straight to the Glens. Connie can say what she likes, I have never fingered a human gizzard; my lot in life would no doubt have been easier had I delved deeper. But am at peace with that now; can skin & mount any bird carcass I care to, & most small to moderate game. Yet I know little more about breaking a fever than taking lemon juice & keeping the windows open.

Besides, these are famine times. If Connie's broadsheets are to be believed, so great is the count of the Irish dead, whether by starvation, disease or misadventure, the constabulary is likely so inundated with the tallying of mortalities, it is hard to imagine they would find motivation to investigate an infant death out here, half-submerged in the Atlantic. Even if it came down to it, so casually & whimsically has she been thrust into my care, it would be McGonigle's word against mine, & such a dispute would hardly take long for the courts to reconcile.

The child's death, shd she die, will be his responsibility.

The waters of my conscience run clear.

Still, monstrous as it sounds, as I hefted the box onto the boat, angling the damp edge away from my britches, it did occur to me it would have been the kindest thing to tip her into the sea.

Who knows I might catch some plague off her yet?

But I am not a monster. If anything, I am generous to a fault.

The day worsened as it brightened.

This my first time taking the rowboat out to sea, & the rowboat is itself a monstrosity.

I do not believe it has been used for anything but housing chickens these last dozen years. There are chicken feathers & faecal matter worked into the wood, & visible cracks above the water level, & altho no obvious hole in its base, it is poorly sealed & leaks, albeit slowly enough you can bail with a cup that has been attached to the seat by a length of twine for precisely this purpose. But the real issue is the rowing. The crutches are ill-set in the hull & rattle in place, at times hanging off entirely shd the oars jolt, which, in these rocky seas, they do constantly.

McGonigle assured me the boat was rowed here by one of his sons. I may not be as precociously skilled in small craft as these toothless islanders—half of whom resemble sea-otters in their hirsuteness, weak shoulders

& sloped brows—but I rowed four grown women across Windermere as a young man, & misspent a large part of my youth in country tarns, & can hardly be considered a novice when it comes to water, if not the sea. It is my honest belief I have been mis-sold a vessel of death, if not quite with the deliberate intent to drown me, then with a genuine ambivalence to my survival.

What shd have taken less than forty minutes brisk rowing took the grosser part of three hours, bailing at intervals, staring into the near-horizontal slant of the northern sun & telling the child to quit her damned noise. For as we were over halfway there, her silence broke to chanting. She had finished her water, demanded more *wishke* thrice then thrice again & when I had nothing to give her, started keening. The repetition of but one syllable: *Ai, ai, ai. Ai, ai, ai. Ai-ai-ai, ai-ai-ai, ai-ai-ai*, over & over, even tho I shouted, cajoled, rattled, mollycoddled, cursed & threatened to throw her overboard.

Midday saw us moored on what Liam McGonigle calls the Blind Rocks, a submerged outcrop of metamorphic granite maybe two-hundred yards off Portmore. The rocks lie close to the surface, expanding to a width I cannot easily tell, but try as I might I could not come off them. So choppy was the tide, each time I pushed us off the outcrop, the waves lifted & dumped us back, much to the hilarity of three wretched islander children pulling in crab boxes on the rocks.

ISLANDER CHILDREN: Fear More! Fear More!

This their name for me. *Fear More*. According to McGonigle, it means Big Man. I cannot tell if he is lying or not.

MYSELF: Fetch me McGonigle. Get me McGonigle. Don't just stand there hooting. Go get McGonigle!

I berated them as they waved at me, in their thin white shirts, but could no more escape the rocks than hurl the child's basket the two-hundred-yard stretch to the shore. The savages cackled; they are ugly thin-faced children. But eventually, thru my repeated shouting, they worked out my demands.

AN ISLANDER CHILD: McGonigawl! McGonigawl!
MYSELF: Yes! McGonigle! Get him!
THE OTHER: (laughter) McGonigawl! McGonigawl!

By the time they clambered inland to help, McGonigle was already striding down the grassy hill to the cove with an entourage of at least two families of islanders & a braying infant in his arms. Rather than try to close the distance to the shore & risk further depraved hilarity, I waited as he pried himself from the gaggle, climbed into a little three-man rowing vessel almost twice the size of my own & made his way out to me, aided in the rowing by the same two frail coughing nephews of yester-eve.

The boys were wan yet capable rowers.

That is an understatement. Their skill was unnatural.

Even as they hacked & shuddered, white as dough, they could control the boat against the tide with barely a tug of the oars. I could find no egress from the rocks; indeed, could barely stand for nausea & the lifting & dropping of my vessel, not a little afraid my vessel might be staved entirely with a sudden knock; but those bare-chinned boys never once got lifted onto the promontory, keeping the boat close enough for McGonigle to stand & converse, but all the while just out of reach of my oars.

It was unnatural.

McGONIGLE: Are you having bother with the Blind Rocks, Mr Green?
MYSELF: (hissing) McGonigle, you are a thief.
McGONIGLE: Excuse me, sir?
MYSELF: You are a thief & a kidnapper. First you steal my goods; now, your antics have nearly cost a child's life.
McGONIGLE: Sir?

I had anticipated feigned innocence, but not my own rage at his performance. Clutched where I was to the basket, I could barely lift her but grabbed the girl's arm in one hand & waved it at him. A genuinely surprised man would have gasped, or started, at the sight of a child's arm. McGonigle committed to his role like a veteran of the boards, but his feigned astonishment never met his eyes.

McGONIGLE: Is that a girl, Mr Green?
MYSELF: Damn you McGonigle! You know full well—full well!—you delivered this child to me yesterday. Take her back!
McGONIGLE: A girl? Among your deliveries?
MYSELF: McGonigle, I will see you hanged!

I had to modulate my voice so the rage would not get the better of me, as the women were lined on the shore, & I did not want to incur further laughter. I tried to stand, but the tide jolted me afresh, & I sat abruptly.

McGONIGLE: You are absolutely sure she was in the box when we delivered it?

MYSELF: You will hang, McGonigle, for your dissimulations—this is unchristian!

McGONIGLE: Now you say it, sir, there was a scent to one of the boxes. An off-scent, aye. Was that the girl so?

Etc. Had I been able to reach him, I would have throttled him. The more he appeared unfazed, the greater my agitation: my language less dignified than I care to record—with such terms contriving to crack his shrewd islander heart. Threatened to go inland for the constabulary. Told him that unless he took the child back immediately, delivered Sir Phillip my missive forthwith & supplied me a new, seaworthy boat, I would see him in gaol.

To which, his response:

McGONIGLE: That I might understand you, sir, you want me to take your girl into my household?

MYSELF: She is not my girl!

McGONIGLE: (abruptly laughing) Sir! I can barely get my wife to feed these boys sir, & they my own flesh & blood! I could no more take in another child than I could fly!

MYSELF: I don't care if you feed her—just take her!

McGONIGLE: You could try the workhouse, sir, but I do not think they will take an Englishman's child.

MYSELF: She is not an English child!

I am incensed to even write it. He repeatedly interrupted me, with his sorry-for-your-troubles, are-your-studies-with-the-birds-progressing-well-sir, either-of-these-boys-here-can-row-you-back-if-you-lack-the-knack-sir. Whatever I said, he maintained his chicanery of ignorance.

The girl, all the while, had given up her *ai-ai-ai*, gone utterly passive in the box.

I must confess, I saw red. At some point, I steeled my legs & between peaks of the tide, when I was lodged with some steadiness on a high submarine ledge, I managed to stand upright & heaved the girl aloft by one arm. My stomach lurched, but I raised her into the sun, where she hung like a shot deer.

MYSELF: Take her or I'll let her drop, McGonigle! Take her now or I'll throw her to the fish!

There was shouting, then, from the womenfolk on the shore.

McGonigle dropped his guile in a flash.

If my actions were rash, my situation was also extraordinary. I would not have drowned her; I was simply trying to draw the yokel's bluff; my variation on Solomon's paradox. But even as I swung her, McGonigle reached forward, not to grab her, but to point.

McGONIGLE: Mr Green sir! On her chest! A letter, sir! A letter with your name on it. Look!

MYSELF: I will drop her!

McGONIGLE: On her chest! Mr Green, on her chest. A letter!

So much did he gesture & tap his own chest, I swung the child around to me, now fully beholding in the light of day what I must suppose has become my temporary ward, flopping like an unstrung puppet, her eyes fitfully closed.

But what he said was true.

There, attached to a bedraggled ribbon on her pinafore, was an envelope, secured with a knot thru a rough-cut hole in the paper.

On the envelope, writ large in jagged handwriting, mired in filth, was my own misspelt name.

For Ignashus Green.

I jerked as a wave knocked us off the rock, & I stumbled, nearly tumbling from the boat; the girl's weight an unexpected ballast in the opposite direction; with a lurch forward, I dropped her into the basket & fell to my knees again.

In my disgust, it seems I had not examined the child as closely as I might have.

When the boat had stopped lurching, & I could open my eyes again, McGonigle had brought his boat almost nearside mine, his boys holding his vessel in place by jamming the oars against the rocks at inverse obtuse angles, & McGonigle was peering directly into the basket.

McGONIGLE: Have you read the letter, sir?

MYSELF: (flustered) No.

McGONIGLE: Does it explain her provenance?

MYSELF: I have not read it, I said!

McGONIGLE: (pause) Have you let the girl out of the box at all, sir?

I shd have drowned him! But now the situation appeared suddenly more complex. I thought of the trouble poor Edmund had clearing his name.

My mind raced. Men of means are always at risk of spurious claims of bastardry. Before I could abandon the girl, I needed to be sure what was at stake here. Of course I shd have known it was preposterous. Of course it is! But, as it was, I felt utterly exposed, to his gaggle of women, to McGonigle's uncanny nephews, & to the islandman's own apish leer.

McGONIGLE: A bowl of warm porridge is what she needs, sir. Warm porridge is great sustenance for a child & more than my boys will eat tonight.

Confound him! But now nothing would placate me but reading the letter in privacy. But even as I struggled to detach the paper from the dress, I could not fully reconcile myself to taking her back to the island.

MYSELF: Liam. Please. I mean. Fetch me a knife to free this damned letter! She will die on Tor Mor. You do not want the death of a girl on your hands.
McGONIGLE: (oh, his raised brows) Will you kill her, sir?
MYSELF: Liam. Let her join your brood. What is one more mouth to your table?
McGONIGLE: She will be right, sir, she will be right. You have food aplenty. Just take her out of the box, sir, & feed her.

So knotted the ribbon, I could not undo it without risking tearing it contents.

Ultimately, he was simply more stubborn than me.

At length, he & his spluttering nephews towed me off the Blind Rocks, & he tipped his hat, & sang a tuneless ditty as they rowed him to his island, & I began the long heave back to Tor Mor.

I shd have rowed after him.

Dumped the basket on the cove & see if the skinny islander women dared lampoon me within thumping distance.

But it is all pish.

Let him think he has got the better of me.

I am more resourceful than he supposes.

The row back opened the blisters I had been earning all morning. Had I a sail, I could have managed the trip in half an hour. At least the wind was behind me. But as it was, an hour into the journey the child picked up her *ai, ai, ai* once again. To the North, I spotted whales cresting & spouting. Greenland whales to my guess, far astray from their patrols, spraying bright rainbows over a low daylight moon.

Cut it loose at the cabin. A short letter folded excessively on thick parchment, stabbed thru with a knife.

To Ignashus Green,

The child is yours now. Act as her mother until my return, with all the dutees thereby implied. Do not let her starve. Do not let her bee taken by the law. Answer no questions about her.

If she comes to harm, it will not end well for you.

The Canniball, Aisling O'Leary

A girlish hand, but jagged, just shy of unlearned; the letters child-like, but roughly aligned. The spelling primitive. A woman, perhaps? Claiming to be a cannibal?

The whole situation offensive & silly to boot.

A cannibal, in Christendom. A self-proclaimed, female cannibal, in a Christian country? Is Aisling a name? Some Gaelic bastardised version of Alison or Ashley? I thought at first it was another misspelling, & then a cryptic anagram, before tossing it back in the basket in contempt.

But there on the envelope is my name, misspelt, but clear.

Somehow fraudsters have gotten hold of my name!

The only person it can be is McGonigle.

Do I have enemies? Barring scientific rivalries, none of significance spring to mind, & all of my peers are bound by the same chains of propriety as I am. Davies? Three years dead. Schoolyard rivalries, then? Hennessey? If I was indelicate about his essays in the two years following Emily's passing, there has been almost a decade for his bitterness to surface. But even if he had hoarded grievances, none but select members of the Royal Society have the faintest hint of my whereabouts!

It is preposterous.

A scandal, then—some rogue fraudsters dream of tricking me of my property? It cannot be happenstance—it has my name! Someone has targeted me!

McGonigle. It can only be him.

Men of means are always susceptible, but barring the worst manner of drawing room gossip, Edmund's is the only public case I know of—the Scotch hussy—but behind closed doors, perhaps his situation is not as rare as one might suppose?

Some misadventure of my own?

Why then no claim of inheritance? *The child is yours now. Now* implies she is to *become* mine, not *she is your rightful daughter etc.* No claim is implied, either directly or circumspectly; then again, nor is such a claim wholly excluded. But surely—if this was the intent—bogey evidence would be offered? The date of a supposed tryst?

It is ridiculous.

Cannibals!

I knew—of course, of course—that this corner of the Empire would be deplorable, but such a garish attempt to frighten a naturalist of my standing shows a higher degree of idiocy than I would have credited. But to measure the possible culprits in turn:

a) Hancock. He knows my whereabouts. If I was to take McGonigle at his word, the evidence points to him in a roundabout way. But it is nonsensical. He is as English as I am, only latterly come to these shores. Where would he procure a child with no English? & why with no English? & why here? A tithe of a bastard's claim to my estate? Which is only loosely implied herein? This idea I find most contemptible. Hancock is a known operative, has worked for Sir Phillip first in India then in Londonderry. I have dined with him, slept in his house twice, the last time less than six weeks ago. He has shown me a portrait of his pretty fiancée in Lancashire. A Staffordshire man, simple but earnest. Ex-military. He would have at least corrected the spelling of the note!

b) McGonigle. The only believable suspect. He has a base countryman's guile. But, for sake of counterpoint: if he had the intent of blackmailing me with a bastard's claim, would he be so stupid as to leave the child at my disposal? If the child dies, he loses his leverage. Unless he hopes for the child's death to create some scandal? A stretch of the imagination. Conceivably, might he just want the child fed? Against famine? But I do not believe the child is his: as I dangled her over the sea, his concern was less terror than bemusement. His whole manner has a schoolboy's whimsicality. Childish enough to try to intimidate me with a bogey? Yes.

c) Some famine-wildened hussy lacking the fare to bring her child to the New World. A victim of ejectment? Frank speaks of such women; emigrants unable to pay their children's passage. Some dark-eyed starveling short of means to get to Boston? But even the most profligate of women would be racked with guilt at such a juncture; the mention of cannibalism would surely be unbearable? The idea has no merit. This theoretical hussy would have had to have known my particulars, name, whereabouts–with education enough, these might be garnered from stolen nautical documentation–but would still have required prodigious strength, a reinforced basket, & the complicity of either McGonigle or Hancock in hiding the child among my deliveries!

Which, again, can only point to McGonigle!

So slapdash a trick, the scrawl so thoughtless. I will trace this to him! A simple test of handwriting will be sufficient!

But I am more resourceful than he supposes.

Frank is stationed in Londonderry.

I had the wit not to trust my safety to the native population. Frank is but half-native, & my Stoneyhurst companion; his education respectable if as Jesuit as my own, & between the two of us, we have organised a system of long-distance semaphore in case of emergency.

On the 11th of every month for the duration of my stay, or as soon thereafter as his Bishop permits, we have arranged that he will take a horse from Londonderry to the Malin promontory with his spyglass to observe the easternmost tip of Tor Mor. Where I have arranged to leave hoisted a blue flag for All is well!; a green flag for I am lonesome, bring wine!; & a red flag for Medical emergencies, come imminently!

This is nothing if not a medical emergency, at least for the child, if not myself.

He lifted me from my fug after Emily's passing.

He will save me now, once again.

In ten days, he will come riding. No doubt armed with splints & questions. At which point, I will give him the girl, & a note to be delivered to Sir Phillip, & a package explaining the situation for the constabulary also.

Ten days from now.

So I must play mother a fortnight?

It makes me writhe with anger to write it.

The garefowl have laid!

But it is either play mother or traipse to the mainland on a floating chicken coop & possibly a two-day hike inland & the requisite documentation in the workhouse & risk missing the hatching of the auklets.

It cannot be very hard to feed a child intermittently.

She has abandoned her ai ai ai now. It is dark, & the still is not burning, & she has not stirred since we landed. I have tried to shove the bottle into her, first with warm water, then cold water, but she has taken neither.

Our supplies—thinner than they shd be—will be adequate.

I shd rouse her.

The child will not rouse.

I have gone thru her things. Laid her on my spare blanket on the floor. Hurled her stinking basket & the awful rag she slept in out to the shale.

She is running a fever. Her head hot to the touch. So hot to be worrisome? I have a bear's constitution, but shall double my own quinine & lemon juice tonight.

Her head droops & does not register porridge brushed onto her lips. She barely whimpers on being pinched.

My supplies are simple. Camphor & quinine & laudanum & my lemon juice & quicklime & arsenic & soap & for anything more complex I thought to rely on Frank.

Sleep shd do her good?

I am stone tired myself.

WEDNESDAY 2ND JUNE, 1847

Again, the piss.

My spare blanket is soaked thru.

No point in shouting for the child will not register my voice. I had the bright idea of opening the shutters in the night as the rains abated, to soothe her fever somewhat, letting in the cooling wind, but the rattling of my partition, the disturbance of my papers & McGonigle's hateful light flooding the cabin grew rapidly unbearable, & so I shut the elements out.

The child did not stir either way.

Her skin is simply too hot. There are lice dropping off her head nigh comparable in size to houseflies. They crawl onto me if I touch her hair, & I have scrubbed my fingers red with the wire brush.

Sometimes she coughs—a weak sound—& then I wonder if I cannot feel a catch in my own throat.

I have had my coffee. Two doses of lemon juice & quinine & refilled the still & baked four stacks of honeyed oatcakes. Chewed here quietly. I must go to the birds, but the child has not drunk any water, & stinks like meat again.

I cannot bear the smell.

There is nothing for it. I will have to wash her.

Her clothes were wholly soiled & I cut them off with scissors. Washed her in the sea with a sliver of soap. Her undergarments & skin crusted together as a single unit. The sea woke her up. She wailed & splashed but showed little animal strength in the arching of her back, even as I tugged the garments roughly from where they had sedimented to her skin. The last rags of her dress served as a washcloth before I tossed that too into the bladderwrack.

The process gruesome.

Under the dirt, her rash was bright. Spots on the skin. Not smallpox to my eye, but measles? Typhus?

Lice ran off my soapy hands into the Atlantic.

Naked you can see the full distension of her belly. The limbs are formed more or less as one would expect, standard human, but on a miniature scale. Much like a male child but for the absence of genitalia. No wounds or broken bones, & most of the skeleton is visible; the ribs countable, shoulder blades protruding, as are the clavicle, hip bones, sternum & vertebra. Her back, buttocks & legs fully constellated by sores. The spots flat, without pimpling. Where clasped, the imprint of my hand remains indented on her belly, legs & arms: a visible bloating of her skin. The thickness of down on her shoulders & back perhaps merits comment, altho I suspect remains within the realms of normality for a human child of hirsute lineage.

Washed of muck, her face has no discernible abnormality bar the gauntness of her cheeks & pocked complexion, & if the rash & spots were to clear up, she might not provoke remark selling chestnuts at a street-corner. As it is, even clean, she has multiple deep scratches on her face—presumably self-imposed, or perhaps from the steel wiring of her wicker prison—& a great density of the same flat scabby spots on her torso & limbs.

This entire land is said to be heaving with disease, at least according to Connie's broadsheets, a sickness of the body & the crops. But it is a moral & spiritual sickness to allow a child to wither thus. The negligence of the populace entire may be witnessed in the grievous state of this child.

It would be easier to be moved were the process of cleaning her not so repulsive.

Frank would call me hard-hearted.

I have not seen the blight myself. It is said the potato grows black & rotten, leaf to tuber. Who knows but these starvelings might eat the rotten crops, & absorb some germ thereof into their own body?

No. I cannot credit it. A human can surely not take on a plant diseasc any more than a bird can. Plenty of birds are brought down by botanical poisoning—*exempli gratia* the culling of Sardinian crows by oleandered corn—but to be poisoned is not the same as catching a disease proper to the plant itself.

The child has some regular human illness, then?

I know not what.

At least the washing shook her out of sleep. She was strong enough to stand a few moments while I wiped myself of her grime with the last of the soap. She watched me, her legs feeble on the shale, her arms outstretched.

CHILD: Ai ai ai. Ai ai ai.
MYSELF: Hush child. I must wash myself too.
CHILD: Ai ai ai.

In the cabin, I poured us each a shot of quinine & lemon juice. She would not touch it: I tried warming hers on the stove.

MYSELF: Drink this. This is good for you. Drink it up.
MYSELF: Come now. You need this. It is good for you. Good *wishke*.
CHILD: Ai ai ai.

She is sitting now on a square of tarpaulin, wrapped in my towel. Her lips a shade of purplish blue.

She has collapsed.

I have shaved her.

I took pity on her on collapsing, but the more I propped her the more the lice dropped off her. So big I could crush them in my fingers without the application of the thumbnail. When I pulled back the hair, her scalp seethed, but the damn girl was so shivery & off colour, I wasn't sure another sea-rinse wouldn't kill her. So I tried combing her, but the knotting was impossible; then I tried picking them live from her one-by-one with tweezers but this barely dented the swarm, so eventually I filled a tub with warm water from the belly of the still & tried combing her hair thru with soap.

She lay placid in the tub, albeit whimpering as the comb yanked the knots & matting, & at first I thought to use the razor just to cut out individual clumps. But the further I combed the more infestations I revealed, until eventually I folded a cloth to the side of the tub & leant her head on it & fetched my taxidermy scissors again & after clipping tight to the skull, there was still a crust of grime & lice on the skin, & I trimmed first by her neck & behind her ears & now it appears I have shaved her as bald as an egg.

I have polished the remaining grime & filth with a cloth.

Some of the sores on her scalp I have cut open. There are two nicks on her left ear, but they did not cause her to stir.

Trimmed the fuzz on her neck & shoulders to match.

I think I have done an admirable job.

The cloth I used to wipe her was disgusting with grime & insect matter & fizzled in the belly of the stove when we were done.

She will not suck the bottle. Will not take a spoonful of quinine or lemon juice. There is a whistle in her breathing.

I have tried spooning the water into her mouth. Putting it in her teated bottle. Dripping it with a clean cloth over her parted lips. Tried to get her to suck the cloth. Murmuring nonsense all the time:

MYSELF: That's nice is it? Little wishke wishke, yes? Take a drink. You need a drink. It is good for you.

Some got in her mouth, but most got in her windpipe & caused her to splutter & struggle for breath.

But thru the coughing she has taken in some water?

I have set up a pallet for her below the window, where there is a decent draft, & placed her under a sheet to protect her from chills & tucked it about her so her legs cannot kick it off.

Bald, wrapped, she looks much a mummified cat.

I must remember that she is under the sheet if I rise for the outhouse in the night. It would be easy to step on her in the darkness & break her ribs.

Wary of her pissing over my floor again, I have contrived a swaddle of sorts, with a towel cut in half, & bound into a tight garment with bent taxidermy hooks, looped so as to avoid piercing the skin. The binding is sound; if she spews now, it can only be from her mouth.

In honest moments, I do not consider her odds of survival to be betting odds.

Clothes. If she lives, she will need clothes.

I am faint with hunger & have no appetite, but if I am not to sicken, I must eat.

The child refuses solids too. I got a little water into her mouth just now by holding her nose, but this left her wracked utterly with coughs, & a terrible whimpering.

Everything I try chokes her & makes her droop.

I have wasted two days on this!

It is late now. I could break my leg on the Organ Pipes. The stars are infinite, the moons halo bright enough perhaps to climb by. But every few moments McGonigle's lighthouse obliterates the sky & the sea & sets everything stark white & black, & it takes near the entire round of the light for the eyes to adjust.

I am here for the birds!

I will see the birds in the morning.

THURSDAY 3RD JUNE, 1847

So much puke is coming out of her, she will die if I cannot replace her fluids. I have rubbed camphor into her chest. Her arms. It gives no respite. My towelling, my sheets all puke. I do not know what she is puking—this mustardy-orange fluid is a colour I have not seen—but I have no time to wash the sheets.

The gagging assures me at least she is not dead. If there is no gagging for more time than I think reasonable, I check her breathing with a knife-blade placed between her teeth: by the misting of steel, I track her vital functions.

Her swaddled arse is dry, which is good in theory as she cannot spare the fluids, but it cannot be really good, as by my count, she has not passed water in nearly thirty hours.

I have exhausted the entirety of my medical knowledge. It is not smallpox as there is no pus. Beyond that, I am a layman. Force-feeding her quinine is hopeless for anything but vomiting: she spits it out, explosive coughing to phlegmy retching then to intermittent puking again.

Earlier I thought to ease the quickened pace of her breath with fingerful of laudanum rubbed to her gums only to feel the gnash of her limbs go limp; initially this seemed harmless enough, but now I worry an increase in dosage might sink her into a stupor from which she might not wake.

When the lemon juice is spat, she squeals briefly, vomits, then passes to panting in short shallow breaths.

Same for brandy. Same for soured ale.

I must go to the birds, but I do not.

All that works is a slow trickle of water down one cheek. I lay her on her belly & with a spoon drip a rivulet of water over her hot cheek & in this way, let the water trickle into her mouth. The annoyance of the drip stirs her unrest ever so slightly; she chews on the water briefly, with her tongue protruding to remove the irritation, & lets it pool on the inside of her cheek; thus, by & by, a little is swallowed.

Crumbed wet biscuit was a moronic idea.

I slept briefly in the afternoon; took a short trip to the outhouse; got cut short when I heard her choke again.

The day is near gone!

I have eaten yesterday's honeycakes & moved on to a bowl of dried oats with cold water.

I need to light the stove!

There is barely water enough for the night.

I say to myself intermittently it would be a kindness to aid her passage into the earth with an abrupt mercy. Then I go to the still, fill a small tumbler with water, & recommence the drips across her cheek.

from

The Freeman's Journal

FRIDAY 4TH JUNE, 1847

BAILIFF MURDERED

Duncan Cook, a bailiff working for Mr Mahon for the last twelve years, was returning from the funeral of his friend at eight o'clock on Monday, when he was shot dead less than two miles out of Strokestown. According to our informant, the assassin was a lone figure clad in a black overcoat, broad about the chest, with his face covered by a kerchief and a distinctive high-pitched voice. The assailant called out, once, from the bushes; before the victim could draw, the shot came from behind, lodged into his chest and removed him from his horse, which the assailant then chased down and used to flee the scene. The cause attributed to this atrocious deed was the destruction of properties re-entered by tenants who had been ejected therefrom. An inquest was held upon the body on Wednesday, after a verdict of wilful murder was returned.

from

Field Notes on the Final Colony of Garefowl

VOL. II, continued

FRIDAY 4TH JUNE, 1847

Whoever has done this to me deserves hanging.

The more I think on it, it cannot be Liam McGonigle. It is too easily traced to him. The crimes he has hitherto conducted on my person have always left him some kind of alibi—a this-is-all-we-have-received-from-Hancock-sir—& altho I have no doubt his skinny brides produce a steady brood—who knows how many of the women on the island he breeds into or his "dead" brother has—& he lacking the basic sense to feed the children he takes to his hearth himself—it cannot be him. The track is too easily traced, he simply has too much to lose, he is too wily, Sir Phillip owns the land he & all his family live on, pays his wage at the lighthouse as well as the fee for the spurious services he offers me. Sir Phillip who indeed must have scores of examples of the man's handwriting, & we know where to get McGonigle, no matter how desperate he is, he must know he would be hanged for this!

I would pay to see him hanged for this!

But I cannot allow myself to be duped. No: more likely the child's mother is a canny young slut shaking the child loose before the hop to Boston or Toronto or Liverpool, who secured my particulars from an overeducated dockhand in Londonderry. Who knows but my early work on the cattle egret may have garnered wider readership than Sir Phillip supposes, & some dockhand recognised my name & passed the information to a beggar waif for a quick tup in an alleyway? McGonigle either did not find the child among the boxes due to innate obtuseness, or did find the child but trusted in his order with the fastidious obedience of anyone who has worked the tea ships. In which case, the mother is gone fancy free to breed again & again in the New World without consequence, & justice will be evaded, & the hatching of possibly the last colony of garefowl will remain undocumented!

But we can trace it to the dockhand! Some rugged brutish type, a smattering of letters about him; a tradesman's rudimentary learning. A man with access to the manifest & sufficient literacy to pass on my whereabouts to a starveling hussy for a tussle!

Let it then be some dockhand at Londonderry. Some idiot fellow, thick of brow, unusually well-read, easily seduced.

It must be a dockhand.

I will hold them accountable.

The child's skin is like roast pork. The only difference from yesterday is I sometimes think I am more intermittent with the trickle of water & between deathly pauses in breath & coughing fits the child has resumed her drone, but with such acute constancy it seems deliberate. Not a cry, not words, just the steady *ai-ai-ai-ai-ai-ai-ai-ai*. At first, I was relieved & thought it a sign of health. But it cuts thru me. I have told her to stop. I have screamed at her that I will put her outside, that I will let her choke. I have pinched her. I have withheld her water. But then the *ai-ai-ai-ai-ai* returns, then the coughs, the vomit, sleep.

I am losing my mind.

I have not been to the birds.

Today at noon, thought I was done. Went out determined to take notes at least, never mind the easel or sketchbook. But so tired am I with the sleepless constancy of the child's chant & cough, I left my wits at the cabin door. Ascending the Organ Pipes by I thought a shorter route, I passed too close to the nest of the fulmars, & the rain falling heavily on the rocks. I have heard of its defence—of course I have—but somehow, this far south, in my disturbed state, it did not register in my mind to keep my distance. The mother swooped on me, caught me off-guard like some bespectacled novice & the chicks cast their vile demoniac vomit upon me, & I was unprepared, & the stream caught me in my face, in my mouth, in my hair, & I lost my footing & landed hard at the foot of the Pipes on my back.

Nothing was broken but the agony & indignity were sharp. More than that, my whole sinuses filled with the stench of bird & oily puke & fish, leaving me retching & my clothes sodden & filthy.

I had to abandon my plan so as to scour the fulmar's gunk from my mouth & hair.

By the time I was clean, changed & dry-mouthed with a week's ration of tooth powder, the child was choking on sputum again, until I rolled her, hooked a finger to scoop the spit from her tongue, then her *ai-ai-ai*, *ai-ai-ai*, *ai-ai-ai*.

McGonigle's lights have started up.

It must be a dockhand.

But why would a dockhand copy my name incorrectly from the manifest?

Could the name be one he has heard & not read?

Which would lead us back to McGonigle!

O let it be McGonigle. Let it be him.

Let him try to blackmail me. Or taunt me once more! One glance at his handwriting will be enough to lock him up.

I will have him in gaol.
I will have him hanged.

SATURDAY 5TH JUNE, 1847

A victory of sorts.

The child filled its swaddling in the night.

A warm parcel of piss.

Reward for my two days steady trickling.

She was chanting late, long after the northern sunset. The sheets underneath her head soaked with water from the trickling. But I thought the wet sheet might do something to reduce her fever.

Perhaps it worked. She has slept now with relative soundness some four hours or more. I near thought her dead in the night. But then, before dawn, her little croak.

CHILD: (nigh inaudible) Wishke! Wishke!
MYSELF: What? What do you want?
CHILD: Wishke.
MYSELF: Say it again, child.
CHILD: Wishke.

She had not moved from her supine sideways pose. But her eyes not as dull as yesterday. I fetched her a cool bottle from the still & lo, she sucked on it!

I could hardly believe it. Half a bottle. Not air-lapped like a dying lamb but sucked thirstily.

I sat there watching over her, fell asleep so.

After maybe half an hour, I jerked awake, touched her cheek with the trickling spoon, only for her to murmur & push me wanly away, sucking afresh on her rubber teat.

She slept, & then, I confess, so did I.

When I rose, she was still asleep.

I had a biscuit, & got dressed, all without her stirring.

I have just now fed the still, & fired it, & listened until it started bubbling, & she is still here, & unwoken, & her breathing has held, & is steady.

Her bottle is empty.

But why am I still here?

I will refill her bottle.

A bundle of piss awaits me, but I am going to the birds.

The wind low enough to risk the easel but I am not going back. I will make notes here, & in the sketchbook.

The crab baskets empty.

All four nesting pairs now have laid, each with a single egg on the unadorned rocks of the Organ Pipes. The nest arrangements now appear settled, as follows.

a) Othello & Desdemona the highest, near the marram & herring gulls, towards the top of the Pipes just under the windline, easternmost;
b) Antony & Cleopatra in a mini-ravine, two yards above the tideline, the central pair;

c) Canute & Boadicea almost four yards inland, at slight elevation over Antony & Cleopatra, their nest the most established, a shocking white mess of guano;
d) At furthest remove from the colony proper, Macbeth & Lady Macbeth, perhaps an eight-foot drop above the water, in a sheltered position with a clear diving spot, but most awkward on reascent;
e & f) Closer to the edge of the sea, Lear & Falstaff, their own roosts, with easiest access to the water, diving more regularly than the other birds, hunting mostly with the males but on occasion the females, with no eggs of their own or partner to preen.

Of the latter, Lear & Falstaff remain close enough to attempt wooing the other females, occasionally causing a joust even this late season with hooked bills at the changing of the guard. Falstaff seemingly inclined to Cleopatra. He mooned for her as Antony left, to no avail.

No lethal blow is ever struck; they are cautious in both attempted adultery & violence.

Nesting much more separate than accounts of Eldey; rather than clustering, they have left ample space between their sites; their reasons unclear. To avoid confusion of the hatchlings? More likely the steepness of rock makes the alignment of nests impossible. It is improbable the mega-colonies of Eldey & Funk are historical outliers caused by overcrowding, but in remoter regions, perhaps smaller colonies have always supported greater nest-dispersal? The sites not so sheer as to lose eggs to slippage.

They climb in short clumsy hops, better suited to shuffling. Gives much comedy in their ascension. Fall, hop again, fall again. Five distinct calls, which I will record here.

a) Male preening mate: Wheee, wheee, wheee. This whistling of the throat, both before mating & on return to the nest, combing the female's chest feathers. Wheedling: sometimes heard at night among the brooding auks.
b) Garefowl, either sex: Grrrr, sometimes Grrrrr-uh, twice. Guttural, scratchy; reminiscent of the razorbill. The more common response to a returning mate; preceding but not during grooming. An acknowledgement.
c) Garefowl, either sex; a hollow whoop: HOOOwk, HOOOwk; like the herring gull or a wounded child; denoting excitement/distress.
d) Male garefowl; Chit-chit-chit-chit-chit. A warning, issued by a rapid chattering of the beak, comparable to the magpie. This when a young mateless buck–Falstaff or Lear–approaches. Sometimes followed by;
e) Garefowl, either sex, imminent threat: CLACK CLACK CLACK; at first mistakable for a missed bite, but repeated twice after. Rarely does Falstaff venture close enough for Antony to CLACK him. The birds CLACK me, shd I overstep their boundaries in observing eggs or collecting guano.

But their boundaries exceedingly permissive compared to any bird.

Tragedy has struck: at least one of the eggs is cracked. Canute & Boadicea. A small fissure near the point, barely noticeable but for the greyish colour of the shell, as opposed to the pale squiggled ivory of Cleopatra's or Desdemona's. I still have not been able to get a clear view of Lady Macbeth's egg without causing inordinate disturbance; its state of health is unknown.

Two healthy eggs, one dead, one unknown.

The loss of even one egg is a human loss.

Canute oblivious. Bristles when I get close, CLACKS at me. CLACK CLACK CLACK. Stands as if to rush me. Poor fellow.

Sketchbook 2:

pg 11: Cursory Map of the breeding sites; pen on paper.

pg 12: A sketch of three eggs, two living, one dead, pen on paper.

pg 13: The auk's awkward angle of brooding, Canute; charcoal on paper.

They lie not horizontal on the eggs like swans, nor vertical like Cape penguins; contra Longfellow, at rest, they incline their bodies at perhaps 30 degrees.

I could stay here all day.

McGonigle & his men roving the bay in the distance. I know his boat from the others now; larger; always accompanied by his pasty entourage of nephews.

Charon, putting the souls of misers to work.

I must tend to the child,

I have left her sleeping.

Much at peace with myself I came back to the chanting at the cabin. *Ai-ai-ai.* The child lying on its side, wet with tears, on the bottle. The tears genuine, by all appearances, rather than sweat.

MYSELF: No chanting. Stop it! Stop that noise.

CHILD: *Ai-ai-ai, ai-ai-ai.*

MYSELF: You are lying in your own filth.

No idea how long she had lain like this, but her bottle was dry. Changed her swaddling, tho neither of us care for the procedure. She showed some partial strength as I lifted her, by kicks & screams. A different beast altogether than before. No excreta, but her arse roseate with open sores, the skin cracked & bleeding.

On her upper back, the rash unchanged.

Bloating of the skin is notably faded. The mark of my palm barely lingers where I lift her.

The sores are troublesome. Camphor seems to sting them. I tried to let them dry in the air as I scrubbed myself & ate a biscuit, before reswaddling. Her howling did not abate a long while. A bottle of water silenced her briefly, but as I turned my back on her, the chanting began afresh in three note bursts.

CHILD: *Ai-ai-ai. Ai-ai-ai.*
MYSELF: No bloody chanting. Do you hear?

Cooked a simple repast: oats, suet, apple & raisins. As the oats boiled, the child pleaded for *wishke* again. Much inured to ignoring her noise after the last harsh nights, I did not respond immediately. Then, a curious thing.

CHILD: *Ai-ai-ai. Ai-ai-ai.*
MYSELF: I'm not listening.
CHILD: *Wishke. Wishke!*

This she followed with a tirade of either Gaelic or gibberish. I ignored her.

CHILD: *Ai-ai-ai. Ai-ai-ai. Ai-ai-ai.*

MYSELF: (waving the knife at her) *Ai ai* bloody *ai*. No bloody chanting, do you hear? I will get you a drink presently. I am cooking now. No bloody chanting.

There was a longish pause, as I sliced apple. Then:

CHILD: No bloody chudding.

MYSELF: What?

CHILD: (quieter) No bloody chudding.

No bloody chanting. She had taken my unguarded speech & rendered me an approximation of my own sounds. I knelt by her, looked in her eyes.

MYSELF: No bloody chanting.

CHILD: No bloody chudding.

She can repeat what she hears.

I got her some water, & she drank.

Before I ate, I set a bowl out for the child also. Her hand reached out to touch it & recoiled, the porridge clearly too hot.

I got a biscuit from the chest & approached again.

MYSELF: Want a biscuit?

The girl flinches when I approach & would not take it, so I dropped it by her pallet.

MYSELF: No bloody chudding. Eat it.

She drank, stared at me, stared at the biscuit.

She is clearly getting stronger. Hallelujah, I suppose? But I cannot have her running about naked as a piglet so after the dinner dishes, I prepared two sets of tools: my oils for the auks—*enfin!*—& sewing equipment for clothes for the child. By the time I had started clipping the seams of my spare pillowcase, I looked up & saw she had sucked the biscuit down to a paste in her fingers.

No chanting. Just a quiet medley of sounds: the child's breath; the steady mulching of the biscuit in her jaw; gull-cry; the sea; the bubbling still & the hiss of the lamp.

Wonderful.

She is asleep now. I have rinsed her swaddle in a tub, set it to dry above the stove. We will have a spare for the morning, but I must do her bedding too, & indeed, all my own phlegmy clothes.

I must set up the semaphore too. Frank will be here in six days. But first, clothes.

SUNDAY 6TH JUNE, 1847

The child fitful all night. Two refills of her bottle. Coughing; a deep rattle broken by snorting, but even at peace, her sonorous little rumble. Then waking, first to weeping, then *ai-ai-ai*, & chuddy-bloody, chudding blood too.

Her head is hot.

Maybe less hot?

My sleep entirely ruined since her arrival.

Five more days to go.

Child watched me at prayer. I showed her the fragmented host, as if to offer it. But she scowled, did not trust it, pulled back.

MYSELF: Today is Sunday. This is the body of Christ. Would you join me for prayer?
CHILD: *Wishke.*

I did not heed her, but continued my ritual.

CHILD: *Ai-ai-ai. Ai-ai-ai.*
CHILD: Bloody chud. Bloody chud. No bloody.
CHILD: *Wishke*! *Wishke*!

This last a squealing. I let her wait & when I was done, I changed her swaddling again—moderate wetness, still no excreta—& she opposed me with noise & partial vigour. Water would not pacify her, but then I brought her another biscuit.

As she set to sucking the biscuit, I laid out her outfits.

MYSELF: These are your clothes. Look. I made them. See?
MYSELF: Pretty dresses! Cover your bottom. Nice clothes. You'll be a lady.

Two pillowcases, sewn deftly to a fair approximation of her size. Took me late into the night, used up two of my feather pillows, their innards emptied into an oatmeal sack.

This she gave me in thanks: a single slow bovine blink.

MYSELF: Damn you so.

Manhandled into the outfit, she stood briefly. A thin thing, slightly shrunk in proportion to her new pillowcase dress. But it covers her belly & her arse & the hideous rash. Not enough for the rock–unless there is some unforeseen summer warmth yet inbound–& she could use an overcoat. But, if it were not for the shaved head & her nicked ear, & the cake of sores on her face, she could pass as one of McGonigle's spindly brood. Give her a fine set of ringlets & liberal buckets of rosewater & she could almost pass as English.

Shaved as she is, the effect is more simian.

MYSELF: Stand up straight. You needn't be afraid of me.

MYSELF: Pleased to meet you. Shake my hand.

CHILD: (*sotto voce*) *Ai-ai-ai.*

MYSELF: Keep your hand so. Pleased to meet you anyway. My name is Ignatius Green. I am a naturalist, an Englishman. In my heart, an ornithologist. A redeemed öologist, if you will.

She looked pained.

MYSELF: Redeemed öologist means I no longer collect eggs. Live ones at least. I am Ignatius. Ig. I am also something of an artist. At least, I have a good eye. What is your name?

Might as well have chatted to the garefowl.

I was entirely correct though. What agues her is not smallpox. Not with this recovery. I offered her a small tumbler of quinine & lemon juice again.

MYSELF: Nice water. This is good. *Wishke*. Drink it up.
MYSELF: Open your mouth. Come now. It's good for you.

She slumped, despondent, & tho I tried to make her drink, she turned her head. At least now she has strength to push my hands away, like a sheep at shearing, but then her sobbing passed to a coughing fit. The best I could do without her compliance was apply camphor to her chest & the neck of her new nightdress, before she screamed excessively & wrung herself back under her sheet.

She is staring up at me as I write.

There she goes. Her bloody endless chanting.

CHILD: *Ai. Ai. Ai-ai-ai-ai-ai. Ai. Ai. Ai.*

I am off to the birds.

The crab baskets empty.

I witnessed the changing of the guard as I arrived. Canute has become the sole parent to his grey egg. When the womenfolk return from fishing, the other men growl & cluck, preening. Then, the switch: the ladies shuffle to the nests, while the men head out. But not Boadicea. When she landed, she showed total disinterest in brooding, walking near but not to their nook, holding her distance. Canute sat where he was, growling softly to her; then rose, combed her chest-feathers, tried to nudge her nestward with the top of his head; at this, she CLACKED him & moved almost two yards apart.

She knows the game is up & senses death.

He has hope.

Poor beast.

The wind muted sufficiently to set up the easel.

Have been experimenting on mixing auk guano with my white. Gathered fresh from the rocks before it dries & mashed in a cup to form a thicker grainy gouache. Dry samples are too hard, almost limestone in texture, but have a cooler greyish undernote than the zinc or even the lead white. The zinc white mixes well with guano & loses its glare for a warmer grey, as of cygnet-down: a colour particularly apt for the skies of Tor Mor, the blazing greys of Atlantic afternoons, sun-thru-seaclouds.

Artwork: Tor Mor Skies, oil & guano on canvas.

Canute pleading with Boadicea, oil & guano on canvas.

All garefowl on Tor Mor between six-&-twenty inches up to Antony, who at rest is almost a full three feet. The stubby wings approximately six inches long, useful crutches on an incline. Woolley's proposition they perform only as rudders appears incorrect: in my limited observation from the Pipes, the wings are thrust also for subaquatic propulsion. Legs protrude so obtusely from torso, they appear squat at all times except on diving & in defensive displays, such as Falstaff's approach, when Antony stands nearly chest-height. Proportions make them ungainly & stupid in waddling.

Confirmed: all have white eye-patch fully visible now. Summer plumage. Beaks rival the ornateness of the puffin, albeit in monochrome black.

My measurements currently remain approximations. I could easily snatch one dozing on the nest, bind its stabbing beak. But I once saw Olafson crush three razorbill eggs to bring back one intact specimen in Arbroath. There are but four garefowl eggs left on the island now, a maximum of three healthy. One struggling mother, one slipped boot & another egg may be lost.

There are plenty of alcine skeletons in private collections. Let the purveyors of bones declare their quarter inches. I shall observe the living at a distance while I can.

Poor Canute is morose. He just let out a sorrowful whoop. The other menfolk gone, he is likely hungry, & his estranged spouse dozing on the ledge.

He CLACKS at her now & again, but she will not brood.

He will not leave the dead egg.

On my return, I found the child covered in crumbs & the still left running.

MYSELF: What the devil is going on here?
CHILD: Aaaaaah!

No chanting. In fear she screamed & darted her eyes, like a cat trying to judge the space between me & the door, then scampered to her pallet, bashing her bald head on the table, whimpering.

But this new vital energy!

MYSELF: The water! The water!
CHILD: Aaaa-hah, aaaah-hah, aaa-haw.

She'd got at the spigot & managed to turn it on. The overflow tub was spilling over & tho the boards were not entirely wet, we suffered a substantial loss of the day's clean water.

MYSELF: Don't touch the still! This is mine! Do not touch the still!
CHILD: Ah-ha-aa-aa-aa! (or thereabouts)
MYSELF: We will die if the still breaks, do you understand? Do not touch the still. No bloody still!

No indication of apprehension. At some point she bolted for the door: I stepped before her & she leapt back howling.

But she leapt!

MYSELF: You don't have to go anywhere. I am not throwing you out. But listen to me. Just don't touch the still!

Etc. It ended with the child mewling on her pallet & the door firmly closed. But she had managed to access the biscuits: unclear how. The suet & butter rest on the chest, & given the weight of the lid, the child either has more vigour than previously appeared or—as the mess & torn grease paper would indicate—her theft took much time & clawing.

We will need some medium of communication.

But the child was clearly hungry, so I set the still to cycle again, a full hour's work cleaning the salt chamber & fetching the water & setting it to light, & then set to cooking a light gruel with tiny slivers of bacon.

MYSELF: Listen. My name is Ignatius Green. Iggy. What is your name?
MYSELF: Everyone has a name. What is yours? Susan? Elise? Some pretty Irish name?
MYSELF: Look, my point is, you cannot touch the still. Do not touch it. You hear? This part of the

room—no actually, behind the partition too. In fact, anything on this side of the room—do not touch. You don't go in here, see?

It was quite fruitless. I am Fear More, & she fears me.

She did eat the gruel: only after I had eaten mine, & when my back was turned, & it was cool. Chewed one small piece of pork rind too. Then, as I busied the preparations for the morning & went outside to the sailcloth storage & dug out the semaphore, her refrain.

CHILD: *Wishke.*
MYSELF: What?
CHILD: (flinching) *Wishke.*
MYSELF: Here. Good. Drink up. You must ask if you want water. The still is for me, see? My still. Mine. We have five more days.

I changed her swaddling again. Still no excreta. The child screamed but now sleeps, after some bloody-chuddy & her ai-ai-ai.

MONDAY 7TH JUNE, 1847

Child woke for water twice, then slept soundly after dawn.

The day glorious. Set up the semaphore on the eastern tip. The wind shall not take it—the spot sheltered from both the North Wind & Easterlies by the Organ Pipes—& shd, by my calculations, be visible from land. The pole I have set two feet deep in shale; hit solid rock below. Dug three small guy ropes on wooden poles into the shale around it, much like the design of the cabin. It will of course need checked in high winds & if the tide lifts.

The whole world is bright & windy.

The seals have returned. Two in the sea, one basking. The basker definitely male by the thickness of his neck & discernible brow. Likely all three males. Shall take my rifle on my next outing & shoot them if I find them basking.

But not this morning. The world is too alive.

When I got back I found the child sat on her pallet. Watching me as I moved. I made place at the table, gestured to the chair across from me. But she would have nothing of society. We ate with her squat on the floor, me at my chair. Man & his dog. Leftover gruel & a biscuit.

MYSELF: Try some lemon juice. It makes you strong.

She pulled her disgusted face. I smiled; for a miniscule moment thought I saw my smile mirrored in her face? Might the smile in itself be considered a primitive form of communication?

Perhaps her grimace was trapped wind, nothing more.

MYSELF: Hear me now. I must set about washing my clothes & your smelly swaddle. The bedsheets too. Then I will watch the birds. You can stay here. But you must not touch anything.

As I talked, I set up her daily food rations to stop her grubbing fingers. Eight biscuits will hopefully keep her out of the chest. One handful of diced dried apple, one handful of raisins, a waste of my delicacies but some protection from rickets if she will not take her lemon juice. Had some leftover tea, left her with two big tumblers, honey-sweetened, & her pewter bottle filled with water.

She was munching at her pallet when I came back from laundry & had clearly helped herself to the apple cubes.

MYSELF: Good. You like apple, do you?
CHILD: (nothing)
MYSELF: Now listen to me. I have to go away to paint.
CHILD: (nothing)
MYSELF: This is the study. Don't go in. Say it. No go in here.
CHILD: (nothing)
MYSELF: I won't leave until you say it. Don't go in the study. No bloody study. Say it. No bloody still too. Say it.
CHILD: (murmuring from her pallet) No chudding.
MYSELF: Good girl. Good girl. Say it. No touching the still.
CHILD: No bloody still.

One week together & we can communicate!

I am off for the birds.

Seals attacked today in a three-man team. I was aghast.

I needn't have been.

The garefowl outplayed them marvellously.

Two seals tried repeatedly to circle the auk flotilla, pushing inland from the ocean as the third rose from below. They clearly know the garefowl cannot fly away. Trying to get the birds panicking in the shallows to snatch them. But garefowl are masters of the flotilla, with at least one on lookout above & one below at all times. At any approach of the seals, either one of the sedentary or submerged auks would perform a full flurry on the surface, a signal simultaneously visible below & above. Thus did first LM, then Desdemona, then LM again, fan the water with both wings as an alarum, then they dove as an entire group.

Each time the seals went for the kill, this performance: the splash, the whole flotilla disappearing.

On each assault, I stared anxiously over the sea.

Only for first Lady Macbeth, then the other ladies one by one, to reappear minutes later, far from the shore.

This repeated thrice, upon which point the seals abandoned their sea assault. To which it may be noted: alcine underwater speed & agility is clearly superior to the pinniped.

After regrouping, the seals tried briefly to climb the Organ Pipes, possibly drawn by the stink of guano for the garefowl eggs? Unheard of. Curiosity? New basking spots? Regardless, it was folly afresh. Antony & Lear & Macbeth hopped to the higher stones spearing the seal-heads as they came close.

Garefowl. Geir-fugl. Spear-birds.

ANTONY: Clack-clack CLACK. Clack-clack CLACK.

The seals could not weather the blows from above & the treachery of the rocks, & their land assault was short-lived. One of them sporting a lively gash on his nose for his troubles.

I have never seen a seal attack a bird, but then, most birds fly. They can distinguish the garefowl from other birds, then? Nevertheless, it appears to me the only real danger the seals present lies in the ten-yard zone between the shore & the deeper ocean; thus the seals corral them; but in the shallower water, their smaller size must give the birds the advantage. They dive too well, & on rocks hop too high, to come to harm.

The seals dallied the long afternoon here, long enough for me to consider fetching my rifle but not long enough for me to do so, & occasionally they harangued the guillemots to the south, & were harangued in turn.

I witnessed the changing of the guard again, much delayed.

I will gather seaweed on the southern rocks before I return. The locals eat it dried, & I miss vegetal matter terribly, but even shd it prove tasteless, it may be useful to shore up my supplies of tinder.

It is like being robbed. If a ransacker had come with the sole intent of deliberately sabotaging me, I hardly see what more he could have done. The entire still—a full week's supply of desalinated sweet water—has been emptied onto the floorboards. The sacks of Indian meal & the pease are soaked thru. I will lose at least one fifth part of the meal, if not a third. Suet & butter cast down in the water, the butter trodden on. Biscuits quite ripped out of the chest, the grease paper torn back. My tinderbox rifled, the tinder sodden. A dozen biscuits left dampening in the spill. A shitty swaddle pulled from the child & hurled yolk-down on the floor.

Behind the partition, my study, ruined. My Bewick, both volumes, left open, spines neatly cracked, soaking through on the boards. Humboldt's *Views of the Cordilleras* upended, face-down. Montague's *Supplement* the same, trodden on–a wet buttery imprint of a child's foot. 12 pages torn loose to one side. My guillemot skeleton, unwired, its sinuses cracked. My lepidoptera case open, smeared with handprints; nigh half of the specimens in disarray.

I saw her as I returned from the crab baskets, my arms full of seaweed. Saw her darting from the outhouse back into the cabin. Was impressed. Thought she might have learned base humanity.

When I got to the door, the full bedlam dawned on me.

In the centre, she sat.

A half smile on her skinny face.

A charming Satan in the ruins of Babel.

I was rendered speechless. I dared not step into the chaos.

She saw the thunder in my face.

Her half-smile dropped & she ran for the study.

MYSELF: No! No! No! No! No!
CHILD: Aaaaaah! Aaaaaah!

My aim was not to beat her, tho she would have deserved it, wholly. My aim was to hold her, make her bear witness to the destruction she had wrought. But the weasel has grown fitter & faster than I could have believed. Into my study, stamping on the books, leaping onto the desk, knocking the lepidoptera. Ducking past me thru the gap, my fingers clutching air. Leapt on the bed: as I reached for her, leaping onto my chests. But here she was cornered. I had flung down the last handful of seaweed & stretched my arms.

She made as if to leap onto the still.

If she got hold of the top of the still, she risked bringing it down.

MYSELF: Not the still! Not the still!

CHILD: Aaaah! Aaaah!

Her energy wholly other. The wan milquetoast now a cornered fox. I watched, incredulous, as she coiled & flung herself.

I caught her by the ankle.

She swung in an arc, hit the table's edge with her face, & fell like a sack of meat to the floor.

I thought her killed. Screamed. Stood staring.

Seconds passed.

Then the remarkable.

The child spasmed, grunted on the floor, turned utterly feral. There was blood on one side of her head; from where the blood was issuing I could not see. Only one side of her face visible, but her visage twisted into a rictus, clenched, all bared teeth & scowl.

She leapt at me, & I could have sworn her more heavy than before, her torso more massive, for her weight threw my balance.

In surprise—no, fear, if I am honest, fear—I tried to hold her out of reach. She coiled, turned, bit hard on my hand. I cried out, as I felt her teeth ripping the meat of me. Trying to pull her off I ended up slipping on the butter, landing heavily on my side.

Still she bore at me, pulling at my jacket. Recoiled; grabbed my good knife from the table. I had to grab her arm to stop her running me thru. In a flash she switched knife-hands like a barroom Spaniard, & if I hadn't managed to grab her other wrist, I have no doubt I would have lost an eye.

Even held wide, crucified by the wrists, it did not stop her. She twisted her knife, trying to cut my wrist. When she could not angle the blade into skin, she tried to bite my face, gnashing at me, like a rabid hound with blood on her teeth, her blood or mine I knew not.

MYSELF: Stop! Child, stop!

I met her eyes. Small black holes. Fury.

I saw a brief spark of recognition.

Then she put both feet on my chest & kicked hard so hard I had to let go, her little dirty toenails scraping my throat, wringing herself so I could not hold her, & in a moment, she was out the door.

I sat there for longer than I shd have. Utterly bewildered. My jacket was torn thru. Only minor damage to the sleeve, but the collar she has quite tugged from its seams: further split seams in the left sleeve & armpit from when we fell, but in the back, somehow, there is a long gash in the tweed itself.

Blood on the edge of the table.

The whole cabin in utter disarray.

It has taken me all late afternoon to put the room right. The butter I have moulded back into form & resealed, having lost perhaps a third to grit & smearing. The floor is drying. I could probably rebind the books but I have not the spirit, & have just jammed them loose-leaved & damp in the bookshelf.

The wet sacks I have left drying in the sun. The wet grain I have spread on my bedsheets.

The still, thank God, is intact!

She could have scuppered us wholly.

Nothing appears permanently broken but the guillemot skull. Perhaps two thirds of the butterfly specimens will be fit for repinning. Some have been rolled in her fingers to dust. Some I can only conclude she has eaten.

My jacket is beyond saving.

Likely the girl's face is damaged.

Her jaw is not broken, that is for sure.

The thud she made was awful.

About halfway thru tidying, my bewilderment turned back into rage, & I stood at the cabin door, trying to see where the girl had got to, but the shale was featureless.

MYSELF: Go on, you orphan. Run from me.

MYSELF: Don't come back. I never wanted you here. Go.

MYSELF: Stupid dirty Irish whore's daughter etc.

By the time my throat was raw, it seemed to me the girl must be in one of four places: somewhere on the Northern Wall, up at the Organ Pipes, in the rock constructs to the west, or drowned. I checked the Pipes–lest she shd wreck her havoc on my garefowl–but by their chitters & soft moans, they sounded unharangued. The rest of my search was utterly futile. Every corner of Tor Mor is nooks & small peaks; not five hundred yards long & half that in width but there are hundreds of places a child her size could insert themselves.

I have scraped out the salt chamber in the still, stinging my hand where the skin is broken. Fetched brine, cleansed my wound, refilled the still, flooded the belly & set it burning with my spare tinderbox. Cast out handfuls of wet biscuits to the gulls. Reassembled the display case & polished it. Made an envelope for the broken butterfly specimens.

Cleaned her blood off the table.

Cleaned my wound a second time with gin.

She has torn the skin deeply.

MYSELF: Child! Where are you? Where are you?
MYSELF: Child? Are you hurt?

I am much aggrieved. Frank is coming soon to take her off my hands. I cannot believe the strength in her.

I hope she is not hurt.

She is not my responsibility!

Oh, let it be McGonigle. Let it be him. I will have my retribution!

I have been calling for the child.

The low clouds threaten rain when they are not throwing brief shock downpours but at least they hold back the bitter cold of the open stars. The child is wearing but a thin slip, a pillowcase. But the sweep of the lighthouse & my own little lamp reveal nothing but shadows.

MYSELF: *Wishke. Wishke*! *Wishke*!
MYSELF: Come back. I am not angry.
MYSELF: Never touch my water again!

She will come back mewling for biscuits & water in the morning, a recalcitrant dog. I am being taken for a fool.

MYSELF: Come back. Come sleep in the cabin. I command it!
MYSELF: Cannibal! Stay out here & freeze for all I care.

Twice I thought I spied her on the ridge in the flare of the lighthouse. I have left gruel & a biscuit just outside the door, with her bottle of water. I have left the door unlatched, & propped up the sacks of dried grain against the wind; she will be able to push her way in if she needs shelter.

If she can open my chest, she can open the bloody door.

Even if McGonigle is not the sole culprit, he knows more than he has said. Frank will get the constabulary, & we will get the truth out of him.

Whoever has done this to me shd be hanged.

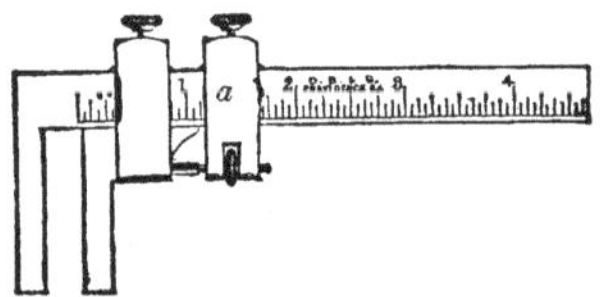

from

The Nation

MONDAY 7TH JUNE, 1847

SHERIFF FOUND DECAPITATED

The body of Richard Cunningham Esq. of Carrick-on-Shannon, landed proprietor and sheriff, was discovered without his head attached in the most gruesome of circumstances in the early hours of Saturday morning by his wife at the southern edge of his estate. He had left his house on the previous day after eating his lunch, and no tidings of him had been received until she encountered his decapitated remains prostrate in a ditch. The body had been savagely rendered by dogs, with the flesh peeled off his neck, upper shoulders, and limbs, and his spine protruding, but his identity was ascertained both by his clothes and the handkerchief in his pocket. There were no witnesses, but several tenants have been recently evicted, and the police immediately went in search of them. No cause has as yet been attributed to this gruesome deed, but this is the third case of most cold-blooded and savage murder related to the ejectment of one Martin O'Leary in February of this year.

from

Field Notes on the Final Colony of Garefowl

VOL. II, continued

TUESDAY 8TH JUNE, 1847

The girl slept in a sheltered nook on the Northern Wall.

Dragged her basket up, laid on one side for shelter. Little legs sticking out, wrapped in her filthy blanket. Must have dragged it up after midnight, or I would have heard it scraping the shale.

I spied it from the cabin doorway as I made coffee. Managed to creep close enough to hear her faint snore. Her face & the front of her nightdress are blood-smeared. My good knife lay by her sleeping hand. Her mouth open; her teeth apparently whole but an almighty bruise on her face & a cut on her jawline.

She has, indeed, taken her water bottle in the night.

I contemplated lifting her to the warmth of the cabin but thought better of it. By the time I had brought her out a bowl of soured porridge, she was gone.

Her basket was filthy. Unfit for a pig, never mind a child. But I am not sure I shall be able to cajole her back to the cabin, so I have dislodged it from the wall, & wiped it out thoroughly with brine. Crumbled a crust of filth & her own hair from the wires into the sea.

She was watching me from the Northern Wall.

When I rose to acknowledge her, she ducked the ridge.

I left her basket back in her nook, with a bowl of porridge & biscuits & a thin slice of pig under a heavy plate. A basin of sweet water alongside it for drinking. I have washed her stinking blanket & pinioned it with shale lest it blow away.

Three days until Frank reaches Malin.

Can she sleep with only the basket for protection? The nights are cold. I have no idea what conditions she is used to. But summer has not touched these rocks & she is still in recovery from a fever.

I am not a wetnurse!

I will not risk her destroying my study again. I shall take one of the padlocks from the chests & secure the door when I leave.

To the birds!

Artwork:

Light on dark clouds, watercolour on canvas (begun).

Lear afloat with the womenfolk, watercolour on canvas (abandoned).

Sketchbook 2:

pg 14: Bladderwrack & Guillemot; charcoal on paper (begun).

pg 15: Return of the She-auks, pen on paper (unfinished).

pg 16: Canute stares into a squall of *Larus argentatus*; charcoal on paper (begun).

❊

I cannot finish anything. The paintings utterly lacklustre.

Still no sign of the seals. I do not believe they can have left. Tomorrow early I shall take the rifle, see what I can get. Might carve a steak off them if my aim is true.

The girl would come at the smell of fried steak.

Butter. The last of the onions. Pepper.

What ho?

Here comes McGonigle.

He is headed straight for me. In his rowboat. On his own?

I'm getting the rifle.

❊

McGonigle lives. In freedom. Still.

But he did not set foot on my rock.

I stopped him twenty yards from the shore, the rifle trained on him. I could see him well enough. His thin white shirt. But on his own; deftly manning his sailboat without his pale rowers.

I called out to stop him in his tracks.

MYSELF: Come no closer, McGonigle.

McGONIGLE: (grinning) Are you aiming a gun at me, Mr Green?

MYSELF: What does it look like?

McGONIGLE: Would you shoot me, sir?

MYSELF: Do I have a reason to, McGonigle?

McGONIGLE: A reason to shoot me? What reason might you have, sir?

His face as always, mock-surprise, ill-shaven: his tone, pretending to warmth, even as he slackened the sail.

His very smile irks me.

MYSELF: State your business, McGonigle. Have you brought the rest of my goods? My beef?
McGONIGLE: Delivery is once a month, Mr Green.
MYSELF: Once a month. That's right.

I once shot a doe at seventy paces in the neck, leaving the jawbone intact for mounting. In Barrackpore, I was considered something of a sharpshooter. Had I wanted, I could have sent McGonigle's hat spinning into the water & left him with a hot new parting.

MYSELF: Where are your wards, McGonigle? Your lank toothless boys?
McGONIGLE: My nephews, sir?
MYSELF: Your gaunt apes. Those little wheezing rowmen.
McGONIGLE: It is very kind of you to ask, sir. They are not fit for the boat right now, sir.

Does he think to move me with ashen glances? What does he know of suffering or loss? Had he but turned his head, I could have taken the nose off his face & left his moustache.

MYSELF: State your intent.

McGONIGLE: (clearing his throat) I just thought to inquire about the wellbeing of your charge, sir? Might I ask how she fares?

MYSELF: What do you mean?

McGONIGLE: You mentioned my nephews, sir. They have a fever & cannot shake it. The child in your care, sir, had the same, did she not?

MYSELF: The child, McGonigle?

McGONIGLE: Your ward, sir.

MYSELF: Why she is dead, McGonigle. I sent her to sleep in the rocks, & she died.

He flinched at my words. That was good to see. No pall fell on him, as of a bereaved father, but an unease I relished.

McGONIGLE: You are joking, sir. You are joking with me.

MYSELF: Am I?

McGONIGLE: You are joking with me. I appreciate the wit, sir. But I know you are joking with me.

MYSELF: State your business, McGonigle. I am a busy man, & as you say, deliveries are once a month.

McGONIGLE: (taking off his hat) I will leave you, sir. I can see you are occupied. Only. The boys have a fever, & I was wondering about your medical supplies. Only, we normally rely on a fellow in Portronan, but he has gone back to Leitrim, & the doctor in Malin Town is recently dead. I was wondering about your medical supplies, sir, your medical understanding?

I shot, then. Not to hit him, I am not mad. Any fool could see that it was a warning shot, angled clearly into the water. But there was some sharp pleasure in seeing him jump & crouch in the belly of the boat, letting his arm off the boom & cowering under the sail.

I knelt & reloaded the rifle.

MYSELF: I must apologise, McGonigle. My medical lore is sorely lacking. I was not always the student my father would have liked me to be. But there it is. I became an ornithologist, you see, because I love to record the doings of birds. I would kindly ask that you let me do so, without further interruption.

McGONIGLE: Are you shooting at me now, sir?

MYSELF: (my own mock surprise) I am cleaning my gun, McGonigle. It is a good gun. It shoots straight.

I hefted it again to my shoulder.

He watched me. Afraid to stand or turn his back.

I aimed at his head, then his stomach, then his head.

McGONIGLE: My nephews, sir. They are sick.

MYSELF: My condolences. Have you tried porridge?

He watched me for a while, not averting his eyes.

I did not lower my weapon.

Eventually, he stood upright, fumbled the ropes on his sail, hefted them aloft. But before he let the wind fill them, he shouted once again.

McGONIGLE: You have flags up, sir.

MYSELF: What?

McGONIGLE: Flags, sir. To the east of the island.

MYSELF: Yes. I am testing how the birds respond to colours.

McGONIGLE: The flags are for birds, sir? You are not trying to signal the coastguard?

MYSELF: What if I was, McGonigle?

McGONIGLE: Well sir. If you want to be sending a message to the coastguard, you don't need to be bothering with flags. The coastguard is one James Quigley, my brother-in-law. I can deliver him any message you might have.

The brazenness of the man! Even as he turned from me, even as he felt my sights on his shoulders, my gaze burrowing into the square of flesh where his hair met his collar, he dared speak with his cauled threats, sailing off like a vicar riding a pony home from a garden party.

I could have ended him with a twitched finger!

He thinks me his prisoner?

I have more wit than him!

Frank, come to me, my saviour!

Knifemarks are scored around the lock.

She tried to get into the cabin while I was away. She will break my good blade thus. Her bottle is gone, & the pig & the biscuits eaten, but the gruel she has spilled with seeming deliberation on the shale, & her dropped stools beside it.

She has dragged her basket higher, half up the Northern Wall, like a robin abandoning a nest after a schoolboy's touch. Her new position offers her more protection from the wind.

I spied her sitting in a nook above it, trying to make fire in the manner of the Indians by rubbing two sticks together. Fire, out of my purloined outhouse almanac & its wooden holder.

I did not fancy her chances in this wind.

I thought to coax her in; my encounter with McGonigle had got me enthused: I wanted to celebrate with another human being. But when I got to within twenty yards, she stood, dropped her fire kit & threw a rock at me. Not half the size of my fist, sailing over my head.

CHILD: Aaaaaah! Aaaaaaaaaah!
MYSELF: There is no need for that. Parley! Parley! There is no need.

She dropped to her knees, picked up another stone. Her recovery is marvellous. What was parboiled leeks is now brambles. Her vigour grows day by day. The bald head, raised in a scowl.

CHILD: (waving the knife) Aaaaaaah! Aaaaaaah!
MYSELF: Come to the cabin. I am sorry I hurt you. I am very sorry.
CHILD: Aaaaah!

She threw another stone: I skipped away as she scrabbled for another.

Could I have manhandled her in? What would have been the point? I raised my palms, backed off to my cabin. I will write to Connie with a tumbler of gin.

No. The coat.

⁂

The hail started before dusk.

I took her out a bowl of pea-and-suet broth, bearing a lantern before me so as not to startle her.

> MYSELF: I am sorry I hurt you. Come back.
> MYSELF: I have food. Food.

No response but the wind.

At a loss, I left the bowl & a spoon at the bottom of the ridge.

I have spent the last few hours drinking gin & cutting up my torn green jacket. By the time I am back in England in reach of decent tweed to fix it, I shall have my entire wardrobe. No man needs two jackets south of Aberdeenshire & if the child insists on sleeping outside for her last few days here, I can at least send her back to her mother in a half-decent overcoat.

If the rural Irish can be convinced to wear coats at all.

Shortening the sleeves is easy. Cutting the lower half so it only reaches her knees, then hemming it to avoid fraying; this I can do. Reshaping the shoulders is beyond my skill, but with a basic loop at intervals for a belt just below the armpits, she can cinch herself at the middle.

It is a shoddy green thing.

But it will be warmer than her pillowcase.

She was snoring as I approached, long after midnight. The pea-suet broth she has eaten. I cast the little overcoat in on her. Caught a glimpse of her bruised head in the gleam of the lighthouse.

WEDNESDAY 9TH JUNE, 1847

She was sat outside my door when I awoke. In her new overcoat, left untied, so it hung around her.

I have misjudged my measurements. The coat is ankle-length & quite ridiculous. It trails on the shale with the slightest of stoops & makes her look altogether like a miniature bailiff, bald to boot.

I laughed when I open the door, & she was not amused.

MYSELF: Oi sor, Jesus, Mary & Joseph, have you come to take me house & all? Only me potahtoes are surely all rot & me babbies all starving & there's no money in the house—o plais don't eject me, sor!

Etc. I was trying to make her laugh.

She beheld me with disdain & threw her bottle at my feet.

CHILD: *Wishke.*

She did not respond to further horseplay. Her scalp was wet & her face washed of blood & her nightdress soaked to her skin. I suspect she has dipped herself in the sea & put dry clothes on her wet body. The bruise a full black mark down one cheek.

She kept her face turned away, a mark of disrespect. The knife she holds loosely, in one hand, more an afterthought than a threat.

CHILD: (again) *Wishke.*

MYSELF: Alright, cannibal.

I filled her bottle at the still. Took fours biscuits & placed them both on the shale. She sniffed & deigned to take the biscuits, but sucked hard on the water & retreated to her box.

☼

Something has killed one of the grey seals. I suspect a mid-size porbeagle shark–*Squalus nasus*–altho I am surprised to find one this far north. Normally I would lay the blame on an orca, particularly with a bite this large. Olafsson swears there are orcas in Iceland big enough to take a young seal in a single gulp. But I have seen no orcas about, & they are not shy beasts. The wound is uncustomarily clean, perhaps even for a porbeagle? Definitely not the ragged carcass left after an orca has tired himself playing with it.

The carcass is what has been enthusing the gulls.

Its death a curiosity. The body bigger than a yearling pig. The original wounds have been shredded somewhat by gulls, but it appears the entire head has been removed, & not much else. The neck hole worried hollow under the skin, but other than the scrapings of gulls & the excised head, there are no toothmarks.

There is a fair chance it died to disease, more's the pity; but by all appearances, the kill appears still relatively fresh.

The gulls are harpies. I had to go back to the cabin & fetch my brown jacket to rebuff their beaks, & use both my inferior knife & the rifle to club them.

The seal would have been a mighty beast had I shot him myself. We could have eaten of him an entire week. I have dreamt of seal steaks in my pit the last few days. But now to find him killed–only weak or sick seals are brought down by predators–& to eat a diseased kill risks all manner of gutrot.

I am a sturdy specimen, but not a hyena.

Nevertheless, our pork is getting ragged & the carcass was terrifically fresh in colour & smell, at least as far as my salt-caulked nose can discern.

As I dithered, mulling, I saw the child watching me from a nook among the western rocks. Trying to make fire again, hunkered in an alcove.

Waved again. Got ignored again.

Likely I shd have let the carcass rest. In normal time I would be disgusted at the idea. But seal is an oily meat. If you cook it long enough, even boot-leather can be edible. I have eaten older meat on ships.

It is not rancid or spoiled, I am almost sure.

The gulls grew aggressive as I prevaricated; then, as I cut the meat, they rioted in the air about me. But I have taken two large steaks from the fins, where the skin was untorn, & then waded the rest out & heaved it into the sea, beyond temptation.

I have fired up the still, & my steaks are frying on the griddle.

The smell is like buttery heaven.

The steaks were marvellous.

One I cut in two, smothered in butter & lemon juice, fried it crisp. The larger I cut into thin strips & boiled up with pease. Grog in both. Sourness & the heat to sear any lingering foulness. Left the door open as I cooked, the scent whipping off in the wind.

My mouth juiced enough to set me coughing.

Of course, it worked. Soon enough the child was at the door, a wounded deer.

MYSELF: It smells good, doesn't it.
MYSELF: Go on. Try a bit.

I cut a sliver off the frying steak, held it out on the tip of the blade to the child, who winced, at first feigning to look away, but then gave in, snatched it, hunger overpowering pride & the heat of her fingers.

She tore it in two with a bite & stuffed both in her mouth.

MYSELF: It's good, isn't it. Do you want more?

She nodded to my gestures.

I cut her a plate of seal slivers. Made a gesture to my good knife that she still holds, but she snatched it back. So I took my time with the bad knife, then offered her the plate, just inside the threshold of the cabin.

She would not enter, but I could see the hunger in the hold of her mouth.

So I put out one stool for her at the doorstop, & pushed the table to the door, & for the first time we ate together like Christians, albeit on either side of the threshold, as I cut up more rich sour strands of steak, which she clawed, at first overstuffing her mouth so chewing was impossible, but then more slowly, piece by piece.

MYSELF: Grog?

She looked up, grease-faced, as I poured her a tumbler.

She tried it, twisted her face, spat it out & threw the cup down.

I could not help but laugh at her expression.

MYSELF: Do not—do not throw the cup.

Her glare met me.

MYSELF: *Wishke*? You would rather water, yes?

I fetched her a second tumbler & she drank water, never putting down my knife, & we ate on in silence. She learned to chew it slowly, as the meat was gamey & hard to swallow. She licked her bowl afterwards.

MYSELF: Your face. It's dirty. Wash your face.
MYSELF: Like this, see? I dip the cloth in the water & wipe my face & now I am clean, see?

I fetched her my shaving mirror for her to behold her face. She blinked. Held her bald head, stroking the fuzz on it. Touched her bruised cheek.

MYSELF: You try. Take the cloth.

Keeping my gaze, she took the cloth & threw it very deliberately on the ground. She rose, knocking down her chair, reached over to my plate & took the rest of my steak in her hand, & walked back to her box in the North Wall.

I could have shouted after.

Tried to wrestle my knife from her.

Instead I watched her climb the ridge, to where the gannets nest, where the rocks are too treacherous for me.

She will be gone in a few days.

It is better so.

I have taken the stew off the boil: experimented & made Indian meal flatbreads in the griddle, as an unleavened pie-top to the stew. They are not as crisp as I would like, but it will be hard to ruin a fresh pie.

I will lock the door now & go to the birds.

Artwork:

Canute's egg & Canute; watercolour on canvas.

Child sat on rocks, watercolour on canvas (unfinished).

His nest unsettled. Canute is obviously distressed. Hunched brooding on the dead egg. Sometimes sitting beside it, as if it burns him, as if he can finally smell death in it. Boadicea sits apart, when she isn't foraging, & snaps at him when he comes near.

He does not go foraging with the other males.

Falstaff notes Boadicea's solitude, occasionally struts near her, to no avail. He does not push his luck overly, but nor does Canute chase him anymore.

At the changing of the guard, Canute followed Boadicea to the water. It gave me an ideal chance to get close to the egg: even a stillborn nest is a source of knowledge. The guano is thick, & there is a smattering of down around it, but no concerted effort has been made to cushion the egg with leaves or plant matter. Much like with pigeons, the egg rests on the hard stone, decorated with no more than sparse snatches of grass & a gouache of dried guano &

down. Likely this inability to cushion is an indirect cause of the cracking? However, with Desdemona & Cleopatra, & the brief glimpse of Lady Macbeth's egg—a fine living ivory specimen, I am happy to report—theirs all likewise rest on the bare rock yet remain intact.

Saw the child observing me, at a distance.

In a fit of whimsy I thought to paint her.

She spied me & spooked, ducking the ridge.

The child has returned.

She was at the door as I arrived. Hunched shivering in her little greatcoat. Big streaks of tears down her cheeks.

MYSELF: *Wishke*, yes?
MYSELF: You want water?

She stood holding out her bottle, waiting for me to unlock the door. I took her bottle & filled it. Then she raised her hand & pointed at the still.

CHILD: No bloody water.
MYSELF: What?
CHILD: No bloody water!
MYSELF: Yes. No bloody water. The still is mine. You do not touch the still. Yes.

She grunted, & then strode in past me & has flung herself on her little pallet, bound herself tightly in her sheets & overcoat, where she lies face down now, the material balled around her.

Remarkable.

The cold has brought her inside.
I will cook us a feast.

I fixed us seal pie, warmed on the griddle. She did not move, but watched me with her face cowled under her arm.

When the table was set, I waited for her to join. She needed a nudge so I raised a glass.

MYSELF: To your good health.
MYSELF: *Wishke*? Do you want a drink?

At which point she rose, face downcast, but took the stool opposite mine. We ate in silence. After, she went to the tub & washed her face with the cloth.

In silence, I placed a small handful of raisins on the table.

She pinched them singly & when they were done retired to her cot. For my part, I kept the stalemate, not daring to feel her head or suggest a swaddle.

I only broke the silence when I rose to arrange my canvasses.

MYSELF: Don't go into the study either. Do you hear me?
MYSELF: Did you hear that, child? The study is out of bounds.
MYSELF: I said—
CHILD: (in a single shout) No bloody study!

Then she buried her head in her arms, & has, just now, resumed her gentle snore.

Remarkable.

Two days until Frank's arrival, & we have achieved some base level of communication!

THURSDAY 10TH JUNE, 1847

Canute is dead.

A sorrow.

A scientific & human loss.

I found him this morning. Belly down at the tide's edge. His body crumpled. Boadicea out hunting with the womenfolk, lacking any sense of ceremony. Falstaff was poking him, & uttered a solitary whoop as I approached, before he shuffled away.

He did not bother me as I first prodded, then lifted, the carcass. The other menfolk kept to their nests.

Poor Canute.

No sign of violence. I approached gingerly, hoping in vain for some small chance of his convalescence. But no. His limbs stiffening, sandhoppers already set in around his eyes. Comparable to the child in height, incomparable in weight. They look so big one expects the weight of a dog, but the most part is feathers. I know this of course, but still I am moved to find his body so light.

Brought him back to the cabin, having snuck out to catch the early sky in watercolours, when the girl was still sleeping. Of course, I did not paint.

Him & his sorry egg.

I must preserve what I can.

The girl has woken now & is watching every move I make.

☼

His body is soaking in a butt filled with lukewarm saltwater from the evaporation chamber of the still.

Must confess to feeling unreasonably distraught, & responsible for his demise. I knew he wasn't hunting. I tell myself there are no records of a human successfully feeding an auk, that Gough force-feeding his captured specimen resulted swiftly in the bird's death. It gives me no peace. I watched him pining & made no effort, & now he is dead, & I let it happen.

There are small mercies. Sir Phillip will be delighted with another specimen. The egg–bar the crack & discolouration–is well preserved, & has not grown putrid, & I have formaldehyde enough & a jar of appropriate dimensions.

Small mercies.

Perhaps better than this is the total dissipation of the child's fever. Her damn chanting has gone. She defecates outside too. I have seen her stools, dotted about the shale.

I slept like a well-fed bull seal, but woke to this.

The child herself stayed in all morning, watching me prepare his carcass, first at a distance but drawing ever closer.

MYSELF: This is Canute. Say hello, child. Heartbreak has killed him.

MYSELF: That is a joke in poor taste. Starvation killed him. Feel the weight of him. Feel him.

She would not take him, so I immersed him in the brine, & put the tub in my study.

MYSELF: Do not touch him. He is like my study. Do not touch him.

CHILD: (thru a biscuit) No bloody study.

MYSELF: Yes. No bloody study. Exactly so.

He will have to steep a few hours.

Checked on the semaphore. Washed her clothes, set up the still. Baked oatcakes. The honey is all but done, & the brandy. I have checked the auks, witnessed the changing of the guard. The female auks returning.

I watched Boadicea hopping up the rocks.

She flapped a little, settled near her nest.

She did not check for her egg.

Her behaviour not markedly different to any other day.

A sad but necessary task.

Canute's skin naturally much resistant to soaking; brine his natural medium. But I have concocted a makeshift Bécoeur's solution from camphor, salt, the warm brine & a tablespoon of arsenic & half a bar of flaked soap to soften his oily feathers.

Some hours of this, warmed below boiling by heating stones in the stove & dropping them hissing into the tub, & his skin was much softened. I cut him open carefully, prepared him for full anatomical dissection. At least now we shall have another set of measurements for Sir Phillip.

entire length, 29 inches
the stubby wing, 5 ½ inches
longest black wing feather, 3 ½ inches

bill: (dorsal), 2 ½ inches; (at nostrils), 2 ¼ inches; (in the gape), 4 inches; depth, 1 ½ inches
humerus, 3 ¾ inches
ulna, 2 inches

Sketchbook 2:

pg 17: Canute, opened. Throat to tail. Scale 1:5: Pencil on paper.
pg 18: Canute, skeleton & wing-joints, measurements. Scale 1:6: Pencil on paper.

He makes a small but not outlandish specimen. Stubby thing. His skeleton entirely intact. Beak oddly chipped at rim but the damage far from extensive, all ridges intact: 7 upper, 11 lower. His irises warm hazel; the bladka present, just under eyelid, a fragile inner lid. Wings, skull, even ribs & toes all whole.

No discoloration of the organs to suggest poisoning or disease. No injury or foreign objects in the crop or windpipe. Hard to tell if the gizzards are discoloured without established precedent but they are very comparable to a puffin's or guillemot's in colour, pale purplish-pink & crusty with shell fragments. But the entrails are much shrivelled. No guano, fluids or semi-digested materials present in lower intestines. Possible bleaching of the bladder. Again, I lack sufficient precedent. Stomach empty but for fluid & traces of semi-digested seaweed.

Altho this is my first garefowl dissection–indeed, the first systematic dissection overall of garefowl entrails to my knowledge–the emptiness of the digestive tract must clearly be the prime cause of death. It shd by all accounts be as full of fish & shellfish as would a gannet's.

He has starved himself.

In mourning.

His whole demise depressingly predictable.

Skin removal complete, I have it suspended, drying on hooks in my study. Salt, camphor, & a much concentrated solution of my makeshift Bécoeur's rubbed thoroughly into the endodermis to initiate tanning. Will apply hourly, hang at middle distance from the still to prevent cracking.

It shd be ready by the time I have the frame built.

Both the skeleton & the skin are remarkably intact specimens.

Sir Phillip will be delighted. Of course he will.

There is much afoot with the girl though.

All day, she watched. Standing just outside the partition, but as I began dissection, she crept forward by inches, until eventually I coaxed her in by the angling of my body.

MYSELF: Come on in, then. Have a look.

I said this, but we both hesitated as she crossed the threshold.

MYSELF: It's all right. You can come in now. Not later. But now.

I doubt she understood my full nuance but the gestures she could grasp. By-and-by, I began narrating my dissection with an odd childish babble.

MYSELF: So we must separate all the elements of life. The heart sits in the middle, see? That directs the blood about the body, here to the brain, here to

> the lungs. These, the ligaments—see, they connect bones. You & I both have ligaments.

She was much enthralled as I held the parts up for her to observe, & cut the meat away from the skin & bones; pointing out the parallel structures of muscle & bone either on my own arms or on her bare legs. She sniffed the entrails & lifted the stomach from my hands, the closer to inspect it.

While I initially found her presence unnerving, I grew at ease with her. Even let her touch the heart when she reached out a hesitant finger. But as I turned my back to get more hooks to suspend the skin, I returned to see the heart missing, & her chewing, chin dripping blood & likely, traces of arsenic.

> MYSELF: No! Don't eat that! Don't!
> MYSELF: No bloody bird. No bloody auk!

She made as if to bolt.

The whole atmosphere—previously studious & practically drowsy—was suddenly as violent as the day she leapt the still.

My precaution was not just for the specimen—I will of course preserve the guts in formaldehyde—and while the loss of the heart would have been a scientific tragedy, the main issue was the strength of the Bécoeur's. I did not want to poison the girl—have never heard of it ingested. But nor did I want her running off to her basket, yanking my specimen & the whole pelt asunder.

For a moment, wild-eyed, we both stared at each other.

I could believe she was a cannibal's daughter, heart-blood dripping from her mouth.

> MYSELF: (lowering my voice) It's all right. It's all right. I'm not angry. I am smiling. See? But we can't eat this. This is bad. Phlah! Bad meat! No bloody bird!

I had, in my fixation, left us both unfed since we broke fast.

> MYSELF: (awhisper) Don't run, little cannibal. You want meat?

I went to the living quarters, giving her wide berth. I cut a long thin slice of the smoked pork, a biscuit, & brought them into the whale-lit study.

> MYSELF: (holding out the food) No bloody auk. Eat this. Eat this instead.

I gestured spitting into my hand, & then put my palm out below her mouth. Slowly, keeping eye contact, she spat the raw auk heart into my hand. Then she snatched the pork & biscuits & darted out to her pallet.

I did not know what to do.

By rights, I shd have forced her to take an emetic. The salty gunk from the bottom of the still would have purged her system. But I did not believe for a second I could force her to drink it. On the other hand, I had not treated the inner organs with Bécoeur's, beyond warming the entire bird, & thus there was a chance the heart was unpolluted? But it takes only a tiny amount of arsenic to kill a man.

I followed her out to her pallet, watching her eating the pork.

She was uncomfortable with my gaze.

I scooped out some of the thickened hot brine from the still, & offered it to her, alongside a scoop of the seal pie.

She smelled the concoction, eyed me strangely, & ate the pie.

I did not know what to do.

She does not look poorly.

She is right, of course. We could have eaten Canute, had I removed his meat before applying the Bécoeur's.

Now I have the innards bobbing in formaldehyde, his half-chewed heart moulded & stitched back in shape, & have buried the jar of guts in the bookshelf behind my Humboldts, lest she shd come in in the night for a snack.

Surely the smell of the formaldehyde would disgust her?

I will warn her again.

The child is not, as far as I can see, poisoned.

She was up late in the ridges of the North Wall, by darkness, where my spyglass couldn't see her, where I dared not follow, & I could hear her hooting & cavorting, & now she has come back, finished the pie crust & is snoring gently on her pallet.

Thank the Lord.

I have resoaked the skin in yet thicker concentrate. The skeleton I have in a large pewter jar for bleaching.

I will finish the frame tomorrow.

I will rise early, to get it done before Frank comes to relieve me of my visitor!

FRIDAY 11TH JUNE, 1847

My spyglass shows nothing.

The rocks around Malin Point itself are far too treacherous, but there are plenty of launching points along the shore.

Heaven knows, he might easily charter a small vessel from some famine-starved family for a handful of pennies? He is of course more likely to leave from the far side of the peninsula, as the islanders do, tipping around the head to Portronan, or even as far as Malin Town, in which case there is no reason for nerves & he will be here before noon. My flags are upright, the day is clear.

Perhaps there is a chance the Bishop has him delayed?

But Frank knows he is my lifeline, that I would only summon him in the severest of circumstances, & am not one to whine over a bruised rib, & that this must be the very pinch.

He will be here tonight, at the latest.

It is time to celebrate.

※

Sketchbook 2:

pg 19; Lear & Falstaff; charcoal on paper.

Falstaff eating crab; oil on canvas (unfinished).

The girl, swimming; oil on canvas.

Now, on her last day, I do not feel so frustrated observing her. Indeed, when she sees me watching, she behaves merely diffident rather than actively hostile.

She could be fit as a mainland child now, I believe. I'd say she is eight. Ten, factoring in malnutrition. Her rash has faded almost to nothing; she barely scratches, the spots visible if you look closely, but by no means prominent. Her face is bruised, yes, but she can walk, & speak even a few words of English, tho I increasingly suspect she understands more than she pretends. I tried to engage her at breakfast, laid out a mighty feast of grog, raisins, almonds, & the last of the seal pie.

MYSELF: Frank is coming! My old schoolfriend.
MYSELF: Do you know what school is, child?

She ate contentedly, but drank neither grog nor lemon juice.

CHILD: *Wishke*.
MYSELF: *Wishke wishke*! More than a week you have lived on my hospitality! It's called water!
MYSELF: Let's try this again. I am Ignatius Green. Your name is?

She watched me, chewing, inscrutable.

MYSELF: You have to say it. Say your name. My name is Ignatius. Mr Green. Tell me your name. Me Ig. You?
CHILD: (sipping water) You.
MYSELF: No. Me Ig. That's me. You?
CHILD: You.

Enough to drive one quite mad. Her impious twinkle.

She appears this morning quite taken to the island. She has been here long enough, likely knows its nooks better than I do. She has abandoned her attempts at fire, & when I gathered my almanac from her little basket this morning for my ablutions, & found the knife stashed, & put it back in the cabin, she noticed, but did not raise her hackles.

A beast of the rocks she has become, in her little green coat. Still coughs. But the mark of her face is subsiding to a mustardy green.

I think I have quite saved her life.

Her sport for the day: swimming. She tugs out of her clothes on the southern shore in a midday sun. Checks to see where I am & if she sees me, I avert my gaze. Paddles in the water first. Then: her whole body ducked, comes up spluttering. The water is cold, but undaunted she submerges & ruffles like a gannet. This is repeated much, until she finally dives in proper; let waves lift & drop her, unafraid they will take her too deep. Then she dries herself on the rocks, at which point I give her her modesty.

This noon, I saw her taking eggs from the guillemots.

She climbed the lower rocks to the west. It is sheer there, but the day is dry & she gathered handfuls of shale & folded them in her nightdress, held as a clasped pouch with her mouth. The birds did not like her climbing & harangued her. This they maintained as she stood on the plateau, but from there she could pelt them repeatedly, & they shrieked & she moved closer, guarding her head with an arm, until the birds retreated from the nest.

She then sat & ate the eggs, while the birds watched on mournfully.

Sketchbook 2:

pg 20: The girl climbs the North Wall; pen on paper.

pg 21: The girl & the guillemots; charcoal on paper.

❂

The girl has just slept.

I have been at the gin all day, & dozed all afternoon, & Frank is still not here, & my head is sore. The Bishop cannot have stopped him! He knows I am desperate & he is my only lifeline!

My skin is red from dozing all afternoon in the Organ Pipes. Woke to the girl stood watching me, & reared, in sudden panic.

MYSELF: What are you at, little bitch?

But I was all right, the girl was all right & even the auks below us, growling & unfussed. She was only looking at the pictures I had made, of birds & herself.

It is night now. McGonigle's light is sweeping. There is a larger ship passing north from Londonderry, bound for Boston.

No sign of a boat carrying Frank to me.

I am Napoleon rotting on my St Helena. The frame for Canute is nearly done, but my head is too wretched for any more & my fingers are slow.

Frank, come to me. Where are you, man?

from

The Newry Telegraph

VOL. II

FRIDAY THE 11TH JUNE, 1847

FOURTH O'LEARY BAILIFF DEAD

In the early hours of Wednesday morning, an officer of the law was summoned to the premises of Simon Murphy, a bailiff associated with the violent ejectment of Martin O'Leary in February, whereupon he discovered the body hanging by the neck from the rafters. There were no signs of violent entrance, or further wounds or harm to the body, other than those caused by the noose. It was surmised that he got the noose around his neck of his own accord: but as the officer left the premises he was accosted by a destitute, who made incredible claims about the visitation of a woman in the night, who took the man's horse, which proved nonsensical, as no evidence could be found that Simon Murphy was in current ownership of a horse. The destitute's claims were dismissed after several hours of questioning. The jury returned a verdict of "found dead in consequence of suspension by a rope."

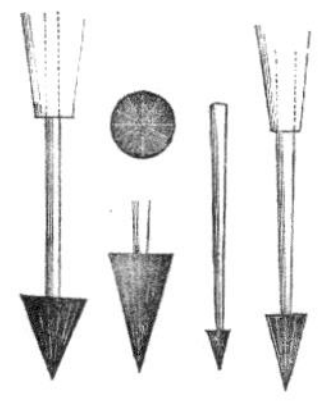

from

Field Notes on the Final Colony of Garefowl

VOL. II, continued

SATURDAY 12TH JUNE, 1847

Frank may disdain the positivist focus of my studies but the whole practice of naturalism, he has often said, belongs to the celebration of the glory of God & is not in itself to be shunned in its entirety. It is the red flag I have up. I have checked it multiple times. We were clear about the red flag!

I am beloved by him, & he will come.

The child tries my patience. She is out more & more at night. Cavorting & hooting on the ridges. Leaves the door open as she goes, slamming to & fro, & I shout at her.

MYSELF: Close the bloody door when you go out.
MYSELF: I can lock it if I have to!

When I rise to latch it, I can hear her howling. Like as not slipping on rocks as the wind blows piss back on her. Howling like a tomcat in spring. Whatever she is at, she comes back unharmed.

Still, there are small mercies.

I found, hallelujah, two huge crabs in the cage this morning, the colour of rust.

I will leave them submerged till tonight. Keeps them hidden from the girl. She may eat raw eggs & survived trace amounts of arsenic in an auk-heart, but I do not want her sickening with uncooked crab in her belly before Frank takes her back.

The little bitch!

She whined for biscuits after breakfast; I ignored her, & chased her, retired to my study, where I have been working all morning at Canute's frame. The wire is ready; a good approximation of his shape; his leather still supple enough. I lack substantial wood for shavings to give him bulk but there is leftover cloth from my overcoat & dried seaweed too. But the room was too dark & the wind was abated so I threw back the shutters.

The bloody girl was headed to the auks.

Hitching the hem of her skirt for a pouchful of shale.

MYSELF: No! No! Don't! Child, get away from there.

She did not turn, so I ran out skittering & shouting with a grazed elbow before she was at the top of the Pipes where she turned to watch me from on high.

MYSELF: Don't touch my auks! No. No. Don't eat this. No bloody auks. These are the birds. No bloody auks.

She eyed me, a lump of shale in her hand, half-raised.

MYSELF: Don't eat this. No bloody eggs. The auks are good birds.

Did she really mean to eat my garefowl eggs? Her eyes narrowed. She was not impressed. But I still had the spine of the pig, & not a little meat left on its last three ribs, & the crabs in the water.

MYSELF: Come. You want more food. Come.

I gestured her down off the Pipes. After much coaxing, she dropped her stones & leapt down to the shale beside me, & I cut her some small morsels of pig.

She scooped them, chewed briefly, eying me.

GIRL: Birds. Eat birds.
MYSELF: No! No eat birds. No!

It is in the way she holds her chin that she expresses defiance. I went into the study, got out some of the finished canvasses, & spread them on the table in front of her.

MYSELF: Look at the birds. These birds. I draw them. I draw these birds. These birds are good birds.
GIRL: Draw birds.
MYSELF: Yes. I draw good birds. Don't eat them.

I am pretty sure she got it. But then it took a turn.

GIRL: Draw birds.
MYSELF: Yes. I draw birds.
GIRL: (shaking her head) No. Draw birds. Draw birds.

She was holding the canvas, almost shoving it at me, & there was a growing urgency in her motions. She began to mutter gibberish, in Irish & it slowly dawned on me what she wanted.

I shook my head.

MYSELF: I cannot draw birds today. I am occupied with Canute.
GIRL: No. No. No. Draw birds. Draw birds.

She was getting increasingly irate. Tears were forming in her eyes for the first time since her fever passed. So I pulled out Sketchbook 2 & some fresh charcoal, & handed them to her.

MYSELF: You draw birds. You want to draw? You do it. Here you go.

Cautiously she took the charcoal. Held it hamfisted, like an assailant wielding a knife.

MYSELF: No, not like that. Like this. The finger here. Like this.

It took much trying. But she let me touch her hand, & eventually, drew a long line.

MYSELF: That's it. Draw. You draw. Like this.
MYSELF: This is a line. This is a circle. Draw a circle.
MYSELF: Look, it's a face. You have drawn a face.
MYSELF: Here are the eyes.
GIRL: Draw face.

Sketchbook 2:

pg 64: Lines & circles; charcoal on paper.
back pg 63: Girl does faces; charcoal on paper.
back pg 58-62: Circles & maybe a dog?; charcoal on paper.

I left her with the charcoal & slivers of pork. She filled the page with dark scribbles & mewled when I told her not to use the rest of the book, but she dared not go on without checking first with me, & between fetching new charcoal & keeping her stocked with what little oddments we have, I have finished Canute's frame.

I do not believe he will voyage on a Sunday, which is why, of course, we agreed he shd come on the bloody eleventh!

I gathered the crab; made soup, pease, apple.

The girl, much fascinated by my cracking & boiling of the crab. Sucked the shell as we emptied the pot, tried crunching it too.

MYSELF: Your teeth. Don't eat the shell. For your teeth.

GIRL: Teeth. Teeth.

Her speech is getting better. At least the ability to parrot my own words back to me. But comprehension of complex sentences is still absent. I tried to explain to her about the door at night.

MYSELF: You're pissing outside, that's good. Good. But close the door. Close the door. Or it bangs & I cannot sleep.

My words accompanied by basic charades. No clue what she understood, but she found much hilarity in my gestures.

There is, I suppose, some satisfaction in making her laugh.

SUNDAY 13TH JUNE, 1847

Before dawn, shouting from the shore. The girl beside me, eyes black in shadow.

I thought it must be Frank, ushered her away, grabbed my trousers, went out bleary-headed in the darkness. But as I got down to the shore, the wailing was garbled. I found myself stumbling over the rocks, to where a boat was floating in the bay, before I realised McGonigle's light was not spinning.

The boat & the voice were McGonigle's.

I thought to return for my pistol but was almost at the shoreline. I could see he was trying to stand, rocking his vessel wildly. A little rowboat, not much bigger than my own vessel. The craft was slowly revolving, & he had not cast the anchor.

MCGONIGLE: (drunk, howling) Fear More! Fear More! Mr Green. Fear More!

MYSELF: What in the devil do you want, man?

MCGONIGLE: They are dead, Mr Green. My brother's sons. They have died.

His nephews. I thought again of my rifle, but it was clear he was a wreck & I had nothing to fear. It took me a while to decipher his speech, but from what I could piece together, the fever had taken the boys earlier in the night.

I despise the man. But I know what it is to lose a child & could not bring myself to berate him.

MYSELF: Go home, Liam. Your family need you. Go home.

MCGONIGLE: They are dead, Mr Green. Fear More.

MYSELF: Go home, man.
McGONIGLE: (gibberish or Irish)
MYSELF: What avails you this? I am sorry they are dead. Go home.
McGONIGLE: (gibberish or Irish)

So we conversed. His wails & gibberish, my remonstrances. After a while, his rantings grew fainter, & he collapsed on his rump & his breathing grew heavy. An oar splashed into the water & he did not fish it out. When I heard him snort, I realised he slept.

Sleep too long out, & the tide could suck his boat out to the Atlantic, & that would be the end of him.

I was in no fit state to swim out to his rescue. My shouting availed nothing, so I tried throwing shale at his boat, to clunk him awake.

MYSELF: Liam. Liam McGonigle. (thunk)
MYSELF: Wake up, man. (thunk) Wake up, damn you! (thunk) You must go home! (thunk) Your other children are hungry & need their father! (thunk)

I think one of my stones must have struck him, on the arm or the head, & that brought him to.

McGONIGLE: Aow. Mr Green. Aow.
MYSELF: Liam. Liam McGonigle!
McGONIGLE: What?
MYSELF: Go home, Liam. You are drunk on your boat. Go home.

I heard him, splashing about. It was beginning to brighten, & I could see he was leaning out over the water, so far that the whole boat tilted, as he tried to fish out his dropped oar.

> **MYSELF:** Be careful, man! You could fall in!
> **McGONIGLE:** (inaudible rambling)

Perhaps the cold water served to rouse him. By the time he retrieved it, he managed to fit it back into its crutch the third time. The sky had the coldness of pre-dawn, & my bones felt heavy, as I watched him row first in a circle, but then southeast, roughly in the direction of Inishtrahull.

But as I stumbled back toward the cabin, he called one more time.

> **McGONIGLE:** Did you kill her, Mr Green?
> **MYSELF:** What?
> **McGONIGLE:** The O'Leary girl–is she dead?
> **MYSELF:** She lives, McGonigle. She lives. Go home.

Even with the sky half-leavening, the stars were immense. A line of blue had begun to mark the horizon, & my eyeballs ached. I cannot say for certain if he returned to his island, or if he fell asleep again & is now lost at sea.

He will get his justice soon enough, one way or the other.

This land is degenerate. Sadness rolls over it like a blight.

Artwork: Boadicea, side profile, yawning; oil on canvas.

The bladka on Boadicea's eye gives a muted veiling to her blinking, a retractable milky rheum. Her tongue–all their tongues–a warm yellow, the inner mouth orange-yellow, like *Alca torda*. She hunts with either sex now, like Lear & Falstaff, three quarters of her time on the water. Other than this, I find no awareness of the tragedy that has taken her family. No widow's lament.

Nature is unsentimental.

No sign of Frank.

Have had pease three days in a row. Crab & pease. Pork bone broth & pease. Pease & pease.

Pease are not a civilised base for a meal.

I cannot master the Indian meal.

The girl cannot tolerate it either.

But I must explain her our situation. Our supplies are not infinite, & she is constantly ravenous, & has all but done for the pork.

I beheld a new trick today. The girl knocking limpets off the rocks. Prising them from their shells, sucking them raw. There was a mastery in her method, knocking them off with a single unequivocal blow, but they need cooking. By the time I climbed down the Organ Pipes to warn her, she had abandoned the limpets for skimming shale.

Her idea is good–we have limpets aplenty–but unless we are to be poisoned, we must roast them.

She wants to draw regularly now. On waking. After breakfast. Just now. I have no second easel, & grow impatient as she vies for my stool, so I have set her up a little studio at my dining table.

Her hand is crude. She gets frustrated at her failures & drags the charcoal on the page so as to tear it, & licks it overly, gets a black tongue & lips. But she has a quiet concentration, & if I keep her stocked in paper she becomes quite tame.

It gives me an opportunity to teach her more words.

MYSELF: We are running out of pork. When the neck is bare we will have no meat.
GIRL: Meat.
MYSELF: Yes. Meat. This is meat. (I draw a pork shoulder.)
GIRL: Meat.
MYSELF: Yes. This is meat & these are limpets. (I draw limpets.) But we must cook limpets, on the stove.
GIRL: Stove.
MYSELF: Yes. Like the crab. I know you are hungry, but we must cook them. More food is coming.
GIRL: Coming.
MYSELF: That's right. Frank is coming, & he will bring carrots & turnips & take you back to your mother.
GIRL: Mother.
MYSELF: That's right. Frank is coming. Frank is coming.
GIRL: Mother is coming.

She speaks in a dull monotone, her head flat to the page, earning a charcoal-blackened cheek.

If Frank does not come, I still have my fishing rod.

Sketchbook 3:

pg 1-2: full black charcoal on paper (the girl's).
pg 3-8: Circles, lines, faces, plants; charcoal on paper (the girl's).

Sketchbook 2: pg 23: Second study of the eye of the auk, Cleopatra & Antony; charcoal on paper (mine). pg 24-25: More eyes: Falstaff, Macbeth, & the girl's eyes; charcoal on paper (unfinished, mine).

The girl helped prepare supper. Set the table, stirred the crab soup, used the spigot on the still correctly, preserving the supply. Took her first glass of lemon, gagging at first but after much coaxing, drank it down, her face balled like a hanky. In return, I have gifted her her own sketchbook–hereafter, Sketchbook 3–so she will no longer be haranguing me for my own.

No doubt she will be howling all night again. One glass of gin & I retire.

MONDAY 14TH JUNE, 1847

I have had something of a breakthrough.

I am confident Tor Mor is a new nesting site. By which I mean: these birds are recent immigrants. Which means: the garefowl can adapt, can change their traditional sites.

Thus, speculation of resettled colonies of garefowl is not without merit.

This I realised on waking.

It occurred to me to check the bones around the island, including old guano heaps among the herring gull nests & the guillemots, looking for bones comparable to Canute's skeleton; & indeed, it is my conclusion that there are no garefowl bones in significant numbers on the rock.

It did not occur to me before due to the density of bones on the rock of comparable proportions to the garefowl by the naked eye: the lack of great auk skulls I assumed was merely due to the relative fragility of the premaxillary & nasal bones. But I have compared poor Canute's ulna, radius & metacarpus to all other samples on the island, including the lower northern ridges & in the Organ Pipes. To a specimen, all samples I salvaged are much finer in proportions than Canute's: & Canute is–was–not a particularly stout or heavy bird at his death.

Which shows, to my mind, the other alcid bones belong to the razorbill. Given the rarity of razorbills on the island–I have only seen seven mating couples, & all on the far side of the Northern Wall–it had not occurred to me before to make the comparison. But my measurements appear conclusive.

This is a new nesting site.

I estimate it cannot be more than three years old.

St Kilda was hitherto–indeed still is according to most scholars–the southernmost nesting site in Britain of the garefowl, & the absence from Eldey has been interpreted as a sign of impending or actual extinction. Hopes of relict populations in Newfoundland or the Breiðafjörður have grown more desperate by the year, & reports of sightings in the Arctic Circle have proven spurious.

But here, on Tor Mor, we may have some actual hope for the species. My colony of four nesting pairs–three now–is hardly Eldey in its heyday. But if satellite communities can find new breeding grounds, the great auk might yet avoid becoming the dodo of modernity.

❊

Bridget! That is the girl's name.

A day of breakthroughs!

I cannot guess at the native spelling. Bridgit? Broibhjet? But by ear, the girl's name is Bridget.

She was bothering me for charcoal as I measured bones. The day was so bright & windless I thought I would take the dining table outside for her drawing. For a while, I put apart my bones, had a sour ale in the sun & bribed her to take a tumbler of lemon juice with a handful of raisins.

She gets enthralled in the page so quickly.

It occurred to me to draw myself; then draw her alongside it; my big pale beard, her bald head & bare legs. Little monkey ears on her, my overalls & boots.

MYSELF: Look. This is me. Ignatius. Ig. That's my name. Ig.

I wrote my name beneath it, underlined. Then pointed to the picture of her.

MYSELF: But who is this? Who is this?
BRIDGET: (pause) Me.
MYSELF: Yes! It's you. Now. This is me–Ig. This is you–who?
BRIDGET: (nothing)
MYSELF: You–you–who?
BRIDGET: Bridget.

Just like that. Bridget. She went back to her page, the looping lines, vague bird-shapes, jagged spires.

Bridget.

She went swimming shortly thereafter. I had to weigh her sketchpad down with shale when the wind picked up. Then watched the islander boats & went back to measuring bones.

Artwork: Guano, bones, a ruined nest; oil on canvas (mine).

Sketchbook 2:

pg 24: Razorbill bones in comparison to Canute's; pen on paper (mine).
pg 25: Bridget diving from a rock; pen on paper (mine).

Sketchbook 3:

pg 10: Bridget & Ignatius, caricatures; pen on paper (mine).
pg 11-18: Circles, spires, two stickmen, a goose, a dog's head; charcoal on paper (the girl's).

With the wind & hail in abeyance, one could almost believe oneself in Kent.

We cooked limpets on the griddle. I still have all the coal a man could want. We tried chewing the dried seaweed too like the islanders do. Dulse, they call it. Sweet, it is not. Raw, it is innocuous enough—a wet crunch to the leaf, comparable to shredded cucumber skin. Dried, like the islanders eat it, it tastes like a salty scab. But I thought it might enliven pea stew, & there is still butter enough as I have been inclining to suet when I can.

Fried in butter, if I squint, I can nearly make myself believe limpets & seaweed is a distant cousin to bacon & leek.

Two boats leaving from Londonderry tonight. We are sitting out & watching them as the lights pop on onboard, the natives fleeing, to new lives in the New World.

Perhaps the girl's mother is aboard.

The girl is singing a song in Irish. Repetitive, but charming.

I have laid too heavily into the gin.

I have no desire to spend my days fishing! It takes all day & is tiresome & leaves no time for painting!

The air is chilly & the girl asleep at the table. I will carry her in, before McGonigle's damn light sets the world ablaze.

TUESDAY 15TH JUNE, 1847

Frank is inbound!

I can see his boat rounding Malin Point, in a straight line for Inishtrahull. If there was any doubt, I can make out the sheen off his dome in the spyglass! If only I could signal him somehow to avoid the islanders!

He is too imposing a character to be waylaid!

Bridget, poor girl, seems rather put out.

I took her to the shale, held up the spyglass.

MYSELF: That is my friend. That is Father Francis Kelly. He is bringing us carrots & turnips!

BRIDGET: Coming?

MYSELF: Yes! Frank is coming! To take you back to your mother!

She struggled with the spyglass, kept closing the wrong eye, but when she grasped it, her face did not brighten.

Perhaps she understands better than I thought? It dawns on me, if the constabulary cannot locate her mother, in the not-unlikely event the woman has indeed fled to Boston, the child herself will no doubt be headed for the workhouse if they cannot locate her relatives.

Perhaps the girl fears this?

She needn't worry. I will talk to Frank. He has the church behind him. He will have options. No doubt a convent could take her in, perhaps even offer some form of rudimentary training for the cloistered life. If they have not the means to raise the girl themselves, they will at least be able to house her until suitable fosterage is secured.

We are saved! Frank is come!

I cannot sleep. I am too full of bile.

I will hereby make a full account of what has transpired–is yet transpiring–for Frank yet remains behind the partition, stretched out in my bed.

He thinks me a bugger.

Frank. The man who lifted me from my fug after Emily died. My schoolfriend. My longest friend. I loved him once, & love him yet, despite all this.

He thinks me a bugger! His imagination has become depraved in the church!

I had not thought I could ever write such words. I was overjoyed as he pulled into my bay, waded out to greet him, embraced him in the little one-sail he had hired in Malin Town & again in the water, grinning & full of gusto.

FRANK: You look fine & fit for a man I had thought to find crippled!
MYSELF: I am much improved for seeing you!

I held him, to fully take in the vision of his face, but already a note of querulousness, even sternness, entered his voice.

FRANK: But why did you set up the semaphore? You are not injured?
MYSELF: (laughing) I will explain it shortly. But come. You must be thirsty.

He has brought cursory supplies with him, much less than he might have, namely:

one small goose;
one gallon flask of gin;
a one lb pouch of tobacco;
one bag splints & sundry medical supplies;
one small bag of personal details;

As a restock, it is desperately short-sighted, if not outright cavalier. The goose is fresh, yes, but it is neither salted nor smoked & thus will not keep, & he knew we have not the means to smoke it. On top of this, he has brought no new staple to offer variety for digestion. No vegetal matter of any kind, but tobacco! I cannot reasonably take issue with his thoughtlessness; he is not a serious traveller, indeed, I had no thought of griping initially—who could turn his nose up at fried goose breast & gin? But now, after all he has said, I cannot but consider his lack of imaginative depth to border on negligence.

I helped him disembark the goods, attempted chit-chat, but from the outset, his demeanour was humourless.

MYSELF: How goes the parish?
FRANK: (pause) It is severe, Ig. I mean, severe.
MYSELF: You speak still of the potato harvest?
FRANK: (sucking his teeth)
MYSELF: It cannot be worse than the winter? What of the soup-kitchens?
FRANK: (rubbing his face) Let us not talk of it. It is dire. Tell me why you set up the semaphore.
MYSELF: No, come. I am all ears. Tell me of the mainland.
FRANK: Ignatius. You cannot hope to understand unless you have seen it. There is destitution you cannot imagine. There is death all over. Houses lie empty, whole communities dead or ejected. The workhouses stink of the dead. On the road this morning, I passed two dead bodies, separated by maybe three miles. Two roadside deaths, apparently unrelated. One a child, one a woman. Just abandoned at the roadside. None had taken care to move the bodies. Crows were at them.
MYSELF: That affected you gravely, did it?
FRANK: (pause) Did it affect me gravely?
MYSELF: Such sights were commonplace in Barrackpore.
FRANK: We can talk, Ig. But explain yourself, how you saw fit to drag me from my duties.

I led him to the cabin. But an iciness was there from the outset. He has always been a sharp wit, & until now I never thought there was anything but schoolboy viciousness in his barbs. He was born in the locale, speaks their tongue, despite his education. We have in the past jousted over politics, religion & my studies, but if there is sincerity in his rejection of my enterprises, I always believed him as much a man of rational thought as he is of the cloth, & more than this, he loves me.

I still think so. I can only think so.

But after he changed his sopping trousers, I offered to take him to the auks, & he showed no desire to move from my dining table.

FRANK: You are excitable, Ignatius. What is your emergency?

MYSELF: I am coming to that. Will you not first share a glass of gin with me?

FRANK: I will take water. Food, if you have it. But tell me—please—why the summons?

So matter of fact. I started to clarify the situation, beginning from the initial meeting with McGonigle in the weeks preceding the expedition, & how the theft of supplies jeopardises the expedition, & the importance of the garefowl.

He listened, hands crossed on his belly.

FRANK: McGonigle. Would that be a Liam McGonigle?

MYSELF: That is him.

FRANK: I believe I met the man this morning. He seemed affable. Is he in mourning?

MYSELF: He is mourning. But he is not affable. He is a thief, Francis. He stole my food & I want him arrested. I want him in gaol.

FRANK: (long pause) Ignatius, if you say the man is a thief, I believe you. But I do not think you appreciate quite how desperate the people are.

He gestured to the stove. I was cooking a pea stew, having cut both legs off the goose, & he talked of the suffering of the peasantry again, blackened stalks, the rise of Irish revolt. We have broached our disagreements on the Relief Act & the soup kitchens before, & I can not fathom his failure to comprehend how flooding a market with free grain would itself do untold harm to any future Ireland he might care to live in. I tried to circumvent this familiar ground, but even then, he was growing curt with me.

All the while I had been checking the doorway, waiting for Bridget to evidence herself, my surprise exhibit. For her to explode in, so I might reveal her in a humorous crescendo. Such theatricality is perhaps childish: but Frank had nothing but impatience & equivocations, so I blurted it out.

MYSELF: You are missing the point, Frank. This is not about a sack or two of meal. Your affable McGonigle has delivered me a child. A human child.

FRANK: What?

MYSELF: A child. Liam McGonigle has marooned a child with me—a girlchild, no less—in a pig's basket.

I gestured to the girl's pallet on the ground.

He stared at me, incredulous.

So I retrieved her pinafore note, gave it him.

He needed the light of the doorway—his eyesight is weakening—but he stood there, perplexed, reading.

FRANK: Is this some crude joke, Ignatius?
MYSELF: I do not find it funny, Frank.
FRANK: Ig. Come on. Aisling O'Leary? The Dogwoman of Roscommon?
MYSELF: Shd I have heard of her?

He spluttered over his words, looking from me to the paper & back again, with an indignance bordering on hostility. Truth be told, I was getting irritated by his whole lack of sympathy.

FRANK: Ig! If you do indeed harbour the daughter of Aisling O'Leary, you are harbouring a dead girl. Aisling O'Leary is a fiction. I mean, was there a real flesh-&-blood woman called Aisling O'Leary? There must have been. You have not heard of her?
MYSELF: No.
FRANK: You are being honest here.
MYSELF: Why would I not be?
FRANK: (exasperated) *The Examiner* tells of a woman in Roscommon, whose husband was shot during their evictment. Was in the *Freeman's Journal* too. But the story has been taken up by the gossips with lurid abandon—how a woman tried to bite an officer of the law; how the sheriff who sacked her home was found two weeks later with his head removed. Neither the woman nor her child were found, & in the alleyways they whisper Aisling O'Leary ate both her husband & her daughter. The story has spun out of control & become but one further symptom of the darkness benighting the populace.
MYSELF: How am I supposed to know all this? You know I do not read the Irish periodicals, Frank.

FRANK: It is in the English papers too!

We were both leaning across the table, impassioned.

MYSELF: So the woman is a popular bogey?
FRANK: Ach, Ig. In the market, it is said she transforms into a hound, or a swan, flying over Ireland in search of her child. My own mother has said she hopes Aisling O'Leary will devour all the English from Clare to Donegal. Your beloved *Punch* ran a hideous comic of her, urged on by simian paupers to devour John Bull. The last official report, I believe, was in the *Newry Telegraph*; had a woman of her description stealing a horse in Monaghan Town, but at this point even the broadsheets muddy the line between fact & embellishment.
MYSELF: So. That is it. She is a bogey, meant to scare me.
FRANK: If Aisling O'Leary is real at all, she starved to death in a moor. But as long as the papers have a way of describing Irish unrest as a primitive barbarism, they will run with the story. All the while, real Irish women starve to death in the fields.
MYSELF: I don't care about the bloody papers, man. I mean. What is this to do with me? Why would someone pretend to be her, & deliver a child unto me?
FRANK: What child, Frank?

I pointed again to the pallet.
His eyes narrowed. His blood was up.
I got the girl's sketchbook & slammed her drawings down onto the table.

MYSELF: The bloody child who drew these, Frank. The child who sleeps there. Do you think I am deluding you?

FRANK: I see you are drinking again. (gesturing to the shelf) I see you have laudanum. When did you last shave?

Curse him! I shd not have left us both to hunger so! Of all people, he shd know my dark days are behind me! But now my blood was up too, & I went to the cabin door, & started shouting.

MYSELF: Of course I have laudanum. I have camphor, & quinine too. You think I lie here De Quinceying? With this small bottle? You think this single flask would have lasted me a week in my fug? Those days are gone, man! You saved me from them. You! (calling out the door) Bridget! Brrrridge-ette!! Come here, child. Come here. When you see her, you will see. This is not some fantasy.

I threw her spare nightgown to him; medicine bottles; her unused clogs. He paused, looking at the outfit, feeling the seams. His voice was quieter when he spoke.

FRANK: Ig, you have asked me to leave my parishioners in utterly desperate times, against the advice of my Bishop, & I am hungry & tired, & I have yet to see anything that merits my visit.

He softened then. Perhaps I shd have too. Instead, I downed my drink & marched him up the Northern Wall, showed him her basket wedged in the western ridge, the chamber pot still in it. I tried to climb the rocks, but a light rain had started up, & the rockface was slippery.

MYSELF: Bridget! Damn you. Frank, will you not call out to the child in her own tongue?

We got wet. The bloody girl did not pop her head above the parapet. Eventually, he touched my arm.

FRANK: Ignatius. Come. I apologise. If you say there is a girl, there is a girl. Let us eat.

He was right. We were both getting beside ourselves. We went to the cabin where the goose-pea stew was only beginning to char to the pan, & I put out two big bowls before us, cutting one of the thighs in half, & two stout glasses of gin.

FRANK: Do you have water, Ignatius?

I got him a tumbler. Before I could start eating, he began intoning grace, catching me in my delinquency. After, we ate in silence, staring across McGonigle's letter.

The stew tasted more burnt than it looked.

Eventually I spoke.

MYSELF: I know I have asked a lot of you, Frank, interrupting your institutional rigmarole. But I put it to you that this is an emergency, & I am very grateful you have come. Whether the girl is the daughter of a bogey is immaterial to me. There is a girl here—there is!—& she does not belong here. You are a priest & have a certain position in the community. As far as I see it, you are well placed to take her to the mainland & relocate her with her mother. Who, I would wager, is not a wildened swanwoman but some half-starved slut trying to rut herself the full fare to Boston.

FRANK: (rubbing his face) Ignatius, do you have any idea how many destitute children I passed on the road?

MYSELF: Well, what do you propose I do, then?

FRANK: (sighing) If you have a child, I can take her to the workhouse in Culdaff. But it is terrible there. They have built a fever barn. The bodies pile outside faster than they can bury them.

We both went quiet.

MYSELF: That's your answer, is it? The workhouse?

FRANK: (pause) Yes.

MYSELF: What of the convents?

FRANK: The convents are out of the question.

He kept looking at my glass, but I did not let him shame me. I had expected high spirits. Now we were done eating, & I was thirsty.

MYSELF: You cannot be serious.

FRANK: You have no idea what it is like. The convents are exhausted.

MYSELF: Frank. She is but one child.

FRANK: Every child is but one child.

MYSELF: The convents will take her, Frank. Say it is so.

FRANK: Ignatius. Tell me. How long is it since you celebrated the Eucharist?

MYSELF: I pray daily, & do your little ceremony on Sunday.

FRANK: (pause) I know we have just eaten, but will you put down your glass & celebrate again with me now?

So I knelt, he intoned, & unfolded the pyx from his bag, & we prayed together. I grew aware of the sound of my own breathing. When we were done, I rose to fill my glass again, but he put his hand on the bottle.

FRANK: Tell me, Ig, are your studies progressing?

MYSELF: I am making marvellous discoveries.

FRANK: (pause) What are they?

I told him of the bones, & the auk's ability to find new nesting sites. I showed him Canute's frame & skin. His understanding is a layman's at best, but mentioning the dodo always makes an audience sit up. He obsessed, as people do, about the prices.

FRANK: How much?

MYSELF: One full skin in Hamburg last year: £9. Just the skin, unmounted. The eggs generally fetch about one fourth of that, depending on condition.

FRANK: The islanders have no idea of their worth?

MYSELF: They are simple as oxen, Frank.

Eventually I convinced him to climb to the Organ Pipes. He has grown flabby over time, but the sun was yellowish & slanting & I managed to heft & tug him to the top.

MYSELF: This could be the last colony of garefowl, Frank, south of the outer reaches of Iceland.
FRANK: They are indeed larger than a goose.

Before we climbed down, I called again for Bridget. She was nowhere to be seen. I was growing unsteady with the gin, & let Frank cajole me back to the cabin to refill my glass.

MYSELF: You will stay until morning so?
FRANK: I will have to now, yes.
MYSELF: Good. Then you will take the girl.

I was hungry again, picking at the cooled goose stew. I had the door open, hoping the scent would draw Bridget. We talked & tried to make peace. I spoke of McGonigle's trickery, the need for investigation. He of the starving & the dead. I spoke of civic duty, he of market protectionism. Even then his imagination was lurid, describing ever more grisly tableaus of his parishioner's starvation & poverty; at my suggestion that the poor must not grow dependent on the indulgent pap of the state, he countered that Ireland was the starveling wetnurse, robbed of wheat; spoke of Dame Bitch Britannia encouraging her ravenous merchant pups to gnaw Ireland's teats to the bone. He was ever thus. But eventually, as we leant towards one another, gesticulating in lanternlight, he looked up & gasped.

Bridget was at the door.

MYSELF: Bridget! Bridget, child, come in. Francis–there's your bogey! Young Miss O'Leary, say hello to the priest!

They were both rapt.

MYSELF: Bridget, do not be afraid. This is Father Francis Kelly. He is a good man. Say something to her, Frank. In Gaelic. Go on.
MYSELF: Speak to the girl!
FRANK: Ignatius, what have you done?

She looked odd enough in her little greatcoat, yes! Her legs were of course smeared in filth, as is wont to happen, as she is careless in defecation, but that would be cleared by her swim in the morning. I grant the head of a shaven child by lamplight is somewhat startling, & she is somewhat gaunt, but as Frank looked from her to me & back to her, he did not speak.

I held her out a plate of goose-&-pea stew.

MYSELF: Come, Bridget. Here is your supper.

But she was spooked. Ran in, snatched the tinderbox in one hand & a goose leg in the other & bolted, leaving me & Frank staring after her into the darkness.

We gave chase with the lantern. But she had fled like an oryx, her coat flapping. When she passed out of lantern light, we could only catch glimpses of her in the swathes of the lighthouse, her bare arse hanging as she swung up the ledge of the Northern Wall, her little bald head.

MYSELF: You shd have talked to her, man! Why did you just sit there staring at her?
FRANK: Ignatius. Ignatius. What have you done?

I had not looked at him as we ran. But his voice seemed to me oddly morose, & when I turned & saw in his face, there was wetness in his eyes.

MYSELF: What is wrong, Francis?
FRANCIS: The girl, Ignatius. The girl.
MYSELF: What of the girl?
FRANCIS: What have you done, Ignatius?

I saw he was weeping.

MYSELF: What do you mean? I clothed her. Took care of her.
FRANK: Clothed her? Her arse is bare!
MYSELF: Yes. When she climbs. Just when she climbs.
FRANK: (shrill) She is filthy & half naked!
MYSELF: She'll clean up after a swim.
FRANK: What about her hair—what have you done with her hair?
MYSELF: I shaved her. She was crawling with nits.
FRANK: You shaved a child? You! You shaved a child?
MYSELF: Of course. She was infested!

He audibly sobbed then.

I know exactly where his mind went.

We were both boarders. Had gone thru the wrungs when Father Hendrick was the housemaster, a vicious & intemperate bugger. We all suffered under him, but Frank was his favourite, & never quite put it behind him. As a young man, before he entered the seminary, Frank could grow apoplectic in his cups, about the evil that lives in men's bodies, & indecencies that are allowed to fester silently in institutions.

Frank thought me a bugger. I could see it in his eyes. I grew furious.

MYSELF: Tell me what you think I have done. Say it. Go on.
FRANK: (nothing)
MYSELF: You want to know where she sleeps? On her pallet! Some nights out here, in her basket! Likely in the rocks now, after you have terrified her!
FRANK: You make her sleep in a basket?

I do not know what I said next. I said a lot of things. I know I had taken enough gin & abuse to fan the fire in my heart. He stopped short of outright giving utterance to his grievance; but none of my answers were good enough to shake the remorse from his face.

When I told him the church had twisted his mind, he took the lantern inside to the cabin & left me alone.

The ridges were empty. Dark, light, dark, in the turning of the lighthouse. I called & called for the girl. She would not come.

When I came in, Frank was kneeling at prayer.

I strode in past him, behind the partition, stopping only to lift the gin & take my own lamp & a tumbler into the study.

For the best part of two hours now, I have endured his silhouette thru the canvas, his mutterings broken off & renewed. Heard him taking off his shoes, kissing his beads. Once he came round to me.

FRANK: Ignatius. Would you like me to hear your confession?

MYSELF: What is it you think I need to confess, Frank?

FRANK: (nodding) I will pray for you, then. It is good you summoned me. I will take the girl with me in the morning.

More muttered Latin. Heard him get into my bed while I sat on a wooden chair in my study.

I have not stopped writing since I came in.

He is snoring now. He jolted awake as the girl did her howling in the ridges & muttered his own private blasphemies. It took him another round of the rosary before he could sleep again.

He thinks me a bugger.

Any other man, I would have beaten from my door. Pulled them forcibly by the collar & thrown them into the sea to drown. Any other man.

Francis. Francis.

I will sleep in this chair.

WEDNESDAY 16TH JUNE, 1847

Frank is gone, & with him my peace of mind.

The child is still here.

Bridget. Bridget is still here.

I woke on the chair & heard Frank out on the rocks shouting to the girl. I heard him say the name, *Bridget O'Leary, Bridget O'Leary*, multiple times: also a stream of their guttural tongue. All the sloshy marine anguished cough of the Irish language. I heard her too, answering him shrilly with her sibilant chittering.

They were on the Northern Wall. She had obviously tried to light a fire—she had my almanac all torn up once again & there were shreds of blackened paper blowing in the wind. Frank was trying to climb a sharp overhang, but had neither the strength to haul up his weight nor the wit to survey the wall for an easier point of ascent. She was pelting him with stones when he popped out from the overhang, & there was a small cut on his face above the nose.

FRANK: (something in Irish)
BRIDGET: *Ai! Ai!* (something in Irish) *Ai! Ai!*

I was stiff from a night on the chair & the world was too bright. Bridget spoke twenty words to Frank's one.

MYSELF: What are you at, Francis?
FRANK: Don't stand there, Ignatius, help me get her down from there!

She was on the ledge, the wall's highest point. Frank was coming at an angle without footholds or handholds & would never get her on his own.

MYSELF: You needn't fight her so. She will be harder to take if you enrage her. The child needs cajoling.

He ignored me, trying to get his foot onto a hollow near his chest height, so he could hang like a sack.

MYSELF: What the hell is she saying, anyway?
FRANK: It doesn't matter what she is saying, Ignatius, she is a child. Just help me get her down.

I walked where her basket is lodged, where the ridge can be accessed by a short incline to a series of grassy crenellations, & stood on the edge of the wicker to get a decent handhold. Bridget watched me, & her eyes sparked, & her keening angry chitter grew mournful, a slow animal sound.

BRIDGET: No, Ig. No. Not going. No. Ig. No.
MYSELF: It's all right, Bridget. You have to go with him. Father Kelly is a good man. He will take you back. Back to the mainland.
BRIDGET: No, Ig. No. *Ai-ai-ai. Ai-ai-ai.*

I was making my way along the ridge. Thru the remnants of guillemot's nests she has ransacked. It is treacherous narrow up there. As I inched towards her, she dropped her small pile of shale, & her face sort of crumpled.

BRIDGET: Not going, Ig. Not going. Not going.
MYSELF: Come now, Bridget. It is not that bad. It is for the best.
FRANK: (below the overhang) Can you get to her?

As I reached out to her, the tears started to pour. She had not had her swim yet, her face filthy. She seemed exhausted, like she had not slept the night. At first she pushed back at me, but her strength seemed to drain when I reached out, & she let me pick her up.

So tight & unsteady we were, she clung to me on descent. I had to slide down the western ridge on my backside with her on my chest, scraping up my back on the rockface.

Frank came out from under the overhang, putting his hat back on. He was already dressed in his dry trousers. He must have been up for more than an hour. His personal bag was already down on the shore, waiting for embarkment.

He was taking his flask of gin back with him too.

FRANK: Good man, Ignatius. Good man. Let's get her to the boat.

MYSELF: I see you were good enough to leave me the remains of the goose.

FRANK: Well well well. Let's get the girl on the boat.

As we walked from the wall, Bridget clung tighter & tighter. Her sobbing increased in volume, & with it, the wetness of my collar.

MYSELF: (softly) That's enough, Bridget. Stop that now. That's enough.

BRIDGET: *Ai-ai-ai. Ai-ai-ai. Ai-ai-ai.*

Frank was tutting. I had to leap down the lower ledge as I had no hand free. Even with the child I was nimbler than him, reversing as if he was climbing off a horse.

BRIDGET: *Ai. Ai. Ai.*

MYSELF: That's enough now, Bridget. This is for the best.

Her volume peaked again as I waded into the water. Frank mute behind, watching from the shore. But, of course, it would not work. When I tried to pull her off me, she clung. Her vigour returned, & it was incredible. I had to put my hand on her face just to prise her off my collar & hold her at arm's length. At one point she had a bite on the material, & I was afraid she might tear my last good coat.

FRANK: Get her on the boat. Put her on the boat.
MYSELF: It's easier said than done, Frank.

I couldn't get her feet in. She kept kicking out at the boat, pushing it away. Frank finally waded out to help me, tutting at the wetness of his trousers. Between us, we managed to dislodge her hold on my body with him holding one arm & I the other, but she was wiry, & writhed.

BRIDGET: *Ai ai ai. Ai ai ai.* No, Ig, no. *Ai ai ai.*
FRANK: Come on, Ig. Get her in. Get her in. Hold her!

The rocks were slippery & we were struggling. Between the strength of Bridget, our unsteady footing & the tide, we were wrestling as much with each other as the girl. We were two men; it shd have been manageable. But she bucked like a grazed deer, & finally gave three almighty kicks to Frank's face, catching him hard & knocking him down, & then she bit hard on my hand right where it is scabbed, & I dropped her & fell backwards against the boat, at which point she twisted & ducked into the water.

By the time Frank & I had floundered to our feet, she had splashed to the shore & was running back to the North Wall.

FRANK: Get her! Get her Ignatius, now!

I ran after her, then slowed, then holding my knees to catch my breath. Frank stood knee deep in the water & called out to me.

FRANK: We will have to bind her. Do you have cord?
MYSELF: Cord?

FRANK: Aye. Cord.

The thought of tying her brought out a sudden weariness, & I sat down, soaked, on the shale.

MYSELF: I mean. What is the point of this anyway? You said yourself the workhouses were full to bursting!

FRANK: What?

MYSELF: You want me to tie her now? To bind her limbs & deliver her to the workhouse?

FRANK: Ignatius. Yes. Why? What do you suggest?

My head was hurting. But the whole thing seemed stupid. I had not fully formulated my thoughts.

MYSELF: Will the convents really not take her?

FRANK: They are exhausted, Ignatius, & have not the capacity.

MYSELF: So you will deliver her to the workhouse? Where you said yourself they are dying?

FRANK: Exactly that, Ignatius. That is all we can do.

MYSELF: I mean. I mean, couldn't she just stay here? I have got used to her now.

FRANK: (eyes tightening) Oh Ig. Oh. Oh. The nights are cold here, are they? Is that what you want? A little child to warm your bed? It is a blasphemy you are committing here, Ignatius. An atrocity.

I am afraid to say I rose, pulled him out of the water & punched him in the mouth. He sat down, tide lapping at him, blood running from his nose.

MYSELF: Damn you, Francis. Damn you for a bastard. I have done nothing to that girl!

FRANK: Look at her! Look at her! Look at her!

The girl was near the top of the North Wall, her lower half dangling out of her nightdress, her head a naked dome.

MYSELF: She needs underclothes, I know she does. I have not the knack. But she will not starve here. She will not!

FRANK: You mean to keep her? Here, with you?

MYSELF: Where would you put her, Francis? To die outside a workhouse? If you will not put her in a convent, then what?

FRANK: The workhouse is all we can do, Ignatius. This is no place for a child!

I was confused. Frank was glaring at me all bile & vehemence. I reached out a hand to pull him from the water.

MYSELF: I am sorry I hit you, Francis. I am sorry.

FRANK: She does not belong with you.

MYSELF: I shdn't have hit you. I am sorry. But if you think me guilty of any perversion, talk to the girl. Go & ask her!

FRANK: Ignatius, do you think I am stupid? You think I forget how easy it is to make a child sing if you mix a little tenderness with their shame? Do you think you are the first man to destroy a child for his own loneliness? Emily would die again, & die gladly, Ig, for you to save yourself.

I punched him once more in the mouth, & this time he fell badly on the dry shale, & I backed off.

MYSELF: I am sorry Francis! I am sorry! I did not mean to do that.

His face was quite bloody now. Worse was his expression. I reached him a hand again, but he slapped it away, tried to rise on his own & only managed to stand on the third try.

When he got up, he was sneering.

FRANK: Oh, but the English love an Irish girl, don't they? It is their obedience, is that it? Don't touch me! Don't put a hand on me! Shame on you, Ignatius. I am leaving. I am leaving now. You want your constabulary? I'll get the constabulary.

He had gathered his bags & his gin, struggling to heave them & himself up into the boat.

MYSELF: Frank, whatever you think I have done, it is untrue.

FRANK: God have mercy on your soul, Ignatius. God have mercy.

MYSELF: Talk to the girl!

FRANK: God have mercy on your soul, for the constabulary will have none.

He has more skill with boats than I do, even with a bloodied nose. He unrolled the sail, pulled up the anchor & in a matter of moments, he had caught the wind.

I watched him sail away on the bright water.

I called out to him twice more, but he did not turn to me.

I sat for a while & watched him go. He headed at first towards the tip of Malin, but then turned back on himself, & made his way towards Inishtrahull.

The girl came down to the shore & sat beside me.

Her face was dry, & still filthy with tearmarks, but she smiled & placed two herring gull eggs on the shale beside me. Then she went off down the coast & had her morning swim.

Sketchbook 2:

pg 26: Cleopatra at rest; charcoal on paper (unfinished).

pg 27, 28: Studies: Rocks, weeds, pencil on paper (unfinished).

Tried to focus all afternoon. Too disturbed. Witnessed a short squabble btn Falstaff & Antony over a landed crab.

Bridget came to fetch me late in the noon.

BRIDGET: Eat this. Food. Come. Food.

She tugged at my jacket. I was slow to respond, but was more use as a cook than erasing my own lines. I plucked & boiled the rest of the goose with the last scrapings of barley & an onion I found buried in the Indian meal. Refilled the still.

Then I moved Bridget's pallet into my study. Told her to sleep in here from now on, but not to touch anything.

This needed more than basic charades, it turned out. So as it darkened, I hung our laundry around the still as she ate the goose broth with biscuits, & I told her the following.

She will remain on the rock until she is either removed by the constabulary, or I deliver her back to the mainland.

If I deliver her back to the mainland, I will not leave for England until I have secured her safe fosterage.

Even after I depart, I will use my resources to find her real mother, be she cannibal, whore, or honest starveling.

For the duration of her stay, her pallet will remain behind the partition in the study.

In the event the constabulary do come, she is to be entirely forthright & honest.

It was all entirely ridiculous of course. She could barely grasp the rudiments. She was mainly hungry, for soup & then seconds, & then licking her bowl, & afterwards wanted raisins, of which the supplies are done, because she has been eating them voraciously & steals them when she considers me out of earshot, & the depletion of which she found at first incredible, until seeing the empty grease paper, & thereafter unjust.

I got down her sketchbook & tried to explain our situation again with drawings. This she found amusing at first, but ultimately an exercise in frustration. For the most part, she whined for the use of the pencil. But I pointed to Emily on the picture, & told her of death in childbirth, then I pointed to Bridget's mother on the picture, & gestured, as if to search for her, saying Ashling, Ashling, as Frank pronounces it. But all to no avail; all she wanted was to draw; and eventually I relinquished the pencil & sketchbook & washed the dishes.

Sketchbook 3:

pg 20: Island, house, Bridget; charcoal on paper (rough draft–mine).

pg 21: Island, boat, arrow; pen on paper (rough draft–mine).
pg 22: Emily, pregnant with James, alive; Emily dead, under the earth, James in her arms; charcoal on paper (mine).
pg 23: Bridget looking for her mother, a mock-up; pencil on paper (rough draft–mine).
pg 24: The constabulary & Bridget; pencil on paper (rough–mine).
pg 25-30: Bridget's loops & stick-figures, beasts, etc (the girl's).

Right now she is just tapping small dots on my picture of her mother, her head flat on the blackened page, chanting under her breath.

BRIDGET: (*sotto voce*) Mother is coming. Mother is coming.

Poor child. If she had any chance of understanding, I might try to convey how unlikely it is she will see her mother again. There is no home for her but the workhouse, or here on Tor Mor.

Go out, child, go, howling, into the night.

THURSDAY 17TH JUNE, 1847

I do not believe Frank will summon the law.

I have nothing to fear if he does. I have done nothing wrong.

Besides, he says they are overstretched.

They shd not disturb us, but I am right to be prepared if they do. Who knows but I might rely on them yet, shd McGonigle grow yet more greedy with my supplies?

The child wakes hungry. She made a mess of the biscuits on waking, tearing thru grease paper to scrape the bottom of the chest, wheedling *raisin, raisin* repeatedly, & then looking in my study to see if I had a stash secreted somewhere. I have not. The raisins are done & she must accept it. Breakfast was a bowl of yesterday's cold goose soup, but then she wanted seconds, at which point I refused.

We have remaining:

The breastmeat & remaining carcass of the goose;
one & ¼ sacks of Indian meal;
¾ sack of pease;
¼ sack of oatmeal;
three packets of dried biscuit;
much suet (four lbs?);
some butter (one lb);
salt, two x two lb bags;
½ barrel grog;
¼ barrel soured ale;
¼ gallon gin;
¾ gallon rum;
lemon juice, dregs;
coffee, one & ½ lbs.

In tobacco, coal & whale oil, I am a rich man: a two lb pouch, three sacks & half a bushel respectively. But the food we have depleted. Of tea we have but scrapings. The honeypot bare, licked & pawed clean. The child is an animal.

These to last us 15 days, & while I do not trust McGonigle's men to bring the full list without some degree of theft, I do not expect he will risk his fee outright by letting us starve. The auks, by both Sir Phillip's predictions & my own, shd likely hatch within the fortnight, & if they are indeed precocial, we can expect the chicks to swim within a week, or if semi-precocial, by mid-July. This means, depending on how badly McGonigle fleeces me, these next two weeks will be the driest spell.

We will have to get used to the Indian meal.

I have not the taste for its gruel.

It might conceivably make serviceable unleavened flatbreads in suet? My pie crust was edible, if primitive.

We can experiment with frying seaweed again, tho it is gritty & risks breaking the teeth. We can try to redevelop a taste for pease without lemon or butter, & I can move the crab cages once again.

There are fish leaping in the sea, & I have a rod & line, so even in the direst of circumstances, we will not starve.

But we are at the end of the meat once the goose is gone. When the lemon juice is gone, & the grog, our constitutions may begin to flounder.

Just a fortnight more.

So cry, child, for goose-&-pea stew. It will keep until tonight.

McGonigle's boat is headed to us, from Inishtrahull.

Five other men onboard by my spyglass.

Why would he need five men? It makes no sense. If he has a message, he can deliver it to me alone. He can have no goods to unload until the first.

So why five men?

I am ill at ease. So much that Bridget has noticed my pacing, & came ashore without trying to pull me to swim. Instead, she followed me into the cabin, watched me dig out the pistols, the powder, & stood breathlessly at my shoulder as I loaded them, trying to help, & I had to push her hands away.

> **MYSELF:** Go away, Bridget. Flee. Go to your basket in the wall.
>
> **BRIDGET:** Give me. Give me it. Give.
>
> **MYSELF:** Do not touch that! Go!

She would not leave, no matter how I berated her, but stared intently as I filled the weapons.

She has no fear of guns. Of anything. Oh, for her innocence.

I have loaded both pistols, & set them in my belt, as a precaution only.

Frank has betrayed me to the native populace.

They were after the auks & their eggs.

They have left with nothing.

Supposedly this is a victory; it does not feel like victory. Rather I am shaken. Tho I know myself man enough to take on McGonigle & his hoods, I no longer have full confidence in my safety on this island.

I hereby record our conversation & the happenings pertaining to their arrival, including the implied threats to my life & the likelihood of miscellany.

By the time McGonigle's boat was fifty yards from the shore, the girl had indeed made for the Northern Wall, where to my knowledge, she remained for the entirety of our interchange. I stood alone on the shale. Initially I thought to have my rifle out, to put the fear in them: but such an approach would be to start off on a hostile front; so I kept my twin pistols stowed under my coat, & called out to McGonigle as his men moored their boat & waded onshore, two of them carrying ropes, one a large sack.

MYSELF: How do, McGonigle?
McGONIGLE: Mr Green, sir.
MYSELF: Did you bury your nephews?
McGONIGLE: We did, sir. It was a beautiful ceremony.
MYSELF: I am glad it went well. (pause) Where are you off to today?

The men were walking straight for the Pipes; casually, but not meeting my eye, as if on the way to market. I moved myself in front of them.

Rather than bowl me over, McGonigle held up a hand, & they stopped as one.

McGONIGLE: Let us pass, Mr Green. We are here for the birds, & nothing you can say will dissuade us.
MYSELF: Birds? What birds are you here for?
McGONIGLE: You know which birds well enough. Now, step aside. You do not own this island. There needn't be any bother at all.

Until now, none of the islanders has shown the slightest interest in the birds. They were keen enough to talk about them in the early days, when we first discussed setting up the outpost. Their eyes had lit up when remuneration for their work was discussed.

But now they have realised that there might be some worth to the birds. I can only surmise now Frank has alerted them to this.

I held my ground. Three of McGonigle's men had the decency to look sheepish, but the other two were tall young fellows, with meat enough about the shoulders for a tussle, & jittery, anxious countenances.

MYSELF: I do not own the island, McGonigle. Sir Phillip owns it, & after him, the Queen. The garefowl are protected in British waters, & have been for the last fifty years. It is against the law to take them.

McGONIGLE: Is that right, is it sir?

MYSELF: It is.

McGONIGLE: Well, I wouldn't know much about that law, Mr Green. We are simple as oxen, sir. But I know we cannot eat the law.

He was not smirking.

I reached into my front pocket & unfolded my missive with Sir Phillip's seal on it. Theatre, of course; but it served for me to flounce my coat & make the pistols visible.

MYSELF: The birds are not to be eaten, McGonigle. You know this. Sir Phillip has an express interest in them. Sir Phillip, who pays your wages & takes your rent. He has given me exclusive powers over these birds. Here is my letter.

As I said this, I tried to catch their eyes. I know they can understand some smattering of English.

McGonigle's eyes caught the guns at my belt.

MYSELF: Sir Phillip is a reasonable man. I know you have stolen from me: some light theft he might ignore, given these are extraordinary times. But one thing Sir Philip will not take lightly is harm to his property, particularly in matters of scientific inquiry.

McGONIGLE: Is that the way it is, sir?

McGonigle was never handsome. I watched him shift his weight on his heels, rolling his eyes, but then one of the men behind him whispered something, & McGonigle's face split back into his wide yellow smile.

The whisperer tipped his head to the Organ Pipes.

McGONIGLE: It has been brought to my attention that you have been shaving girls, sir.

I winced, & McGonigle noticed me wincing, as I felt the depth of Frank's betrayal.

MYSELF: Yes I did. A common practice in workhouses. A deterrent for lice & ringworm.

McGONIGLE: (grinning the wider) So the girl is not dead then?

MYSELF: No. She is not.

McGONIGLE: Your priest was very worried about her. He did not find child-shaving a common practice, sir. He says you have been mistreating her in ways that would make a man's eyes bulge. Suggested we get the law involved.

MYSELF: Hah!

My anger got the better of me, then. Not a little heartbroken, I flung open my coat, rested my hands on my pistols & laughed in their faces.

MYSELF: Get the law then. You think to frighten me with the constabulary? Summon them—do so, thief—& show them the child you brought here!

Three of his men were now conferring from the sides of their mouths. McGonigle grinned still.

McGONIGLE: You think to shoot all six of us, sir?
MYSELF: I am not planning to shoot anyone, McGonigle.

McGonigle turned to confer with his islandmen, huddled together. There seemed to be some disagreement; one fellow raised his voice.

I looked around, but could not see Bridget anywhere.

McGonigle turned to me eventually.

McGONIGLE: (mock friendly) Very well then, sir! We will be on our way. I wish you a fine morning, & assure you our little dispute shall in no way affect your supplies. But the men wanted me to tell you, sir—indeed, they voted on it—they wanted me to tell you that we can get weapons too, sir.

He winked at me then, his old manner returning.

I watched them stumbling back over the rocks. Three of them bootless. Sloshing into the waves in their thin shirts.

Before he left:

McGONIGLE: One more thing, sir. I tell you this for your own good. Do not be leaving that little girl out on the rocks. She could die of exposure, & then where would we be? In the name of Jesus & the holy ghost, treat her well. If you knew who that girl's mother was, you would give her the hero's portion of your dinner!

He tipped his hat & laughed, so you would almost not believe he had just made a veiled threat on my life. All the while his men whipped up their anchor, caught a brisk wind & made a path out of the bay, leaving me stood on the stones with bright spume blowing about me.

Sketchbook 3:
pg 30-35: Bridget's stick figures, possibly a flower?; charcoal on paper (Bridget's).
Sketchbook 2:
pg 33: McGonigle & five islanders; pen on paper (mine).
pg 34-35: Monstrous McGonigle, running after Bridget; pen on paper (mine).

I am watching Inishtrahull near constantly in the spyglass.

I could not settle with the birds.

I have sharpened my pencils & drawn the faces of the men with as much detail as I can. At least three of the portraits are reliable; two of the men I cannot recall clearly enough; McGonigle I have from his weak chin to his squint.

The sea is empty. No ships tonight. If any boats were encroaching from Inishtrahull, I would see their sails in the beams of the lighthouse. McGonigle himself is supposedly the keeper, but I have no doubt another of his brood might operate the mechanism, to throw me offguard.

Against my instincts, I set the goose breasts frying in the pan & promptly forgot them, trying to see the island in the half-light. Too late I registered the smell, but Bridget had saved them from turning to charcoal with only a small burn on her forearm to show for it.

The goose breasts only slightly blackened on the outside.

I meant to save some, but she got at the second when I was out again with the spyglass, & rather than berate her, we finished it off, to silence her whimpering.

I tried to settle myself with a glass of grog.

After eating, I quizzed her on her mother. Who was she? Aisling O'Leary? But the girl was stubborn: she wanted to draw. So I dug out my own sketchbook & drew alongside her, breathing in tandem, & held my likenesses of the men up to the girl.

MYSELF: Bridget, these are bad men.
BRIDGET: Bad men.
MYSELF: That is right. They are bad men. If you see them, hide. Do you understand me?
BRIDGET: Hide. Hide.

I don't know what she understood, so I tried drawing the men with exaggerated features, Bridget in the foreground, running. I tried charades too. Which again she found very funny.

I could not impress on her the gravity of our situation.

I have the pistols by the bed.

The door I have locked from the inside.

Most likely McGonigle is just blowing wind. If they had weapons, they could have brought them this afternoon. Stealing a bag of flour is one thing. Assault & the slaughter of garefowl would see them cast from their homes.

I will sit up a little longer.

FRIDAY 18TH JUNE, 1847

The islander boats were fishing from dawn, each with no more than two men aboard, & did not leave the waters around the island.

What need have they of my auks when they can fish?

I tried the corn meal pancakes for breakfast, but struggle to get the consistency right. Without eggs to bind the flour, we ended up sat to thick suet-fried corn porridge for breakfast.

The girl could not eat hers.

I managed half a serving.

Perhaps it will improve with seaweed?

Bridget swims. She leaps into the waves & hassles me to join her in the water.

BRIDGET: Come swim, Ig. Come swim.

MYSELF: Away, you little bastard. I am occupied.

She splashes me, laughs, swims away.

I will get the rod. I am on the strand anyway, watching the boats. Try my hand fishing from the rocks. In a nook below the Organ Pipes, where neither the auks nor Bridget can see me, lest the antics of either scares the fish.

I'll bring the pistols.

Used limpets for bait & caught nothing.

The crab cages empty.

But the boats retired in the late afternoon, the men returning with moderate catches by my spyglass.

I dared a trip to the auks when I saw the boats docking. I can get a vision of Inishtrahull from the top of the Pipes.

I remain ever hopeful for imminent hatching, but no. They spend less & less time brooding, & circulate & chatter at the changing of the guard, a delicate clacking, beaks to the sky, rubbing their chests. Occasional growls—their low guttural burr.

Sketchbook 3:

pg 36: A study of the change of the guard; pencil on paper (sketch—abandoned).

pg 37: Macbeth on Lady Macbeth's return; charcoal on paper (unfinished).

I have brought the girl's sketchbook instead of my own; I will get my work mixed with the girl's doodles.

Seals! At the base of the pipes, two of them—young, blunt-nosed, male—come now between the flotilla & the nesting gulls.

I do not trust the pistol at this distance.

❊

A mid-size buck, healthy & muscular, shot in the neck.

Huzzah!

Bridget saw me running for the rifle & followed me back up the Pipes. At the summit, she saw the seals trying to assail the shore & causing a havoc of herring gulls & shearwaters. The she-auks wary but not yet manning the barricades.

Bridget was much excited.

BRIDGET: Eat this! Eat this!
MYSELF: Hush, child. Leave me be. I must load the gun.

She watched then, breathlessly, as I cleaned & loaded the rifle. Took great interest in the particulars of gun-loading again. I was not a little flustered & my form was off, in my haste fumbling first the powder & then dropping the ramrod, but she fetched it to me, held the powder & the funnel, grinning.

BRIDGET: Good, Ig. Good.
MYSELF: Hush, girl.
BRIDGET: Other one. Other one.
MYSELF: Hmm?
BRIDGET: (miming a pistol with her finger & thumb)
MYSELF: Trust in Ig, girl. We will not need the pistols.

Up the Pipes, Desdemona & Boadicea had started to hop to a ledge above the seals. They were in a line directly below us, so I had to clamber round to avoid clipping the birds. The girl understood, & nodded, gesturing to me that we should climb south of all three; this we did, cautiously.

I had to hang by one hand off the rockface, but my feet had purchase. The seals were distracted by the stabbings of Desdemona.

I got the smaller of the pair with a single shot to the throat.

He thrashed shortly, the heft of the shot turning him onto his side. It took him a moment to realise he was dead; his last throes rolling him into the water. At the sound, his brother disappeared with a tail-flick; I leapt in up to my waist, & waded perhaps two yards out, where floating like a twitching sack, pumping blood into the water, was the seal.

The gulls went wild then, wheeling & screeching. The male auks peered at me from the flotilla; the girl whooped & leapt, & splashed over to me, running & swimming in her coat to help me pull it from the sea

I burst into laughter, as when she caught up with us, she stuck her face straight into the seal's bloody neck wound & came up with a sliver of meat in her teeth.

I had to wrestle her off the carcass & sent her to wash her face. Then we bore the carcass round the tip of the Pipes, giving the auks wide berth. I was gutting it on the shore all afternoon, throwing handful after handful of intestines into the waves to distract the gulls. Bridget would not leave my side. When I paused to wipe my brow & check on the boats of Inishtrahull, she would take my place at the butchery, cutting small slivers of muscle from his body & chewing until her teeth shone red.

I cannot blame the child. So warm the blood, I found myself dreaming of soft white bread to dip into it.

I have it gutted now & it is hanging over a tub in my study.

Desperation is a fine chef. We have eaten two large steaks from the ribs, & almost one-third of the liver, seasoned with a small portion of seaweed, salt & lemon juice.

Bridget is just sitting picking meat from her teeth with a sewing pin. I am still at the stove, setting one haunch to boil with pease & a sliver of butter.

No movement from Inishtrahull.

I have my guns & the spyglass beside me, as I cook.

It seems to me weeping comes in four basic forms, all of them related in some way to an acute state of hope, or the deprivation thereof, namely;

a) Comfort crying; *a-hu-huh-huh*, *a-hu-hu-huh*. A state of lost hope, where no immediate relief is expected; despair. This was the child's crying on her first arrival; akin to her *ai-ai-ai*. Its only purpose appears to be the paltry comfort of making the sound itself.
b) Coercive or communicative crying: *Wah*, *waaah*, sometimes *A-huuuh*, *A-huuuh*, the noise prolonged & purposeful the more the plaintiff is ignored. Communicative crying is when the child has an urgent hope: desire for a thing deprived. As in Make me dinner! or, Let me into the study! or, I want to draw birds! Least likely to be accompanied by genuine tears. Comfort crying can become coercive crying in, for example, thirst. An action of the will.
c) Pained, or panicked crying. *AI*! or *Ha-ha-Ai*! or *Aiiie*! A screaming. When the child first experiences uncommon pain or terror. Often after a pause, the length of which is dependent on the

severity of pain. Pained crying hopes for the immediate removal of the source of pain, & may have a secondary effect of coercing the parent or surrogate to help: also, to induce fear in the intruder. An alarum. Rarest, unless the child falls badly, or fears for its life, or occasionally in the middle of the night with a fever dream, at which it proceeds gradually to comfort crying.

d) Silent crying; no sound, beyond occasional heaves of the breath; often accompanied by real intermittent tears. A state of hopelessness; not hope lost, as in comfort crying; rather the total absence of hope that anything can change. Most usually on waking or going to sleep. The eventual state of all other weeping.

There is of course fluidity between states: in a fever, comfort crying can pass thru all other forms. Pained crying is a high energy state that cannot be maintained indefinitely, & so must pass to comfort crying & then silent crying, &c.

All modes remain into adulthood, but only silent tears in a healthy adult, unless in mourning or gross solitude or unobserved. In field hospitals one is likely to hear both comfort & pained sobs, & I have no doubt coercive crying also, i.e. for pain relief.

Of all these modalities of hope, or rather, degrees of despair, the girl now exhibits mainly coercive crying (when her urgent demands are ignored/refused) & silent crying (at night on her pallet). But the more she has learned to speak, the less she relies on coercive crying. The faculty of language, then, may be considered an alternative for sobbing, a more precise form of coercion? Language as a utilisable sob?

There is perhaps one other form I have not acknowledged.

e) Exultant yawping, night bawling: *AAAA-aaaaah*, *AAAAA-aaaah*, at times, *Ahuuu-ja*! A loud shouting, or halloo, as of a drunk youth, or perhaps a sailor alone on ship deck. Tears wet the face & a howling is indulged. The relationship to hope here is the least clear: what does the young girl want as she screams into the night sea? Defiance in sorrow?

This last most alien to me. But tonight, in the swathe of the lighthouse, Bridget will go out to the rocks & howl into the darkness, & return maybe forty minutes later, wet-faced & ready to sleep.

SATURDAY 19TH JUNE, 1847

My hand is still working.

My eye is sealed shut, & the girl is finally asleep.

They took the garefowl.

I could not stop them.

SUNDAY 20TH JUNE, 1847

I need to set down all that has transpired.

I will do this now as clearly as I can.

☼

The girl woke me yesterday morning, quietly rocking my face in her hands.

BRIDGET: Ig. Hssss. Ig.
MYSELF: What? What is it?

She had a finger over her mouth & pointed to the shutters. I rose, at first thinking it a game, but at the flash of her eyes my stomach bucked.

I pulled the shutters back.

On the shore, McGonigle & the islandmen were mooring McGonigle's larger two-sail boat in the bay.

They were by number five.

I have since recorded their likenesses in my sketchbook, but in case anything shd happen to it, here I describe each in turn.

a) One tall man, over six foot. Lean. Had boots, white shirt, grey woollen trousers. Apparently the leader; more authority than McGonigle. The broadest & the strongest: a new addition to the party. Brown hair, full beard, lightly silvered, close-set eyes. In his prime: possibly early 40s.
b) McGonigle. Narrow-shouldered, a pronounced squint, beard sparse. Wears boots. Approximately my height but narrow in the chest. White shirt. Brown trousers. Chin notably weak. Late 30s, I suspect, but haggard.
c) One youth with a yellow beard. Possibly *Meholl* by name. No boots. Wore a bracelet of beads. The worst teeth: both front teeth missing, top & bottom sets, full lips. Torn white shirt, grey trousers rolled up at the knee.

d) One older man, perhaps approaching fifty years of age, pronounced paunch. Possible name: *Paddar*. Brown hair, largely bald at the back, low set brow, possibly missing teeth in the lower jaw. Grey vest, brown trousers, no boots.
e) Another near-fifty-year-old, similar to the former in appearance; likely they are brothers. No clear sense of his name. Less pronounced paunch than *Paddar*; also brown haired with a bald patch. White shirt, grey trousers, no boots.

Two of these men were new to the party of six that visited on Thursday: three of that crowd, as noted in my sketchbook, were absent.

They disembarked maybe five yards from the shore, wading in up to their waists, likely so I wouldn't hear the scrape of keel on shale. Two of them armed with rifles held above their heads, the yellow-bearded youth holding a long knife, & one of the old brothers wielding a makeshift hatchet, by the looks of it fashioned from a chair leg. The last, McGonigle, held a pistol aloft as he slid over the side of the boat.

Their dirty white shirts clung to their bodies.

The sea so calm, the sky so blue & windless, their clothes seemed nearly appropriate.

Bridget was shaking.

I did not know what to do.

MYSELF: Hide, Bridget. Go hide.
BRIDGET: Hide. Hide.

Her breath panicked. Her eyes trembling, & she held me by the sleeve of my nightgown. I led her to the back of the study, moved Canute off the desk, unbarred the back shutters, & let her slip out. If she went in a straight line, she could make the North Wall without being spotted.

MYSELF: Go. Hide in your basket. Go.
BRIDGET: (tugging my sleeve) Coming. Ig is coming.
MYSELF: No. I'm not coming. I have to talk to these men.
BRIDGET: Come. Come.
MYSELF: No. You go, Bridget. Go now!

I thought for a horrible instant she would start to whine, but thankfully she climbed out, skittered off.

I drank a tumbler of water.

I pulled on my boots. My trousers.

Checked the window.

They were near the lower ledge.

I picked up the two pistols & stuck them in my belt so they would be visible. The rifle was not loaded & I did not have time to reload it. Perhaps I shd have shot at them from the window, there & then. But I thought parley the more prudent choice, & sipped more water, & rechecked the load in both guns & headed out.

They had spread out in a line approaching the cabin.

MYSELF: How do, McGonigle.
McGONIGLE: How do, sir. How do indeed!

He lifted the pistol above his head in a circle, in a parody of a friendly wave. I yawned, stretching my arms overhead, so they might see my weapons.

McGONIGLE: I trust you have slept well?
MYSELF: I slept well enough.

McGONIGLE: That is a fine thing. We are here for the birds, sir.
MYSELF: I know you are.

He was grinning, the men circling out, weapons still low.

McGONIGLE: We have brought guns, sir. It would be foolish to try to refuse us.
MYSELF: Don't come any closer, McGonigle. I am warning you.
TALL FELLOW: (something in Irish)
McGONIGLE: (something in Irish)

The men stopped moving, & looked at the tall fellow, as if waiting for him to speak. Then to McGonigle.

McGONIGLE: Can I ask you to remove those guns from your britches, & hand them over to us?
MYSELF: I will not, McGonigle.

He kept nodding, muttering in Irish.

McGONIGLE: Only I notice you only have two guns sir. (lifting his pistol) We have three.
MYSELF: (nodding) Two of you will die today if you try to touch the birds, or me, or my property. Is that what you want?

McGonigle translated this, I think, to his men. But I saw at least two of them understood me, by the movement of their eyes.

MYSELF: (to them all) I know you men are hungry. Sir Phillip is sending more supplies in a week. You can split the food with me. I do not mind. But you cannot take the birds.

Two of them were smirking. The tall fellow whispered something. McGonigle grinning. The two older brothers were trying to sidle around me, so I could not behold them all without turning my head.

McGONIGLE: Is that how you think this day is going to turn out, is it, Mr Green?
MYSELF: Call your men back, McGonigle.
McGONIGLE: What do you mean, sir?
MYSELF: Call your men back–

But at that point the youth with the yellow beard made a sudden gesture. In retrospect, now, I curse myself; perchance he was merely scratching his armpit. But as he did so, out of the corner of my eye, I saw his knife raised.

I drew both pistols & fired, one gun levelled at McGonigle, one at Yellowbeard.

Both shots went wide.

McGonigle's men all yelped & crouched low on the shale.

The tall fellow stood first.

Then McGonigle coughed & stood.

McGONIGLE: That has made everything much simpler.

I threw the pistols at Yellowbeard. One of the brothers tried to get the rifle up to my head & I grabbed the end of it,

& we scuffled. I whipped it out of his hands but his sudden release made me fall over, & I thought it would go off, but it did not, & then the tall fellow was on me, tugging my vest, & Yellowbeard had hold of the rifle in my hands, & I tried to shoot him in the stomach but the gun was not loaded.

Then we were three tugging on the rifle & with my shirt, rotating on the shale, & I could see nothing as the shirt was lifted over my head, & then I got a sharp knock on the side of my head as of a pistol, & the same blow repeated three times, at which point, I sat down on the shale.

McGONIGLE: For Christ's sake man, at this distance I cannot miss!
MYSELF: Aaaaargh!

I had let go of the empty rifle, & was struggling to stand again, but now two of them grabbed me, shirt-blinkered, & tho they were scrawny I was dragged in a circle on the shale, & then hit multiple times on the head with the pistol again, until three men lifted & set me in a seat outside the cabin.

McGONIGLE: Just sit at peace man. Just sit at peace.
MYSELF: Aaaargh!

I was shouting nonsense sounds. But I was winded & bleeding from my temple & short of breath. I sat & let them pull my nightshirt off me, & tried to shake the dizziness from my head, with the tip of McGonigle's pistol in my face.

MYSELF: (catching my breath) Your gun is not loaded!
McGONIGLE: I loaded it this morning!
MYSELF: You will not shoot!
McGONIGLE: You are making it very difficult not to!

The two older brothers held me. Yellowbeard was trying to bind me but could not hold my forearms together.

YELLOWBEARD: (something in Irish)
TALL FELLOW: Hold out your arms.
MYSELF: Hah! I knew you could speak English!
McGONIGLE: He says hold out your arms. Would you not just hold them together?
McGONIGLE: (gesturing his forearms together) No, like this he means. Hold them like this.

As he held his arms out, I got one of my hands free, & made a swipe for McGonigle's pistol, but the other men pulled me back to the seat.

Yellowbeard held up his blade & shrugged.

McGonigle exasperated, knelt down beside me.

McGONIGLE: I think you do not understand the situation, sir. Think it thru now. If we want to take the birds, your being alive remains a problem for us. But we voted last night, & again this morning on the boat over, & we decided against killing you, three to two. If we reopen the ballot, I cannot swear it will go your way.
MYSELF: I will not let you take me.

I tried to push against them again, but I was losing strength. There was fast talk in Irish. The tall one got his knee on my shoulder, & thus they got my arms in place & bound me fast as rigging.

McGONIGLE: That's the fellow. Good on you.

The ropes were strong enough. They tugged on them, conferred, then four of them went into the cabin, leaving me trussed outside with McGonigle. He took out my other stool & sat in front of me as his companions brought out my belongings & lined them on the shale. Canute. Canute's egg. My fractured guillemot skeleton. My brassware, my spyglass. My rifle & powder. Shot. The flour, my camphor. My laudanum. My globe.

As they worked, McGonigle waved his pistol about, chatting over the array of my ransacked particulars as if we were merely conversing over the sale of cattle. His eyes widened as he picked up Canute.

McGONIGLE: This is one of your big birds, is it not, Mr Green? What would you say a fine specimen like this would fetch over in London there?

MYSELF: You are not starving!

McGONIGLE: Ach, come now. Give me an estimate.

As he spoke, he inspected Canute, stroking his plumage, then scratched at a cut on his jaw with the tip of the pistol.

MYSELF: None of you are starving! There is no blight on Inishtrahull! I see you fishing every day. You are doing this for greed! For greed!

McGONIGLE: That's an unfair simplification, sir. That big fellow there is from the Glenties.

MYSELF: You are an imbecile!

McGonigle shrugged. I watched as the men opened my chests, throwing out my smalls, my sewing kit, pillows. Two of them had broken the clasp on my chest of biscuits. There was little enough left in it, but they gathered around it, munching quite happily, until the tall fellow shouted at them to get back to work.

McGONIGLE: Where's the girl, Mr Green?
MYSELF: You have not thought this thru, McGonigle! What will you do when Sir Phillip hears of this? You will be hanged! What about your family?
McGONIGLE: Oh no, I have thought about this an awful lot, sir. I mentioned hanging myself a few times, to all these fellows. But as my wife says, Mr Green, Sir Phillip cannot see everything that transpires here, & I have the idea that you will not tell him.
MYSELF: (I lost myself to obscenities.)
McGONIGLE: That's terrible talk, sir. Please. Where's the girl?
MYSELF: I will kill you, McGonigle.
McGONIGLE: Me? I am your greatest friend, sir. I have been arguing your case all morning. I convinced these fellows, at great length, you would write to Sir Phillip asking for more supplies. I also told them you had an expertise we are lacking in getting a sale for the birds.
MYSELF: You think I will help you? (spitting at him) Ha! Why would I help you?
McGONIGLE: (wiping his face) That's what they said, Mr Green. Just what they said. But I told them you'd come round.

They had started unloading the canvasses, stacking them on the shale like baking trays. When I saw them break the glass on my butterfly case, a sob escaped my throat.

MYSELF: The priest! You have forgotten Frank!

McGONIGLE: Father Kelly? Oh, I would not count him among your bosom-friends, sir.

Francis would not let me die. I cannot think it.

There was a shout from the cabin. The tall fellow came out & started chattering in Irish with McGonigle. They raised their voices.

McGONIGLE: No. My thinking is, you'll come round, given time. I hope so, for your sake, honestly. But now, come, Mr Green. Where is the girl?

MYSELF: (blinking, looking up at the sky)

McGONIGLE: Where is the girl, Mr Green?

MYSELF: (silence)

TALL FELLOW: (something in Irish, barked)

McGONIGLE: Mr Green?

MYSELF: She is dead. She had a fever she could not shake, & she slept on the rocks, & now she is dead.

McGonigle's eyes narrowed.

The tall fellow spoke short, harsh sentences.

McGonigle turned to him, whispered, & appeared to argue, then turned back to me.

McGONIGLE: Where is the girl?

MYSELF: In the sea. Dead. In the sea.

McGONIGLE: You are lying. The priest saw her. Alive.

MYSELF: I told you from the start she would die. She injured my hand & I would not let her sleep in the cabin & the fever took her after the priest left.

McGONIGLE: Your hand?

MYSELF: She injured me! Look at my hand if you don't believe me!

McGonigle squinted, said something to the tall fellow. They moved cautiously behind me, & I felt them poking my hand where I have the binding on it. The tall fellow grabbed my two arms up behind me to examine the wound & made me cry out with his poking; then he came up to my face & shouted at me.

TALL FELLOW: Where is the girl?
MYSELF: Dead. She is dead.

They conferred more. One of the brothers came out & joined them. They raised their voices. The tall fellow kicked the stack of canvasses over the shale, & punched me twice, hard, on my ear, knocking both stool & me to the ground with the second blow, & then all but McGonigle went back inside.

McGonigle crouched to me, down close to my head, scratching at his beard with the gun.

McGONIGLE: Are you being honest with us?
MYSELF: (silence)
McGONIGLE: You are lying. You have not killed her.
MYSELF: (silence)
McGONIGLE: You had curatives & sustenance aplenty, sir. I know for I brought it you. You gave nothing to help with my nephews. Not a thing, sir.
MYSELF: (silence)
McGONIGLE: Tell me you haven't killed her. You don't want to have killed her. Her mother is a terrible woman. Did you kill her?
MYSELF: I let her die.

McGONIGLE: I did not think you would let her die, sir. My nephews are nothing to you, but you could see the girl. Every day. I did not think you capable of that.

They had brought out all portable goods now. Even the seal carcass. They left them all on the shale, uncovered, & we sat & watched the gulls come down to worry strips of seal meat. They had separated the goods into two piles: one of perishables & fragile goods, one of imperishables. They showed no interest, bizarrely, in the books. These they kicked about, trampled, let them flap in the wind; loose pages let blow away–idiots–the price of the books would far exceed the clothes they took. They flicked thru the canvasses idly, then cast them likewise over the shale. Nor did they take the still, tho I heard them, huffing to lift it, banging it, struggling to unmoor it from its base, still hot & full from the night.

They had no interest in the sack of pease, or the Indian meal.

Done, they turned back to the last of the tack, & munched it stretched out on the shale, conversing in Irish.

McGONIGLE: Tell me when she died.
MYSELF: (silence)
McGONIGLE: When? Go on. How did she die?
MYSELF: Who is the girl's mother?
McGONIGLE: Did you leave her to sleep in the rain?
MYSELF: Tell me of her mother. Is she a cannibal?
McGONIGLE: The girl's mother? A cannibal? Mr Green. The truth is the girl you say you let die was the daughter of a very prodigal woman. A very prodigal woman. Did you make her sleep outside?
MYSELF: (snorting) You mean prodigious, you cretin.

McGONIGLE: Do I? Prodigious then. A very prodigious woman. Honestly, Mr Green, I would not like to be you at all.

McGonigle would not make eye contact with me after that.

Here is a list of what they took.

one seal carcass, gutted;
one wall-hung timepiece (brass);
one pocket-watch (silver);
one barometer;
one sack of feathers;
my two remaining feather pillows;
two diverse sets of medical supplies (bandages, camphor, etc);
a complete set of brass taxidermy tools;
one gallon bottle of spirits (this the last of the rum & the gin, that they mixed into one bottle, the other being cracked in transit);
two bottles of Sydenham's;
one bottle of camphor;
some butter (one lb);
one purse contained £5, 10s;
one & ½ lbs salt;
Canute's egg, in formaldehyde;
Canute, the specimen, himself;
my lepidoptera case, cracked;
one guillemot skeleton (complete & hung);
two sacks, coal;
½ bushel whale oil;

cutlery (all);
cooking utensils (various);
five plates;
two sets of bedsheets;
two pots;
one fishing rod;
two washing tubs;
toothpowder & soap;
one set of rubbered boots;
my good all-weather coat;
various other clothing & particulars;
my globe;
my spyglass;
the remainder of the goose-barley stew.

These they first piled on the shale, then after biscuits, carried barefoot down to the shore, where the balding brothers lifted them & waded out, depositing them in the boat. It took them half the morning. Afterwards they all sat & chatted in their skittering tongue. Yellowbeard kept glancing over, until he righted my chair, heaving me upright. The tall fellow shouted at him then, & then Yellowbeard set me back on the ground, gently as he could. Then they loaded their guns, my pistols & rifle included, from my own supply of powder & shot, as the others took drinks from my brandy/rum mixture, smoking my tobacco as they stretched out, drying their trousers in the sun

They turned to the last of the goose stew, ate it, & there was much discussion. I tried at times to make some sense of it, but could not follow, other than occasional gestures to the Organ Pipes. Finally they rose.

McGONIGLE: Tell me, Mr Green. If you killed her, we will need to provide evidence of the girl's death. Where is her body?

MYSELF: (silence)

McGONIGLE: You said you threw it in the sea, sir. That will not do. We will need the body.

MYSELF: Go tell the fish, McGonigle.

The tall fellow came over & thumped me on the head, into the shale. He has a strong arm. Then they conferred again, & Yellowbeard went off roaming around the perimeter of Tor Mor, as the two balding brothers headed for the boat, & McGonigle & the tall fellow pulled me from the chair & dragged & pushed me up the Organ Pipes, with my hands tied behind my back.

☼

This is how they disposed of the birds.

The male auks were out hunting, & Boadicea too, & the brothers took the boat around to the far side of the flotilla. The water looked treacherous, but the brothers were deft & manoeuvred slickly with the oars & made a commotion clanging my own pots, with my own spoons, to worry the birds inland. Antony & Boadicea dived early, & proved too bothersome to corral with the others, but somehow the commotion of the pots disturbed the diving instinct in the others, & by the time I was manhandled to the top of the Pipes, the rest of the auks stood in the foothills of the Organ Pipes, observing the spectacle of two fat brothers in the rowboat.

I made a ruckus, kicking shale & shouting, trying to spook the birds into the water, but they have grown used to me calling for the girl, & paid me scant heed. They have no fear of land predators. My own presence has inured them to men.

I got a thump in the jaw for my efforts.

Then I witnessed the famed stupidity of the birds.

First Desdemona, disturbed from her nest, was hauled up by McGonigle & bit him on the sleeve & was bound by the legs like a turkey & cast to the ground. One of the brothers had leapt from the boat to spread their corralling powers about the shore, while McGonigle & the tall fellow kept their noise low & moved slowly.

Othello bit the tall fellow on the hand & drew blood, & had his neck wrung for it, a breathy squawk his last sound, & I howled.

Lear & Cleopatra were trussed about the legs like Desdemona. McGonigle bound their beaks to prevent any more bites. His touch had the delicacy one would expect from a farmer birthing a lamb.

The tall fellow stood on Cleopatra's egg & loosed a fit of oaths. Then he took Desdemona's egg with especial care & gave it to McGonigle who placed it in my own leather satchel, wrapped in a section of cloth cut from my bedding for that purpose, & altho I was close enough to kick his legs, I could not bring myself to do so, for fear of harming the egg.

TALL FELLOW: Are these all the eggs?
MYSELF: I knew you could speak English!
TALL FELLOW: (cuffing me twice) Are these all the eggs?
MYSELF: There were two, plus the last, in formaldehyde at my cabin.

Lady Macbeth finally realized the threat, but was unable to find egress to the water. She had joined Falstaff & Macbeth in a huddle at the lowest part of the Organ

Pipes proper, as McGonigle & the tall fellow crept down towards them. There was at one point a scuffle, & Falstaff managed to get out under McGonigle's arm; but the tall fellow grabbed Lady Macbeth between his legs & Macbeth by the neck & beat him to death while pressing Lady Macbeth into the rock with his knees.

McGONIGLE: (shouting in Irish)
TALLEST: (shouting in Irish)

McGonigle rescued Lady Macbeth from the thug's legs & bound her just below me on the rocks, & had I flung myself off the ledge I could perhaps have saved her, but we would have both fallen off the rocks, & likely harmed Lady Macbeth, who was biting for air until McGonigle bound her beak, her eyes blinking wildly.

At this point, it was almost over.

The tall fellow was at this point shouting, & watched one of the brothers take off in the boat after the three remaining auks on the water. Then he went off to the top of the Pipes & yelled in Irish, most likely to Yellowbeard, who was yet to join us.

McGonigle leaned on the wall beside me.

McGONIGLE: Stop sobbing, man. There was nothing you could do.
McGONIGLE: No, but listen to me. Sad as this is, it might play to your advantage. If the girl is dead, we quite own you, sir. You will not go to the law. All the wives of Inishtrahull saw you with the girl, sir.
MYSELF: Go away, McGonigle. Leave me be.
McGONIGLE: No. Don't you see? We need you alive, because Aisling O'Leary will come looking for the

girl. You, in turn, cannot go to the constabulary. Not with a girl's death on your hands, & the testimony of a priest on you. So why would we need to kill you?

MYSELF: Go away.

McGONIGLE: I appreciate it's complicated, Mr Green. But in some ways, the girl's death is your ticket! For a few weeks at least, it's your ticket!

Feathers swirled about us. Desdemona was straining her neck, quite helpless, the only auk alive ashore with an unbound beak, but she could raise no more noise than a few faint clacks at the back of her throat. Her head dangerously close to the tall fellow's boot. I watched as he bent & shoved them one after the other into two large oatmeal sacks.

Then everything stopped.

Far on the other side of the Organ Pipes, someone was screaming.

A man was screaming.

Yellowbeard. Yellowbeard was screaming, somewhere near the cabin, out of sight.

McGonigle rose from my side. The brother in the boat stood up. The brother on the shore was the first to move, clambering up the rocks towards us.

The tall fellow went quiet, & bound the sacks closed. He crawled to the top of the Pipes, peering over; then in silence, he threw the sack of auks down the other side of the Pipes.

Likely that is the moment Desdemona & the rest of them died.

My cries were drowned out by a further scream from Yellowbeard.

I watched as the tall fellow climbed over the ridge, silent, followed by McGonigle & the fat brother.

Then there was a gunshot.

Another scream.

A deeper, man's scream.

Then there was shouting in Irish.

Whooping. The girl's whooping. Bridget. I could hear her voice, whooping, from somewhere over the ridge.

The last brother on the boat started rowing furiously round to the southern shore.

I forced myself to stand. I was utterly confused. My only hope was that someone had arrived: a repentant Frank, the coastguard. My arms were bound & I was dizzy & I struggled with swooning, & had to lever myself up by pushing my face into the rock.

There was much shouting & two more gunshots.

When I got to the top of the Pipes, this is what I saw.

Yellowbeard was wading into the water. His face was covered in blood & he was howling. There were cuts on his face & his left arm had been severed at the elbow, & he was cradling the bloody stump as he waded towards the boat.

Bridget was sat outside our cabin. She was covered in blood up her arms, all over her face & chest. The long knife Yellowbeard had been carrying was on the ground beside her. She had made it to the pile of guns outside the cabin, all freshly loaded, & had shot at the islandmen. The tall fellow she had hit twice, once in the ear, perhaps as he climbed down the Pipes, & once in the stomach, & he appeared to be bleeding quite rapidly from between his fingers. McGonigle was holding the sacks of auks & trying to help the tall fellow stand. The bald brother was standing beside them both, still holding a pot & spoon, prevaricating.

Bridget was reloading the rifle, tapping the ramrod home.

McGonigle started shouting at the brother.

Bridget looked up, whooped, & started deftly reloading the pistols too.

The tall fellow shouted & kicked out at the brother.

I roared & tried to thrust myself down the rocks on top of them, falling from the top of the Pipes. I hit the rocks first with my shoulder, & then my body spun, & I hit my head.

The pain was severe.

With the angle I had fallen, I could only see rock.

There were two more gunshots.

More shouting in Irish.

Shots.

The air smelled of gunpowder.

I blacked out.

I screamed when I came to.

Bridget had the knife & was cutting at my ropes with short stabs. I sat up & found myself too pained and exhausted to stand.

The girl pushed me, pulled me, abandoned me, brought me water, pushed me, shouted gibberish at me, pushed me, but I could not find my legs, or the will to move, or speak.

I was overcome.

I have found my legs now.

But I am still overcome.

The men have gone. My still is broken. The cabin is stripped bare, but for my bed & torn bedding & my scattered books. The men's abandoned cups & their guns & my own guns & my powder & tinderbox & tobacco & my coffee are all I have left, kicked about the shale in front of the cabin.

They ran. Left their guns.

The girl chased them. Bridget.

I have no idea how many of them she shot.

At least she got the tall fellow. In the stomach. At least that.

A shot in the stomach should do for him.

But the rest of my goods they have taken away in their boat.

My auks also.

All the food we have left is half a bag of pease, a smear of suet & half a sack of Indian meal.

The beach is covered with pages flapping in the wind.

I spent hours trying to gather the books again, but now have I given up.

It was near dark by the time I thought of the rowboat & making a last push for the land. But McGonigle's men had considered this too; they have staved a hole in the rowboat's hull.

Limpets! We can eat limpets!

With no pot to cook in.

They took even my rod.

The crab cages they have left. But they are empty.

We have been left to suck the pease dry.

This caused me unreasonable mirth yesterday.

Now I have tried it, it is not so funny.

We have a full tank of sweet water purified in the still. If we are cautious & only wash in the sea, there is a good chance we will not die of thirst this week.

I still have grog. Half a barrel of grog!

They took the whale oil, so I must write during daylight.

I had the presence of mind for one thing yesterday. I went back to the nesting site. Feathers were blowing like my pages to float on the tide. Macbeth's body was there. They had not managed to get him in the sack. So here lay Macbeth, on the shore.

I was quite broken to see him.

His egg was intact in its nest. They had not found it, but killed the father & taken the mother, leaving the egg orphaned, possibly for the last few days before it hatched.

For all I knew, the men had caught the other three auks. I could not see them on the water, or the shore. Falstaff, Antony, Boadicea. The last I had seen them, they made a small, worrisome flotilla, beholding the massacre.

My instincts took over—the reformed öologist—my old egging rituals. I cleansed my scent in the sea, smeared my hands & arms utterly over the elbow in guano from Boadicea's nest. Between my fingers, near up to my shoulders with shed down & shit, to remove all traces of my human stench, so it caked me thoroughly. Then very carefully, I rubbed Lady Macbeth's egg in the same down, glued it on with guano, & placed it on the bare rock of Boadicea's nest.

Macbeth's body I took to my mattress, & fell asleep holding him, lest Bridget seize him in the night.

But I am glad of my instincts.

There are three garefowl alive yet. I am sure of it.

The lighthouse did not come on in the night.

Bridget harangued me for food all morning.

I do not know if she ate last night. I have tried to get her to suck the pease, tried to mix cornmeal into a paste in a tumbler, but she would take none of it, & kept gesturing to Macbeth's carcass.

MYSELF: No, Bridget. No.

BRIDGET: Yes. Eat this, Ig.

MYSELF: Not yet. There is grog. Have some grog.

When I refused to relinquish his body, she went to the North Wall, perhaps looking for eggs, perhaps a live gannet.

I hope she finds something to placate her.

I do not feel particularly sane?

It is like when Emily died. But there is no laudanum & no street corner druggist, no discreet little golden phial. My head hurts all the time. My mirror is splintered, & what I can see of my face is not handsome. I have taken to carrying Macbeth with me at all times, lest the girl bite into him when my back is turned. I have been wandering around all day thus trying to piece together some plan of action & I weep intermittently. My only idea so far is to take off one wall of the cabin, to use as a raft.

But it is unworkable.

Macbeth's eyes are shut. A mercy.

His neck has gone stiff. A mercy.

There is no movement on Inishtrahull to the naked eye, but I have no spyglass & the light slants into my face.

We will end up eating Macbeth.

There are yet two things that stop me walking into the sea.

The girl, the girl, the bastard girl.

The three great auks have indeed survived.

Falstaff was the first I saw. Squat. Alive. I found him sitting on the egg in Boadicea's nest.

This evening. Maybe two hours before sunset. I have no timepiece but the sky.

The other auks were hunting out in the water.

When I first found Falstaff I hid, not crediting my own eyes. I did not want him to see me with Macbeth's body & shoved it deeper under my overalls. I do not think he saw, but maybe he smells it: he was discomforted by my presence, & clacked at me, even tho I did not come within five yards of his nest.

Maybe he thought I would kill him.

Maybe he has learned too late to distrust me.

I held back. But I wanted to stay near him, to lie & sleep up in his presence, but I am worried of drawing the girl in her hungry state.

I do not know the state of the egg, but I know it was intact when I left it. Falstaff is brooding on it. That will have to be enough.

BRIDGET: Come, Ig. Make fire. Make fire.

She has got this idea of fire into her head. She has been building a pyre all day. Broken bits of furniture, the boat, the bindings of books. We still have a tinderbox, & after the ransacking of the hut, the cabin is rich in broken wood from the torn partition.

She is making a great stack of wood & will not heed me when I try to discourage her.

She is eyeing Macbeth, & is plying me with grog, I think to weaken my hold on him.

She plans on eating him tonight.

I know she does, but I do not want to.

Boadicea, Antony, Falstaff.

You escaped.

The girl is not dead.
Nor is the egg.

☼

WE HAVE MADE FIRE.

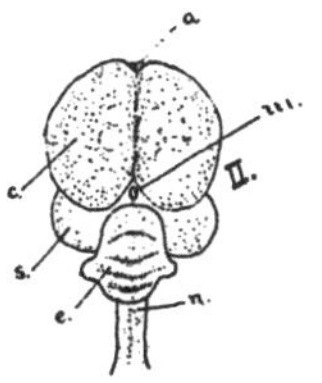

MONDAY 21ST JUNE, 1847

I woke to a herring gull on my chest, looking into my face.

They have been walking around my head, & I think, poking at my overalls. They thought me dead.

The girl was watching & laughed as I started.
I have slept on the shale, like a vagrant.
The day is too bright.
The sea is loud.
The world is loud.
I drank too much grog.
Everything hurts.

BRIDGET: Swimming. Come swimming, Ig. Come swimming.
MYSELF: Piss off, child.

She keeps pulling me by my overshirt & trying to get me to open my eyes to the unholy sun. She laughs when I shout.

BRIDGET: Come swimming, Ig.
MYSELF: Leave me. Leave me be.

We ate Macbeth last night.

The gulls are raucous, tugging at his skin. His empty skin.

I need to patchwork my broken memory together.

☼

The night returns in gelatinous dribs & drabs.

The girl was hungry. I knew what she wanted—Macbeth—but I would not relinquish him. So, she built her fire, coaxing me first for the tinderbox, then making me light it when the wind picked up. I acquiesced; I knew she was thinking to roast him, but I kept myself deliberately obtuse & hoped to placate her with roast limpets smashed off the rocks & seaweed—*Palmaria palmata, dulse*—in sheaves. Offered her grog to wash it down.

But she has not the stomach for limpets or grog.

Kept making grabbing motions at Macbeth under my shirt.

BRIDGET: Eat this, Ig. Eat the bird. Eat it.
MYSELF: The seaweed is good, Bridget. Good seaweed.

I was washing down mouthfuls of the stuff. It was making me nauseous. She kept adding wood to the blaze. Bits of boat, the cabin partition, even seaweed. Every time my tumbler was empty, she would take it & refill it at the barrel. It helped ease the gnawing of my stomach somewhat, but she was not taking any herself.

It was making me drunk.

I tried to engage her in some kind of conversation about her mother. It was pointless—neither of us has the language & I was slurring my words. I tried to draw a woman on the back of some loose pages of Humboldt, pointing, saying "mother" & "Aisling," but it was dark & she was so engaged in coaxing her inferno, we could make no headway, & at some point in our altercation, Bridget threw my scribbles on the blaze too.

MYSELF: Bridget. Your mother. Did she eat your father?

BRIDGET: Eat this, Ig. Eat the bird.

MYSELF: Leave it. Bridget. Tell me. Your mother. I mean—your father. Is he dead?

BRIDGET: Mother is coming.

MYSELF: Yes, your mother. Who is she?

BRIDGET: Eat the bird.

Her blaze was terrific—a terrific waste—of books & resources, but I was addled. Ursa Minor & all the wide constellations were popping in the sky & we could finally see their true brightness undisturbed without McGonigle's damn light swinging.

I asked Bridget if she had shot McGonigle, acting it out.

She laughed at me.

I laughed too & fell over.

I thought for a moment that I could speak Irish, & garbled gibberish at the girl. She spoke back, gibberish, Irish. I imagined we were on the cusp of conversation. I think it was after that she disappeared into the rocks, then, shortly after, she emerged from the darkness, carrying a human forearm.

Yellowbeard's severed arm.

She threw it to roast on the fire.

I picked it out of the blaze, burning my fingers & part of my beard; as I beat the flames down, I shouted at her. Good God. A hand attached to a bone. We both roared at each other. Gibberish. I asked her if she had chewed it already. She started crying.

MYSELF: Don't eat this! Don't eat this!
BRIDGET: Eat this, Ig! (gesturing at Macbeth) Eat this!

I ran stumbling to the sea & I threw the arm into the waves.

Then I got the long knife & cut open Macbeth.

I was lucky not to lose a finger.

I remember throwing the guts hissing into the fire: tugging him roughly from his skin; the surprising slickness of the meat after so many days stiffening. I remember giving up on preserving his head & severing the neck & twisting him roughly apart. Impaling his body on a partition-joist, as Bridget added yet more wood to the blaze. I kept saying I was a cannibal. I think I was weeping. I think I was laughing.

MYSELF: McGonigle! McGonigle, you bugger! I will gut you! I will eat your eyes!
BRIDGET: Mother is coming! Mother is coming!

The girl wanted it raw, but I smacked her hands away, & we sat watching it drip fat into the fire, charring the wings, then its back: then we stuck our fingers in the rich meat, gorged ourselves, pulling off juicy blackened sections of leg, breast, ribs.

The meat was delicious: redder than goose & salty.

Bridget danced in the firelight, howling. I walked into the sea, sobbing, screaming at McGonigle's dark lighthouse.

Macbeth's skeleton & what remains of his pelt has been picked to a thin tatter of leather by the gulls.

I must be clearheaded.

Sir Phillip will not be alerted to my absence for weeks.

Barring the semaphore, I have no means of signalling anyone. Frank will not come back. He will not want to see me again. Nor I him, if I'm honest.

But there is a chance he has alerted the constabulary.

This is, I think, our one shot at survival.

Either they come for the girl, to quiz the cannibal's child, or they come for me, under suspicion of sexual depravity.

Either way, they would take us to the mainland.

Whatever happens, we will need to eat tomorrow.

This must be a priority now.

The crab cages empty.

I checked on the auks.

It is a miracle. Their entire colony is broken. Their fellows slaughtered–spouses, friends, rivals. Yet Boadicea was brooding on the egg.

Falstaff & Antony on the water, in their little flotilla of two.

Boadicea, the absentee mother, who would not brood on her own egg, will sit warming this little outsider. Falstaff, the bachelor, philanderer & would-be adulterer, to my knowledge never a family man, last night taking up his paternal duties with the warmth of his belly. Antony, widower, coward who abandoned his wife to a sack, remaining, their surplus guard.

The colony is finished.

Yet here, in its ruins, they tarry around an egg.

A miracle.

I have taken the broken flask of rum & washed it of fragments & smoothed its sharpness with the rough edges of shale. Much like the clay pot the Indians cook with, I believe we have some chance of a serviceable stew by mixing brine with pease & Indian meal, & heating this little flask-pot in the ashes.

We could well eat nigh a fortnight thereof, had we but clean water to drink with it. We will not have clean water for more than a week, at the most. The coal is gone, but we still have books aplenty to burn, broken wood, & a pile of abandoned canvasses. But they do not provide sufficient heat for a full load; & even had we the coal, the belly is cracked, & I have neither the tools nor the mastery to fix it.

My pot-stew is terrible, but edible.

The girl is cantankerous after her late night & a morning of swimming. She has mooned, cried excessively, rejected offers of paper to draw on, will not be coerced into games of naming things in Irish & English.

At dusk, she waved at the Organ Pipes.

BRIDGET: Eat this, Ig. Eat birds.

MYSELF: (professing to love the stew) No, Bridget. No no no. Eat the stew. The stew is good.

She howled, whined, cried. Tried plying me with grog once again so I might perhaps give in, but I would not touch it. She spat on me then, at which point I roared at her, & she headed up the ridges to howl.

She is back now.

She has thrown herself into her pallet & snores.

I do not believe she will go for the auks when I sleep.

I will not let her.

Her hair is growing back. Brown, with a little curl.

The lighthouse is on again. McGonigle must have survived, & has returned to wind up his beacon.

I will load the pistols in case he returns.

TUESDAY 22ND JUNE, 1847

The chick has hatched.

It sits under Falstaff's wing.

I dare not move closer.

Boadicea left maybe thirty minutes ago, as Falstaff returned with his mouth packed with capelin: the chick whined & peeped much like a guillemot chick, & this gave me a chance to look at it.

Inner mouth yellow. Much bigger than a razorbill hatchling–roughly double the size & plumpness, the down heavy & bright grey, rather than snow-white: the colour of Irish clouds or fresh guano. Fragments of shell still clung to its down, & off-yellow egg-fibres. The capelins were dropped to the rock then fed individually by Falstaff, each swallowed whole by the chick. Boadicea gurgled softly as the chick was feeding: this a new sound. Both Falstaff

& Boadicea preened & cleaned the down as the chick strained to swallow an overlarge specimen.

The entire hatching period thirty-seven days, just over five weeks.

The chick has strength sufficient to stretch itself to feed, a being of pure hunger & high notes, the sheer embodiment of strain; shows surprising extension of the legs, without sufficient balance to maintain its posture: it needs support & correction with wingtip & beak; its wing-stubs fluttering at full extension but otherwise generally helpless: too early to say, but the entire appearance lends much weight to Fleming's formulation of an intermediate fledging period.

Estimated weight: 12 ounces.

All three adult birds notably wary at my approach since hatching. I encroached no nearer than five yards at any point, keeping hard to the grass; I did not move close enough to receive the CLACK CLACK CLACK, but Falstaff notably bristled. This raises serious questions for Davidson's work on the auk's cowardice & readiness to abandon the chick in face of danger; after Boadicea's departure to hunt–she is still on the water–Falstaff did raise himself to a protective display in my direction, even Antony bristling, tho I remain now at the top of the Pipes, approximately seven yards off.

Antony not disinterested, nor was he met with hostility by either Boadicea or Falstaff. If Boadicea & Falstaff do not quite recognize him as a third party in their extra-conjugal tryst, nor is he considered a rival or threat to the chick.

It is miraculous.

Bridget has joined me.

She is much interested in the chick.

I do not let her approach.

MYSELF: (whispering) It is the baby. She has just hatched.

BRIDGET: (also whispering) Baby.

There is wonderment in her face.

MYSELF: Don't eat this. It has just been born. Don't eat this.

BRIDGET: Don't eat this.

I get sideways glances from the girl. I think she understands my import.

I have let the girl's breakfast burn!

The breakfast was barely tolerable. We keep the bonfire going in the morning now to dry the seaweed or roast limpet, & the small clay pot sits on one side of the fire to act as a makeshift oven. Set right at the edge of the firepit, the pot does not boil porridge so much as bake it by degrees: one half of the bowl caked to a dark crust of pea-&-meal biscuit; the other side remained mushy & underdone. We were too hungry to wait for the whole to be cooked.

Regular rotation shd give us an evenly baked biscuit.

The fire was volumes two & three of Humboldt's *Kosmos*.

The idea of a burning cosmos is worthy of some mirth.

If I skip every second meal, & drink but one glass of water a day, our stocks will stretch further, but I have tried & failed to teach the child temperance. She has mastered the spigot long since & she gets thirsty, particularly after swimming, & waits to sneak a drink the moment I am otherwise engaged.

There are hardly any limpets on the rocks now. She is voracious.

Chewing seaweed makes the throat very dry.

It is not easy on the bowels.

I will lecture her again on the water. If we can last a week, I might even get to see the launching of the auk chick.

That would be a fine thing.

To see the chick take to the waves.

BRIDGET: Swimming. Swimming Ig. Swimming.

MYSELF: Leave me in peace.

BRIDGET: Swimming now. Lidohull. Lidohull. Swimming.

MYSELF: Idiot child. I cannot.

The child harangues me constantly, tugging my sleeves. Lidohull is her word for "now," an expression of plaintive urgency. But I shake her off.

I told her I will break the cabin to make a raft.

This is a lie. The raft is but a palliative fantasy.

I know nothing of boatcraft & I barely made it the half-league to Inishtrahull in a rowboat. Our odds of surviving a three-league journey on these waters to the mainland are non-existent.

But I lie now constantly to the girl. In the suppression of my panic; in the optimism with which I serve her porridge. We will die here. I know we will. It will not be starvation but thirst. The girl will likely turn to drinking seawater in the end, & madden & die. I try to stop myself looking into the belly of the still, not for fear of my own pulpy reflection but of seeing the dry base.

We might last the week.

She has no concept of the utter gloom that surrounds us. Now she has fed, she has lost her temper & will make a fool of herself, cavorting up in an angle off the highest rock on the south strand, kicking & splashing in the waves.

Hupla. In she goes.

I go to the birds.

Sketchbook 3:

pg 28-29: Falstaff, the garechick; charcoal on paper.

pg 30: Anthony donates a capelin to the garechick; charcoal on paper (unfinished).

pg 31-32: The changing of the guard; garechick ravenous, standing; pen on paper.

pg 33: Boadicea's wariness & aggression; pen on paper.

It is dusk, & there is a sail coming from the mainland.

I do not know who.

For the longest while I thought the boat was heading to Inishtrahull, but now it is clear they are coming for us.

Bridget spotted them as we cooked. Pease-meal biscuits baked on volume four of the *Kosmos* & Temminck's *Manuel d'ornithologie*. Hunger makes the biscuits almost palatable. But my discipline & patience for the slow rotations of pot-baking leads to fractiousness between me & the girl, who went to the shore, & there started shouting.

BRIDGET: Mother is coming. Mother is coming.

A large white sail, the hull blue, flying a Union Jack.

It is none of the Inishtrahull boats.

The Union Jack could be a sign that it is indeed the constabulary? I dare not hope. Perhaps Frank has summoned them to interrogate the girl? Perhaps a customs boat, engaged in a raid for illegal spirits?

McGonigle said the coastguard was his brother-in-law.

A hoodlum, then?

I have thought much on it & eaten my soggy biscuit.

Whoever it is, when they are upon us, it will be night.

I am wholly excited & wholly afraid. If they are as good as their flag, the girl & I shall be on the mainland soon & likely eating some manner of rich turnip stew. Even if they arrest me, they cannot let me starve. Who knows, but with the help of Sir Phillip's legal aides, it will be less than a week until I sleep on a feather bed, drinking French wine?

Or it could be more brigands, come to finish what McGonigle has started.

His lighthouse has begun already its bright patrol of the sea. But of course, damn him, one of his gaunt brides could easily be working the mechanism.

I must be prepared for the worst.

The girl is giddy & will not leave the shore.

I have reloaded my pistols & the rifle & extinguished the fire as well as I can with the brine from the little clay pot & my bladder.

My heart brims with fear, with hope.

I shall hide this book, as my final testament to posterity, lest we meet our end tonight.

WEDNESDAY 23RD JUNE, 1847

I am alive.

Or not dead, at least.

I have spent the night with my head in Bridget's basket & my legs in the rain. My body creaks. Maybe I got two hours fitful rest, with the shale & the basket digging thru my overalls.

But I am not dead.

It was–is–the girl's mother.

The cannibal, Aisling O'Leary.

Here, on Tor Mor.

As the boat came to shore, I had stowed myself behind an igneous finger of granite. A light rain had started, drawing smoke from my embers, signalling the boat straight to us. She did not moor the craft with the masterful slowing & anchoring of the islanders; rather she crashed the vessel into land, having built such momentum, the boat scraped over the rocks & crunched onto the shale, as if to take a bite out of the island.

I had threatened & cajoled Bridget to make herself hidden, but she would not heed me, so I dragged her to the shadows forcibly, but as the boat landed, at the last instant, she pulled away again.

MYSELF: (hissing) Bridget! Come back, girl!

I could not make out the figure on the boat. Two huge sacks were thrown to the shore, followed by a lone sailor jumping onto land. In a beam of the lighthouse, I could only make out the uniform of an officer of the law, a tall broad figure. Nonetheless, I dared not leave the shadow, but hissed for the girl & raised my pistol.

But when Bridget shouted, the figure turned & called out in a woman's voice.

THE WOMAN: (something in Irish)
BRIDGET: (something in Irish)

I had my pistol trained on her, but I could not make sense of it: the clothes, the hair, even the bulk appeared too big for a woman. But the voice was a woman's. She knelt; Bridget jumped into her arms, ruining my shot & the little composure I had mustered.

They gabbled on the dark shore.

There was embracing & laughter.

The woman–or to my eyes, this huge & dark figure of sex indeterminate–rubbed the girl's head, lifted her, set her down, lifted her again.

I held up my weapon & stepped from the lee of the rock.

MYSELF: Who goes there? I have a pistol on you!

Her head shot up, cap & all. Bridget did not stop talking, but the woman was upright, interposing herself in the way of the pistol.

MYSELF: Identify yourself. Who goes there?
THE WOMAN: (something in Irish)

Bridget laughed, & the woman laughed also.

I still thought her a man, despite the voice & the laugh, due to the uniform & the sheer bulk of her. But then the sweep of the lighthouse caught her profile. Broad shoulders, yes; the hair cropped short; but the cheek & face with no trace of a beard. It seemed the head of a woman, atop the broad uniform of a man.

MYSELF: Put the girl down. I am warning you!

THE WOMAN: Mr Ignatius Green. I do believe you have been playing nanny to my daughter.

I stepped closer.

In the intervals of the light, I could slowly make out the form.

There were great breasts hidden under the loose-fit jacket. The body taller perhaps even than me, the features rough & broad, the complexion weathered. But the face was grinning, & undeniably female.

MYSELF: Tell me who you are or I will shoot!

THE MOTHER: I am the child's mother.

MYSELF: Are you Aisling O'Leary?

AISLING: I am.

MYSELF: The cannibal?

At this, the woman laughed again, as the girl buried her face into her neck, & I watched her bend to the ground, pick up the two sacks in one hand, & then walk past me, with a whiff of sweat & bread, crunching up the shale to the cabin, as if I was not there at all. Carrying a child & two large sacks as if there was no weight to them.

MYSELF: Come back here. Do not walk away from me!
MYSELF: Come back. I command it!

She did not turn, so I ran after them up the beach. But they arrived at the cabin before me, cackling & whispering, & by the time I had caught up–I fell twice in the dark–they had the cabin door closed & bolted from within.

MYSELF: (banging the door with the pistol butt) Listen here. Open up. This is my cabin.
INSIDE THE CABIN: (laughter, hushed chattering)
MYSELF: I do not know who you are. If you are who you say you are. But this is my cabin. I have been given the right to protect this island by its legal proprietor. You will open this door at once.

There was more subdued chatter inside.

I banged again, & the door opened abruptly.

The woman seemed huge in the doorway. I surely must be taller, but her stance filled the space; somehow she appeared to look down on me. In a flash of the lighthouse thru the shutters I caught sight of Bridget, sat on my bed. Before me, the uncowed broad face of Aisling O'Leary, grim, broad & unwelcoming.

I had more to say, but my voice caught in my throat.

THE MOTHER: Me & the girl are taking the cabin. You can sleep on the boat.
BRIDGET: (behind her) (something in Irish)

THE MOTHER: The basket. Bridget says you can take the basket. Or sleep in the boat. I do not care.

I had the pistol in my hand! It is my cabin! Within all scope of reason, I had nothing to fear!

MYSELF: Now listen here. If you are who you say you are, Mrs O'Leary, you are a known criminal...

THE MOTHER: I am The Cannibal, yes, the bandit queen, the Dogwoman of Roscommon! I am scourge of the bailiffs! I am Aisling O'Leary, devourer of Englishmen! If you do not run from me, Mr Green, I will pick you up & split your pretty face on my knee like a loaf of bread!

I felt her shifting towards me more than I saw it—a heft of the shadows—and before I could think, I put up my hands & stumbled onto my backside.

She laughed again, above me, & then the door was closed.

I heard her bolt it, & sat on the ground alone. The rain began to fall more heavily. I could hear more whispering from inside.

The rain intensified from a fine mist to sparse droplets.

I sat there, confounded.

I still had my pistol. I could have broken my way in.

I did not.

Instead I climbed the ridge, & have slept the whole night with my head in the basket, trying to make sense of my situation.

The damn wicker is rough as a rosebush. Steel wires that dig into the back. The ledge is too small for my legs: I spent the first half of the night trying to balance, then moved it down to the shale, which while less precarious, is horribly exposed to the wind.

The wicker did nothing to deaden the gulls' morning chorus or the brightness of the sun.

They have not stirred all morning from the cabin.

I am thirsty.

I dare not disturb them.

Now the sun is high, its warmth merciful.

I will go to the birds.

I have never seen a chick of any species adopted so readily by non-parents without a combination of skullduggery & the presence of live eggs in the nest. Not in pigeons, penguins, definitely not razorbills or any of the minor auks. A pigeon's eggs may be readily swapped, yes, but mistaken identity is not the same as surrogacy in a bachelor & bereaved mother. Nor am I referring to brood parasitism such as the cuckoo, where the parents mistake a chick in their nest for their own, like a crocodile bearing tortoises. Swainson swears his molthrus–so-called New World cowbirds–perform similar hijinks & I have no reason to doubt him. But Boadicea abandoned her own dead egg fourteen nights ago, & Falstaff has brooded not at all this season, if indeed ever.

Now he sits quite restful, the chick peeping from the dark cloak of his down.

I have only heard of this from laymen & sailors. Never seen it. No ornithologist has.

The privilege takes my breath away.

I met a man in Manchester who swore he had a lone bantam cock who lost his swagger to sit on a nest of duck eggs after the drake & the hen were shot & raised the ducklings as if he were the mother. Hens will sit on anything of course, brooding stones or croquet balls even after prolonged infertility, but the comparison is not the same: the nutritional cost of rearing chicks to a hen or a cock is minimal after the laying of the egg; the chicks are precocial & feed themselves.

Chickens are also stupid birds.

Where there is a substantial nutritional deficit incurred by chick-raising, one generally assumes the relationship to the chick to be substantially more fraught.

Falstaff touches beaks with her, makes soft gurring sounds.

She pips ever so slightly at his attentions.

They could feed her twice as fast if they abandoned her at the nest—like starlings or robins or most temperate birds—but of course, like the penguin, they regularly nest in temperatures close to freezing. In normal circumstances, their hatchlings require the parent's heat; although, by the thickness of her grey down, I swear this chick better insulated than any hatchling I ever saw.

Bridget brought me vittles just now.

I heard her climbing the Pipes.

She has brought me my sketchbook, & charcoal too, & lo, a stoppered bottle of water; better, a large chunk of ham—Hallelujah!—& dry bread!

I was famished, & near drank the water in one go.

Bridget turned from me almost immediately, eager to go back to the cabin.

MYSELF: Bridget, wait. Wait. Your mother—is that your mother?

BRIDGET: (nodding)

MYSELF: Tell me Bridget. Your mother. How did she find us?

The girl just waved me off. I tried to ask her more. Where did the food come from? What of her father? Was her mother a cannibal? But she smiled & shrugged, & ignored me, skipping down the Pipes to the cabin.

Sketchbook 2:

pg 29: Boadicea carrying eight capelins; charcoal on paper.
pg 30: Chick grabbing onto Boadicea's feathers; charcoal on paper.
pg 31: Antony, touching beaks with the chick; charcoal on paper.

The woman is a slut &, I can wholly believe, a cannibal.

I ate the ham & the bread much too quickly, I fear, after living for days on a much leaner diet; they have wrecked an abrupt & acute agony in my guts. The outhouse never had a door—I never thought of having to protect my dignity from anyone but a curious gull—& the girl never competes for its use as she drops her waste on the rocks. But the pair had yet to leave the cabin, & I had the pressing & urgent need for the outhouse, so I tried my best to sneak close, dreading the thinness of the walls but hoping the high wind might aid somewhat in suppression of my animal noises.

At first I heard them talking inside the cabin, which was fortuitous for I was in extreme discomfort & could not amply restrain my voice. But then they clearly overheard me & the conversation stopped.

I was horrified.

But then the woman—the mother, the slut!—came outside!

Brazen as a ewe, she stood & watched me!

My condition was such I was no longer able to move, nor had I anything to cover me but my discarded trousers, which lay just out of reach.

MYSELF: What are you doing? Don't stand there!

She laughed. At me, on the seat. I could do nothing but fold my body upon itself to hide from her gaze. But I was in an agony, & powerless to stop my processes.

THE WOMAN: The girl is the same. It takes time to retrain the stomach after a fasting period. You must take it slow.

MYSELF: Stop looking at me!

I had to sit until my shuddering stopped. Observed by a grinning giantess. I could see in the light how ill-fitted the uniform was to her; the jacket clearly had been torn from a much smaller man, & the shirt unmatched, & the hair cut short to her ears.

Then–unshameable! Slut!–while I was still unable to move, without averting her eyes, she pulled down her trousers & squatted, loosing a full flood of piss on the rocks–in the leeside of my cabin!

Without breaking my gaze!

I have never witnessed such as this!

I could not quite speak, partially due to physical weakness brought on by the agony of my bowels, but also due to her utter contempt for the most basic humanity.

MYSELF: (whispering) This is my house. We don't piss near the house.

She grunted, stood without wiping, buckled herself up & turned to go back inside. But despite her depravity, I needed to communicate the urgent practical direness of our situation.

MYSELF: (struggling to speak) Stop. Wait. Wait. You must hear me.

HERSELF: (a swinish grunt)

MYSELF: Hear me. The men of Inishtrahull. They attacked us & they will again. We have their guns, but they will come back. We need to defend ourselves, or alert the constabulary, or flee.

THE WOMAN: (utterly unconcerned) The men of Inishtrahull will not move on me.

She strode into my cabin. At which point I noticed the almanac was gone from the wall. We have used it for lighting bonfires.

MYSELF: (banging the wall) Wait, hussy! Wait! Can't you send the child out with paper?

THE MOTHER: (thru the wall) Wash your arse in the sea.

It occurred to me then, twisting in knots, that I have seen her face somewhere before. I know not where, but I am sure I have.

❋

Sketchbook 2:

pg 32: Aisling O'Leary: brow, eye, nose.

pg 33: Her likeness, various clothes, hairstyles.

Maybe I have seen her likeness in Punch & erased it from my mind? But I can easily imagine her murdering someone. Her husband. With those large hands. Eating human flesh. Not the girl. She wouldn't. The woman's manner is nothing but warmth to the girl. But her hands are so large, & her frame. The bulk of her would not be so disturbing in itself—the shape of her face far from gruesome, handsome even—but the lack of any trace of demureness is uniquely appalling. Even if she were not so brazen, so lacking in base civility & grotesque in her attire, there is something ungainly in her manner—a forthrightness, pride even—the antipathy of everything feminine.

She could have eaten her husband. I could believe it.

The chick keeps trying to climb Boadicea's back. Her little webbed talons clutch into the feathers & she tugs, straining with the same concentrated singularity of muscular yearning with which she strains for food when her surrogates drop capelins into her mouth.

There is such a stark clash in the colour of their coats; the brightest of matte greys against sheer shining black.

Sketchbook 2:

pg 34: Three studies of the chick's head; charcoal on paper.

pg 35-37: Antony, Boadicea & chick; charcoal on paper.

❂

I have banged on the door repeatedly thru the afternoon. They ignore me, or laugh, or talk as if I was not there.

MYSELF: Look here. This is inhumane. I am cold & wet & the rain has started again. This is my cabin. Conceived by me, designed by me, its building overseen by me. I demand you let me in & give me access to the water in my still.

MYSELF: I still have my gun, you know!

MYSELF: Open the door. I will not be ignored. I am armed & unafraid, & this is my property. I will count to five.

MYSELF: One, two, three, four. Five.

MYSELF: I am very, very thirsty!

It is getting dark now for writing, & what little light sources I have for burning are rain-dampened.

They have barely left the cabin all day.

This is an injustice, & I have told them so, repeatedly.

Eventually, after much knocking, Bridget did come out with another chunk of dry bread, a bottle of water & a stack of paper to make a fire; the end of Wood's Ornithological Guide, some dried bladderwrack, & the final volume of the *Kosmos*.

MYSELF: (whispering) Bridget. Bridget. I must come in. I command it.

BRIDGET: (looking back at her mother) No, Ig. No.

She closed the door on me & left me to the elements.

So I have made a little fire beside my basket. Not on the shore, where me & the girl have shared our hearth the last few days. Here, by my miniature kennel, so I may warm legs in the ashes when it burns out.

I could take the woman's boat. This vessel seems fine, has a fine sail. With such a vessel it would be well within my power to reach land, likely in a few hours or less. She must surely realise this. I could push it off the shale by myself, head to the mainland, & summon the law on her. Secure lodgings first, contact Hancock for funds if necessary, a hot bath, beef & turnip stew, then on the second or third day I could summon the constabulary, tell them exactly where to find the cannibal Aisling O'Leary, & her ungrateful daughter, trapped with no boat on Tor Mor, & explain how they have been abetted by the whoreson McGonigle.

I could do it now.

I could do it tomorrow.

THURSDAY 24TH JUNE, 1847

We have had the most bizarre tea-party.

I woke, groggy & aching, from a second night on the rocks. The weather once again warm, & the women had exited the cabin. I watched them moving my little dining table out onto the shale, & set up my stools on either side, the barrel of grog rolled out to make a third place. They laid out the foodstuffs the mother has brought with her, the most surprising feast imaginable. More ham. Half a roast chicken. Plumcakes & red apples & bottles of actual wine & my own tumblers of water.

I did not know what to make of it.

I dared not approach until Bridget came, giggling, to the basket to summon me, tugging my arm.

BRIDGET: Come, Ig. Come.
MYSELF: What theatre is this?

The woman was sat with her back to the sea, wearing a white cotton dress, split at the sides & up the back. It was ill-fitting; barely covered her calves & her outsized men's boots. She was a sight, tugging on the neckline.

Warily I let the girl lead me on.

THE WOMAN: Come, Mr Green, Sir Ignatius sir, won't you break your fast with us? The girl has requested your presence, dear fellow. Sit, by all means, sit down.

I was suspicious. Dry-mouthed & aching from a night in the rain. I had no reason to trust her, nor even the girl, little treacherous witch. But I was very thirsty, & hungry, & I have not seen such a spread, never mind actual fresh apples, in my last six weeks on the island.

MYSELF: What is this?
THE WOMAN: Come. We are simply delighted to have you join us, sir. I can only apologise that we have not found tea, but the kitchen staff have informed me the coffee will be ready presently.

They had indeed a little fire going. I could not see which books they had chosen, but the kettle was sitting in the flames. Bridget had taken her seat, beaming from her mother back to me.

Reluctantly, I sat.

THE WOMAN: Good sir, won't you try a blancmange? They are simply delightful.

She was holding up a roll of dry bread.
I glanced to Bridget, & took it, hesitantly.

MYSELF: What is this?
THE MOTHER: (laughing) This is but apples & cake sir. Apples & cake.

I did not need more of an invitation.

I ate the apples first. Three of them in a row, out of a pile of eight. They were tart & the bruising minimal; they could have done with another few weeks on the tree. They were wonderful. I tried to remind myself not to gorge & overstress my digestion, taking timid little bites, but soon that gave way to hunger. The chicken—wherever it was roasted—was different than I would cook it: less well done, but still cooked to the bone, & juicy, & I cannot complain, as the breast was like chewing a handful of butter.

The girl & her mother prattled in Irish as I ate.

I suspected treachery, but the girl at least was picking at the food too. When the kettle whistled, the girl poured me coffee in a tumbler.

THE WOMAN: (rubbing Bridget's head) I do not mind the little haircut. It makes her look like a bear, don't you think?

I had my mouth full of chicken & could not answer.

THE WOMAN: But you are no tailor, sir. Her dress is laughable.

MYSELF: (swallowing) I had not the tools.

THE WOMAN: (laughing) I can see that.

Her own dress is shoddy & ill-fit, but I did not say so.

I am not used to company when I eat. We had no cutlery. I had not washed myself adequately. There were no napkins, or even plates. The woman was not eating—a tumbler of grainy coffee was all she took—& Bridget was grinning at me the whole time, & nudging different foodstuffs my way, & they both watched as I glanced around in vain for somewhere to wipe my hands or my face, before I wiped myself off as best I could on my sleeves, like a schoolboy.

I could have completed my ablutions more fully in the sea, but more than decorum, I wanted the truth.

MYSELF: Did the girl tell you how sick she was?

THE WOMAN: Hmmm?

MYSELF: Did she tell you how she arrived here? Half-dead & starving? Full of lice? Did she tell you how I thought she would die, & how I lifted her from the fever?

THE WOMAN: (raising an eyebrow) Did she now?

MYSELF: Yes. It was utterly inhumane.

THE WOMAN: (sniffing) She has told me a lot, Mr Green. Said you bashed her face on this table's edge, & nearly cost her a tooth.

MYSELF: (abashed) Yes. There was an accident.

THE MOTHER: So I hear.

I was full, & slightly drowsy on the heaviness of my belly. But I was tired of being constantly wrongfooted, by a woman, on my own island, at my own table.

MYSELF: Tell me. Are you in league with McGonigle?
THE WOMAN: (raising the kettle) Can I interest you in a coffee, Mr Green?
MYSELF: I have had enough coffee. Are you in league with McGonigle?
THE WOMAN: I am not.
MYSELF: Are you in league with the Young Irelanders?
THE WOMAN: (laughing) I am in league with no one.
MYSELF: I do not believe you. How did you find us?
THE WOMAN: (bemused) The girl lit a fire. I have been keeping eyes to the coast of late. The fire was our signal.
MYSELF: No. That is not my meaning. How did you—a brigand, a woman—how did you find me? A lone Englishman on a rock? I am not in the papers.
THE WOMAN: These are famine times, Mr Green. A gentleman on the rocks paying good shilling for deliveries & construction? There's not a drunk between here & Sligo who doesn't know where you are.

Bridget had not stopped grinning, & as her mother put down her empty tumbler, & poured us both another coffee, I pressed on.

MYSELF: No. You are lying. You wrote me a letter by name. You sent the girl to me, by name. You knew me. You knew me personally.

THE WOMAN: I knew you had food, Mr Green. I knew nobody would come looking to find my girl here.
MYSELF: I see that. Yes. But you are not being honest. That is not the matter entire. You knew me. You did.

She looked away then. But something in her face caused again the spark of recognition. I knew her brow. The shape of her head. But I could not recall from where.

THE WOMAN: (looking off to the Pipes) A long time ago sir, when you were living in Primrose Road, before the good Lady Green died, sir, you had two Irish girls in the house. Two of them. One of them was Eileen Sweeney from Monaghan.

She is right. We had Irish girls.

I let them go when the fug descended on me.

But there had been a girl. In the kitchen. Boiling linen, running for the doctor. A voice in the corridors, under the stairs. A fetcher of lost utensils.

The woman watched me.

No doubt my recollections showed on my face.

MYSELF: Are you Eileen Sweeney?
THE WOMAN: (laughing) No. I am Aisling O'Leary. Eileen Sweeney was the other one.
MYSELF: Aisling. Aisling. But I thought you were called Rosie.
THE WOMAN: (laughing) You called us all Rosie, Mr Green. Even Lizzie, the English girl in the kitchen.

Bridget had grown restless. The conversation did not hold her interest, & while the woman was happy to scour my brow to read my thoughts, the girl had risen to poke at the fire.

I did not like being mocked.

Not with my back still sore from the rocks.

MYSELF: So this is what has become of you, is it? After the kindness Emily showed you, you have come here to Ireland to consort with brigands &, &, & devour your husband?

THE MOTHER: Oh eat a blancmange, Mr Green. The only person who ate my husband, sir, was the law.

MYSELF: So you deny it? But still go abroad, writing letters, calling yourself a cannibal? Abandoning your child like an alley cat? What kind of monster abandons her own child?

The smile fell from her face: bemusement became thunder. Her great hand slammed the table. Bridget jerked, suddenly fearful, as did I. Aisling O'Leary swirled her tumbler, took a last swig of coffee & cast a dirty arc of grounds across the shale.

THE MOTHER: That is it. Put the food in the cabin when you are done. I am going for a swim.

With that, she rose, & pulled her dress over her head in one motion, revealing her tall muscular frame in nothing but a man's vest & undergarments. I averted my gaze as she marched down to the shore, & Bridget rose, hurling off her own nightie to follow her.

I sat there awhile, trying not to watch them splash about, until the gulls grew too boisterous, & I put the food in the cabin.

☼

I have taken my pen & ink with me.

Stealing what is mine, from my own cabin.

My hand is not yet fit for drawing though.

I do not like to think back to Emily's last days.

Not in company.

Rosie. Aisling. I don't remember that name. Just her head, really, a certain stolidness, at the bedside & on the stairs. A touch, perhaps, in the months after the funeral. Softness. Maybe. A tall girl, big hands, but somehow less large than this woman.

She was kind, I think, in the last days. I was bewildered. She never talked back.

Not Rosie. Aisling O'Leary.

The girl is her daughter. Bridget O'Leary.

☼

The chick has managed the climb onto Falstaff's back.

Nigh constantly, when she is neither feeding or wheedling to feed, she attempts to climb either him or Boadicea. Her peep for the returning Boadicea is a fantastic grating little sound.

She arches & swallows sprat that look likely to choke her. But after the guard is changed & one parent goes hunting, her high notes disappear, no longer bawling for fish, but learning to navigate the feathers. Sometimes Boadicea helps her up with a nudge of her black nose; sometimes she stares stoically to sea as the chick yanks on her plumage, tugging the little bright blob of her body to her black throne. If she sprays guano as she clambers down, Boadicea combs it from her back with her beak.

Sketchbook 2:

pg 38-39: The chick sitting on Boadicea; pen on paper.

The day is so still I could hear the girl & her mother splashing all morning. Then they laid themselves to dry on the rocks. I did not spy on them, to try to preserve some of the last rags of dignity the woman is so determined to throw away.

But sometime in the late afternoon I heard the cabin door slam, & I peeped over the top of the Pipes.

There, at the tide's edge, a solitary male seal.

Bridget had run to the cabin for my rifle. The woman was crouched behind a long arm of smooth igneous rock, not twenty yards from the seal, & had the long knife of the islanders in her hand, the other hand steadying her as she crept towards it.

The mother whispered to the girl & waved away the rifle.

What followed was a phenomenon of athleticism the likes of which I had never seen. She proceeded to kill the beast, using only the knife, a rock, & her bare hands.

I was very conscious, the whole time, of her state of undress, wearing nothing but a man's vest & smalls; but so impressive a feat, so stark her musculature, I could not look away.

Bootless, feet clinging to the rock, the woman rose to her full height over the ridge. I saw her lift a rock larger than her own head in one hand, & then, with what I can only describe as a mighty twist of her back, she sent the rock sailing in a slow arc nearly twenty yards where it made a solid thud on the blunt head of the seal.

The animal did not die immediately. I suspect its skull was cracked, or its neck, by the stilted manner in which it reeled, but it did not initially flee, just made a single sharp bark, its head at an angle, stunned. At which point the woman leapt to the shale–barefoot!–sending shale skittering as she bolted at him, knife in hand. The seal saw its fate too late & turned for the water's edge. It made it into the waves; dipped; I thought it surely lost.

Aisling O'Leary flung herself in the sea after it, diving in a clean arc, & disappeared.

There was splashing.

For a moment–maybe thirty seconds or more–they both disappeared under water.

Then Aisling returned to the surface, holding the seal against her chest with both arms, working the knife from a long gash under its jaw, blood pumping down the knife blade & over her torso. She gripped it there, spurting, then lifted her head to laugh.

AISLING O'LEARY: (prolonged whooping & shouting in Irish)

BRIDGET: (matching whooping)

She had caught me watching. But rather than covering herself, the woman saluted me with the knife, a squirt of red blood scooting under her chin.

That was late afternoon.

It is not yet evening.

They have been skinning him since, casting the entrails on a rock, where they will stink, & draw the gulls. Bridget has been constructing a fire to rival what she built nights ago & the woman has quartered the seal, & I cannot deny the craft of her butchery. I believe she means to roast the carcass entire on the beach. Her idea is sound. The meat will keep for longer if she cooks it immediately, & we will save firewood too.

She has put on her mannish trousers now.

Seemingly to protect her knees as she kneels to butchery.

I will join them by the fire, if they will have me.

Sketchbook 2

pg: 40: Falstaff, chick underwing; charcoal on paper.

I did not dare approach until Bridget came calling from the bottom of the Pipes. They had set up a good-size blaze, & the smell of the seal-fat was heavenly.

AISLING: Mr Green, let me be your chef again, sir!
Come, good fellow, do not hold yourself on airs!

Her anger at me seemingly gone.

The haunches & the ribs of the seal had been split into four large sections & set up close to the fire: three of the joints she rotated regularly so as not to blacken the meat.

The fourth section—the right haunch—she cut into steaks, roasting them on the far side of the fire, flipping them every few minutes with her fingers.

We stared into the flame & ate with our fingers.

The bread she brought is near dried out now, & even dipped into the sea it is hard to chew, but there is something vastly superior about meat when eaten between mouthfuls of bread.

AISLING: Your water purifier, Mr Green. Is it broken?

MYSELF: Yes. But it is immaterial. We have no coal anyway.

AISLING: (chewing) Surely you tried wood?

MYSELF: It's belly is too large, the furnace chamber too high. The wood does not get hot enough.

THE MOTHER: (nodding) Have some wine so.

She filled me a tumbler. I do not know how many bottles she brought with her, nor where she got them. The girl tried the wine, spat it, & fetched herself water from the still, & we sat eating in silence, until the girl returned & they chatted in Irish.

After dinner, they sang. I poured myself a second glass & the woman did not seem to mind. The woman. Aisling.

Lying there as the light faded & listening to their sad little melodies was almost pleasant. It was not yet dark enough for the lighthouse: a boat was passing off to the west, to Boston, most likely. The girl lay her head in her mother's lap, staring into the flames.

MYSELF: How old is she?

AISLING: Hmm?

MYSELF: The girl. Bridget. Her age.

AISLING: What month is it?

MYSELF: It is June.

AISLING: Then she is ten years old.
MYSELF: You have not thought to teach her letters?
AISLING: Hmmph.

It was drowsy in the heat, as the world turned towards dusk. I nodded at the wine, & she nodded, & I refilled my glass.

MYSELF: So. How did it happen? When you left us in Primrose Road. What became of you?
AISLING: (stroking her daughter's head) I came home. Fell in love. I got married.

I stretched my legs up to the fire. Maybe it was the heat or the drowsiness of a full belly but I could nearly forget who she was, all she is accused of. Even that she was a woman, as she played with her daughter's hair, the girl lying still, watching her fingers in the firelight.

AISLING: Why did you cut it so short?
MYSELF: Fleas. She was crawling with them.
AISLING: (raised eyebrow) What do you mean, crawling?

I told her then at length of the girl's arrival: the basket, the breaking of the fever. I was growing loquacious, & she reached in to open another bottle, slicing its top off neatly, & then the girl resumed humming her little ditties. All the time, she kept her questions short & looked on with dark eyes.

I had become too comfortable, but, as the dusk encroached, I started to question her in return.

MYSELF: No. But tell me more. I mean, what became of you? After you left us. You were but a girl.

AISLING: Hmmph.

MYSELF: No. I mean. You were smaller. Or less. Just less.

I was on my back, & turned to face her, resting on an elbow.

MYSELF: I am not talking of hardship & potatoes! I mean. What happened to you? You seem so different than in Primrose Road.

AISLING: Maybe. Maybe.

MYSELF: So what is it? Did you live with thieves? Where did you learn to hunt?

AISLING: (silence)

MYSELF: I am not asking about your husband, you understand. I am asking what happened to you.

AISLING: (softly) What happened to me is that I learned ingratitude, Mr Green. I learned that the law would not stop when we could not make the rent. Not even when they shot my husband.

I sat up, to face her, to explain myself more clearly.

MYSELF: No. You are not getting my meaning. Not your husband. Frankly, I don't want to know.

AISLING: (nigh *sotto voce*) I learned to stop asking politely for what should already be my own.

MYSELF: No. Listen to me. Look at you. Butchering seals. You did no butchery in Primrose Road, did you? You simply went along to the butcher like the other girls & bought meat. Someone must have taught you this. How to separate skin from meat.

The woman jumped abruptly up, knocking her daughter from her lap & spilling wine in a hissing arc into the fire. She took another swig from the sliced bottle & dislodged the knife from a haunch of meat.

AISLING: I'll tell you how I learned it. A solid diet of Englishmen, one for breakfast, one for dinner! I learned it cutting their cheeks off for the tenderest meat of all!

This she said, holding the knife up against my face. I thrust myself back, quite suddenly sober & ready to box her if it came to it. Only when I was standing with my arms up did I notice her grin, & the girl laughing.

MYSELF: Hussy. You look like a murderess.

AISLING: (shouting) Oh & plenty besides, Mr Green! I am the cannibal queen of Ireland! You're lucky we have eaten tonight, for I quite fancy a little slice of you!

I will not be lampooned. I have left them to their fire. They have passed from singing to dancing; now they are moving from dancing to whooping.

The women & their whooping.

I will lie here in my basket.

McGonigle's lights have started up.

FRIDAY 25TH JUNE, 1847

They were hooting late into the night. They climbed into the ridges when it was dark, as the girl is wont, yawping

& howling at nothing. The waves maybe. The gannets up there, if they have not yet fled or been eaten by the girl.

This morning the girl had a black eye.

She took me food from the cabin. A slice of roast seal & two more apples. I ate them sitting beside the basket, but as she went to sidle away, but I noticed she was holding her head oddly.

MYSELF: Bridget. Child. Stop.

She grunted. Tried to turn again. But I held her by the arm, pulled her to look at me, & she did not fight.

There it was: a full shiner, the skin black with a mustard rim, albeit unbroken.

MYSELF: Bridget. Are you all right?

She grunted. Then she pulled herself from my hand & climbed further up. I sat, breaking my fast, watching as smoke threaded from the cabin's chimney.

The woman is clearly trying to light the stove.

I will go to the birds.

☼

I have been watching the chick.

Her growth is prodigious. Actually prodigious. I cannot be sure of her exact proportions without taking her from the nest–which I will not countenance–but she appears to the naked eye to be a full three inches taller, which is surely as much a matter of the strength of the legs & neck rather than solely down to corporeal increase in mass. She stands now, clacking beak to beak with her surrogates, to receive her parcels of fish; circumnavigates the nest: has quite mastered the ascent onto their backs, altho her descent is still more of a clutching lurch than a graceful leap.

I cannot draw them.

My hand too shaky from a night in the box.

No matter.

I can still scrawl these notes with some degree of legibility.

If I make a noise or throw a pebble near the nest, the chick can be made to cower under Falstaff's wing: it jerks at the noise, scampers; if on his back, clambers to his side; falls, sometimes headlong. The game feels cruel, if comical: I wait until she is sitting like a white queen in her black feather throne, clicking soft beak-kisses with Falstaff, then suddenly at a clatter of pebbles she jerks & silently clutches his feathers & tips herself off, into his plumage.

I have stopped now.

Her agility & strength would seem to indicate she is almost precocial, rather than semi-precocial; however, she is yet to pass more than a foot from the nesting site & the warmth of her surrogates.

At the changing of the guard, Antony came to the nest; he too dropped her a parcel of fish. I have never seen this: a bachelor, uninvolved in the nesting partnership, taking a role in the feeding of the chick.

Surely this must be anomalous also?

One cannot assume communal feeding is the norm in the garefowl, or indeed, any bird regularly laying a single chick: it is nonsensical from a nutritional standpoint. Given the garefowl's ill-defined nest structures, communal feeding could only lead to parents neglecting their own chicks if simply the loudest & fittest can jump the queue; particularly in traditional mega-colonies like St Kilda or even outposts like Eldey, there would be such a disparity of chick-size as to leave a disproportionate number of starved runts.

Antony–indeed, Falstaff & Boadicea herself–are likely confused, either thru mistaken identity brought on by nest loss, or displacement of the parental instinct.

The girl has not returned from the ridge.

Her mother has found my tobacco, it appears, & gone to the shore. She clearly has brought her own pipe.

She heard me approach on the stones but did not turn toward me.

AISLING: What were you thinking with that water contraption?
MYSELF: Pardon?
AISLING: That idiotic device. Your still.
MYSELF: It needs coal, but it doesn't matter now. McGonigle's men have broken the seals in four places.

I sat myself on the rock beside her, & she glanced at me, her expression irate.

AISLING: What was your plan? With the machine broken? Had I not come?
MYSELF: I had grog.
AISLING: Jesus.

MYSELF: I mean, I had ideas for a device to gather rain-water. At the start. But I could not make it work.
AISLING: Hmmph.

She turned back to the sea, & started refilling & tamping the bowl of her pipe, which she lit with an actual match.

MYSELF: You hit the girl.
AISLING: (squinting thru smoke) What?
MYSELF: The girl. Her eye.
AISLING: I did, Father Green. She hit me first.

She pulled up the sleeve of her blazer, to show a bloody arc, the imprint of the child's teeth & a series of scratches the length of her arm.

I know the sharpness of the child's teeth. I showed her my own palm, with the toothmarks still visible. She nodded, & we passed to quietness, watching Inishtrahull's fishing boats.

MYSELF: Why did she bite you?
AISLING: Jesus. Do you not stop?

The islanders had gone back to the water. There must be at least ten families on the island, & my supplies would not feed them long. So they are back fishing.

None of them headed our way. Not yet, at least.

The woman eyed me from the side, as her smoke drifted over her features, picking up & dropping handfuls of shale.

AISLING: She bit me because she does not want me going away.
MYSELF: You are going away from her?
AISLING: Yes.

MYSELF: Where are you going?

AISLING: Away.

MYSELF: Leaving the girl here with me?

AISLING: (agitated) Look. There are two more men out there. I got the fellow who shot my husband & Richard Cunningham who held him & Duncan Cook. Two more of them are out there, free or fled; that is, the one who paid them directly & the fellow in Scarborough who owns the land. I mean to kill them. Are you happy, Father Green? Shd I say a novena?

I did not know what to say. I could not bring myself to look at her. She offered the pipe over to me, nudging me on the arm, but I turned my head.

Eventually she spoke.

AISLING: Lookit, you have fed her well enough so far.

MYSELF: But why–I mean–wouldn't you–take the girl?

AISLING: (exasperated) Are you mad, man? Take a child to kill a man?

MYSELF: No. What? No. I mean. I don't know.

AISLING: Besides, the moon is getting bigger. A full moon is good for hunting. Gets the blood up.

I had barely an inkling of the world she inhabits, but I do not really think I wanted to know more. Nor do I think in all honesty she would have told me.

She watched me a while, puffing, then leant in.

AISLING: So she was delivered to you in that basket. Half-dead, you say. Full of fever & barely fed.

MYSELF: Yes. That is true.

AISLING: (curling her lip) That shd not have been. She left me dressed well, in a little ribboned thing. She had no fleas then. She left me unwilling but healthy.

She sniffed, scratching the side of her face, & then spat a fine glob all the way down into the waves.

AISLING: Liam McGonigle. Shay O'Hagan. The man Hancock. I shall pay them a visit.

MYSELF: Why?

AISLING: I entrusted them.

MYSELF: But. But. Do you mean to kill them?

AISLING: I don't rightly know.

MYSELF: I mean. I mean. What did the girl say?

AISLING: (irate) Jesus, man! Do you not stop? The girl tells me nothing if she thinks it will send me off again.

She sat a while longer. I stayed where I was, out of arm's reach, & she occasionally offered me a puff of my own tobacco. Eventually, when she was done, she put the pipe back in her jacket pocket. One more dollop of phlegm on the stones & she rose.

AISLING: Well well. I better go & beg forgiveness.

MYSELF: Wait. You must tell me. I have to know. Is there no way the child–Bridget–is there any way she could be my own? I mean. In the days after Emily. In my fug. Did we?

She stiffened immediately. Turned to face me front on, the weight of her body in her boots, & the snarl returned to her demeanour.

AISLING: You are a very stupid man. An arse of a man. Bridget had a father. Who looked after her from the day she was born. A strong decent man, who loved her & raised her & sang to her & fed her. The best of men, a strong worker, the love of my life. But he's dead now. He was shot in the head by an Englishman. An Englishman like you. Just like you.

She stared down at me & I thought she was about to strike me, but I did not care, I could not keep silent with the question alive in my gut any longer.

MYSELF: But did we not? If not, then why? Why did you send her to me? I know I had food. I know that. I know the law would not expect your girl here. But I cannot believe you had no better options. Why here? Why did you send her to me?

She knelt down, & I expected violence when she reached out, but instead she took my face in her hands & she pressed her lips to mine & kissed me, strongly, on the mouth before I could think to pull away.

AISLING: You were always so gentle, Mr Green. You were always gentle, & you never tried to fuck any of the younger girls.

She stood up then, & touched my face once more, & turned from me to climb off up the North Wall, after her child.

I sat there a while on the beach after she left. I was on my own in the daylight for what felt like the first time since the child arrived. Their heads did not lift over the ridge. Eventually I went to the Pipes, & washed my body with seaweed behind the boulders, & the same with my clothes, & lay there drying a while.

Not too long. I did not want caught in a state of undress.

The cabin was empty, so I crept in quickly. From a look in her sacks, it appears she has robbed a bakery. There are still two bottles of wine left, & a mass of mixed but dried breadstuffs, & two plumcakes that are yet edible, & a large piece of ham, tho by its smell, I would no longer trust it.

She has made no effort to keep the room tidy.

The still is but one quarter full.

There are still great shanks of roast seal.

With careful rationing, & the dregs of the grog, I reckon we can eat for five days. But the water will be done in two.

We must go soon.

I go to the birds.

Sketchbook 2:

pg 41: Icarus, curious; charcoal on paper.
pg 42: Falstaff nudging Icarus off his back; charcoal on paper.

The women have returned to the cabin. Quietly enough.

I have named the chick Icarus.

Obviously I cannot determine its sex without an internal examination. It is for all I know the only garefowl chick south of Eldey, if not in the world entire, & I dare not touch her. Sexing by behaviour, unreliable as it is, is unthinkable until she reaches adulthood.

But I think of her as a girl.

So Icarus I have dubbed her. A female Icarus. Why not? For she cannot fly.

She is growing less fearful. Willing to step further from their small hollow, while Boadicea watches. Longer periods neither climbing her mother's back nor cowering underwing. Walking, maybe a yard from the halo of guano, turning stones upside-down, testing gravel on her beak-tip or foot.

A fully precocial pelagic bird would be in the water by now.

The Japanese murrelet is said to swim at two days. Closer cousins, including all other large auks, are known to take up to three weeks to launch. But this leg strength, down thickness & the sheer audacity of little Icarus all lead me to estimate two weeks in the nest.

Sir Phillip will be furious.

Hah.

Bridget has just come to summon me.

She climbed the Pipes & stood waiting for my full attention.

BRIDGET: (from memory) Mother says. You. Can sleep. In the cabin. Tonight.

MYSELF: (laughing) Impressive, Bridget. Thank you very much. Tell your mother I am coming soon.

She did not want to leave without me.

I will join them presently.

SATURDAY 26TH JUNE, 1847

Aisling has left the island & Bridget is wild.

I was woken with the sun halfway up the sky by her wailing, utterly forlorn, & I sat up to meet her harrowed face, & she grabbed me & shook me.

BRIDGET: Ig. Ig. Ig. Come Ig. Come.
MYSELF: What? What is it Bridget?.
BRIDGET: Come, Ig. Come. Mother is swimming. My mother.

I rose from the cabin floor—I had slept on the girl's pallet—stunned from a solid sleep. The day was bright & everything looked unchanged. We have the dwindling sackful of goods on the cabin floor, & the still remains broken. The sailboat the woman had brought was crunched up on the shore, its sails rolled up. But the girl was beside herself. Her mother was gone.

The girl wanted me to push the boat into the water & sail out to find her.

I refused, & she would not accept it.

She tried to push the boat off the shale on her own like a miniscule Sisyphus. Since I still refused to help her, she has tried to open the sails, likely hoping they will catch the wind & help launch the boat.

It is hopeless.

Her mother is long gone.

I heard her leave, the door slamming long before dawn.

She has left us the boat.

She must have swum for Inishtrahull.

I cannot believe anyone could make the swim. It is but half a league—I have met men who would boast of swimming such a distance with ease–& Aisling O'Leary had no shortage of bravura or athletic prowess, but the sea here is choppy & deadly & full of rocks. Even the islandmen men don't try to swim here. No one could make such a swim. Not even her.

If I am honest, I knew in my heart she would leave us when she came to me last night. I was lying on the girl's pallet while they shared my bed. The mother had sung the daughter to sleep & I was dozing, when Aisling came down to the floorboards & lay beside me.

She was whispering to me.

AISLING: Tell me you will look after her. Tell me you will.
MYSELF: You shdn't leave her. You mustn't go.
AISLING: Tell me you will not leave her.
MYSELF: I will not.

She lay with me half the night. At some point I felt the floorboards creak & she joined the girl on the bed.

I have never known a woman like her.

Then, shortly before dawn, I felt the creak, & the door close.

I did not rise.

I knew she would leave, but I did not imagine she would swim across the sea in the middle of the night.

That was hours ago.

There is nothing visible on the waves.

The child is running all over the island. Screaming from the shore. She will not stop. Now she is heading up the ridges again.

The sea is empty, even of boats.

She left us her boat.

The girl gives me no peace.

I have come up to the Organ Pipes to watch Icarus, but the girl followed me, pulling my arm.

BRIDGET: Come, Ig. Come in the boat. Come. My mother is swimming. Come.
MYSELF: Child. My poor child. You shd eat something.
BRIDGET: Come, Ig. My mother. Come.

I have tried to calm her like her mother did, putting my hand on her neck, but the child will not stand still. She has screamed at me & hit me & stolen my sketchbook & charcoal & thrown them off the Pipes, & has gone down to struggle with the boat again.

I have tried to shift my focus back to the birds.

Icarus's progress is astounding. She has moved somehow down the rocks, all the way from Canute's high nest to the shore. I did not see her descent. Could Boadicea have carried her? In her beak or on her back?

Icarus dips her head in the water. Boadicea sits on the sea not two yards away. When the chick steps ashore to stand on land, Boadicea nudges her back to water with the edge of her beak.

Bridget is at me.

BRIDGET: Come, Ig. Come, Ig. Come. Come.

She bloody took Icarus in her hand! I was writing & would not budge for her tears or her screams, so she leapt down to the water & lifted the chick.

MYSELF: In the name of God, what are you doing!

Icarus squealed in her face. Boadicea went mad, swimming in circles & clacking, but not approaching the girl. Falstaff & Antony powered in to us from the waves, while I stared down from the summit. Bridget's face was pure mucus & tears, but she held it by her mouth.

BRIDGET: *Kill the bird*, Ig. Kill the bird.
MYSELF: Child, what are you doing?

There was no way for me to make it down to the shore faster than she could wring its neck. I felt utterly paralysed & helpless.

MYSELF: Child, your mother is gone. We have no way of finding her. It is impossible.
BRIDGET: Come, Ig. Come.
MYSELF: Please put the bird down. This is nonsense. You don't understand. This is the worst thing. Please do not do this.

She shook her head at me, & closed her eyes, & tried to put the chick's head in her mouth, as it peeped shrilly.

MYSELF: Alright! I will come! I will come! Just put the bird down. I will come get your mother!

She opened her eyes. Slowly she lowered the bird, where it splashed thru the water towards Boadicea, who swiftly gave up clacking & snatched the chick to her back in her beak, swimming out to join the menfolk.

The chick cannot be ready yet for the water!

Bridget stared up at me, eyes like stones.

I have no way of stopping her getting to the bird.

❊

It would have been a fine thing to see the auks launch!

They are back in the nest. All three milled, bristling, the chick under Boadicea's wing. The damn girl let me check them one last time, but they wanted nothing from me.

The girl is tugging at my sleeve. Tries to knock the pen from my hand. Just now she came in & spat at me, said Kill the bird! & walked out, demonstrably, theatrically, towards the Pipes.

MYSELF: Child! I am coming!
BRIDGET: Kill it! Kill the bird!
MYSELF: I am bloody coming!

It would have been a fine thing to see the bird launch! We only have water for a day & a half, but we might have seen it! We might!

We have a sack of stale breadstuffs. Plenty of roast seal & some dry seaweed. I have drunk some of the wine & poured what I can't to the shale; the last of our water in two corked bottles & the rubber-teated flask of the child.

I am leaving my still. My good still!

Before the auks have launched!

She is throwing shale now!

I have my sketchbooks, my notebooks. Water.

It would have been a fine thing—a fine thing—to see the launch of the auks!

The seas do not look unmanageable.

~~SUNDAY 27TH JUNE, 1847~~

MONDAY 28TH JUNE, 1847

We have landed & found a temporary rest.

Wherever this is.

We shd not have taken the boat.

Launching the boat was a feat. I am a big man, but it had been firmly crunched onto the shore at high tide. I thought this launch would be the hardest part: exerted myself much in the application of my shoulders: found myself laughing when we had her in the water, trying to assuage the enraged despair of the girl.

MYSELF: We'll be there soon, Bridget. We'll find her.
BRIDGET: Come, Ig. Come!

Fool I was. Fool. I am not trained in the use of a sailboat, but thought it could not be that hard: much like a rowboat, except in that the sail would do the hard work. I thought I could just hoist it, catch the breeze, keep at a diagonal to the windface, lie back & man the rudder. The islandmen do it so thoughtlessly, even their children. The hull of this new vessel was intact; no leaks; far superior to the rickety hencoop McGonigle had lumbered me with. If worst came to worst, we had oars, & I thought, shd the sails prove useless in a dearth of wind, I could easily row ourselves out of mischief.

I thought we would have it.

Not catching the mother. I honestly thought her dead. But make it to the mainland. Placate the girl with the journey, perhaps secure further supplies & raise the constabulary to our aid. Perhaps even make it back to the cabin, in time to see Icarus launch.

I thought we had a chance.

After I had punted us thru the rocks with the oars, I hoisted the sail, but the boat spun as I struggled to learn the swing of the boom. Bridget hissed at me, little vixen, thinking I was fooling; but it was not long before I caught a wind from Tor Mor to the southwest, taking us towards Inishtrahull. Then the girl's noise abated, finally, & she kept to the prow scouring the water for a sign of her mother.

We had the pistols, the powder, the shot, shd we meet the men of the island, but I thought caution the wiser choice, & tried to angle her to give the island wide berth.

My angles were wrong.

The current & wind were taking us towards Inishtrahull's westernmost tip.

I tried to adjust our course. Telling & showing the girl how to hold the rudder; myself pulling & straining with the sail.

There was little we could do.

But they had no boats on the water; the wind was strong; even if the islandmen chose to chase us, I thought us so fast we might outrun them.

Our speed shd have been warning.

I had no control of the wind.

As we approached, there were glorious smells of peat off the island–land & earth I never got on the rock–but there was also the smell of burned thatch. Closer to the shore, I could see one cottage had been razed, the husk of the building still smouldering.

That was the first sign that Aisling O'Leary had survived.

We passed Inishtrahull long after noon, too close, no more than thirty yards off the shore; I was shouting the girl to man the rudder properly, rather than admit our trajectory was out of my control. The sun was still high, a glare on the water, & Bridget kept dropping her hold on the rudder to lean out & scoop up the foam. Some of the ghostly children of Inishtrahull spotted us from the rocks & ran up to the village, leaving the hillside empty.

Cursing, I readied the pistols at my side.

But the only figure to descend to the shore was the yellow-bearded youth–Yellowbeard–holding his bandaged stump as he walked down the hill in my rubber boots.

He was carrying a white flag about his arm, waving it when he could. We passed close enough I could see the grimace on his face.

YELLOWBEARD: Parley! Parley!
MYSELF: What goes on the island, man?
YELLOWBEARD: Parley! Parley!
MYSELF: Aisling O'Leary! Aisling O'Leary! Is she there?

When she heard her mother's name, Bridget stood tall on the prow, shouting in Irish. The very girl who had cut off his arm just days before. I could not understand their speech, nor could I stop the continued momentum of the boat, as I wrestled between the sail & the rudder.

They shouted until we passed out of earshot.

MYSELF: What did he say, Bridget?
BRIDGET: Mother is gone. Aisling O'Leary is gone.
MYSELF: Has she gone? Was she swimming? In a boat?
BRIDGET: In a boat. In a boat. This way, Ig. Come.

She was assured, somewhat, returning to her position at the rudder, pert as a gun dog, & we passed the rocky waters around the island, leaving Inishtrahull behind.

I thought to keep clear of Malin Point; thereby to cut a line around the head, & dock in Portronan. We have no money, but surely the constabulary in Portronan would come to our aid; even if they could not supply us with food & water, & protection back on Tor Mor, they would surely put us on a coach to Londonderry. We would find Hancock, warn him of the threat to his life, & collect the funds for our safe transport to England.

The wind slackened. I laid off trying to adjust our path, & sat in the stern, softening hard bread by dipping it in the sea & then gnawing it. The brightness of the day was deceptive: only when we had fully passed the Head did I note our distance from land.

I thought the apparent distance a nautical illusion. I did not panic fast enough, but tried to adjust our path by incremental adjustments of the sail.

The land was growing smaller & smaller.

Fear shifted gradually from intellectual angst to watery nausea in my stomach.

When the sun started going down, I finally gave up on the sail. The little effect it was having was counterproductive.

Bridget had gone silent, but now & again I heard a faint chanting under her breath, the *ai-ai-ai, ai-ai-ai* of her fever days.

MYSELF: Shut up, Bridget. Shut your mouth now.

The warmth of the day had gone. I bound the sails up as best I could. The oars came out. Land had become a long grey line on a blue horizon.

I stared into the setting sun, & tried to heave away from it, back in the direction of land.

The stars opened slowly above & around us.

My left hand's blisters burst first, around my scab.

I used the knife to cut a strip off the sack for a makeshift reinforced bandage. Shortly thereafter, I made another for my right.

MYSELF: Eat, Bridget. Eat the bloody bread & shut your noise.

BRIDGET: *Ai-ai-ai. Ai-ai-ai. Ai-ai-ai.*

There were still lights on the shore. A lighthouse, far in the distance. Not Inishtrahull. It couldn't be. We had travelled so far. But we could not see the land well enough to scour for landmarks. The current had dragged us wildly. In the cold of the night, I grew unsure of myself.

I dared not rest, for if we lost sight of land, we were dead.

BRIDGET: *Ai-ai-ai. Ai-ai-ai.*

The girl had long divined the panic in my posture & the curtness of my voice, & now her chant faded to barely more than a rhythm of her breath. She wrapped her coat tight around her legs; she was shaking with the cold, but I wearied of turning to look at her. At some point I took off my woollen overshirt & laid it on her. But my shoulders could not cope with Atlantic chill, & I was worried the muscles would seize, so I took back my overshirt & covered her with the food sack instead.

The full moon rose, massive & low & yellow.

I do not know how many hours I was pulling.

My hands hurt more than my back.

My left hand seeping blood through the binding.

I worried it would affect the strength of that arm; leave me rowing in circles.

When the sky started brightening, the wind in my face felt wet.

The haar was coming.

I panicked, tried to renew my pace, thought to outrow the haar.

No one can outrow the haar.

It enveloped me, & then saw I nothing: no lighthouse, no land, no sky, no moon.

I no longer knew our direction, & stopped rowing, & sat watching the misty shadow of the girl, & my whole body shook with the cold. I could hear a creaking in the mist, far above us, like bones, or the cracking of space. Abysses yawning. I dared not let myself sleep. I dared not row, lest I was pushing us further into the Atlantic, or winding in circles. Every direction led now to further mist.

I thought we would die then.

But I recalled drinking rum on Arthur's Seat, many moons ago; watching the thick haar boil up from the sea & spilling over Edinburgh in gin-mystical dawns.

Haar blows inland, I thought.

My body was crooked but I hefted the sails again, & they pulled; then I huddled by the sleeping girl, staring into the nothingness all around, nursing my palms, wincing as I lifted the binding to blow on my blisters.

I may have slept so.

I know I jerked as the boat crunched to a stop.

The mist was so thick, when I rose to stand I could see no further than the length of my arm.

I risked slipping off the side of the boat, & my feet touched sand. Not rocks, or stones, but sand, under three feet of water.

MYSELF: Bridget. We are here. We have landed.
BRIDGET: Ig? Ig?
MYSELF: I do not know where we are.

I lifted the girl & the sacks & carried her until the water gave way to dry pebbles.

We wandered a long time. Over sand & rocks. Once we had to follow a rockface with our hands. Then heather. There was mud. A marsh. The water of the marsh was warmer than the water of the sea. When I found a fresh stream I put down the girl & drank; it tasted of shit & we drank of the still water from our bottles instead.

We heard a dog barking.

The haar did not fade whatsoever, but paled with the brightness of a sun somewhere overhead. Eventually we found a muddy road & followed it between the ditches; this eventually led us to a building.

I am sat in it now.

The structure is empty. The hinges on the front door have been snapped. There are desks, & a table. A lamp. A mess of papers on the floor. The girl found a cot behind holding bars.

We appear to be in a ransacked & abandoned constabulary.

Or a coastguard station. Or a customs house. Some outpost of law enforcement. It has been raided by all appearances. Likely by the Young Irelanders.

I slept on the cot.

I think I have lost an entire day to sleep.

Bridget tried to rouse me twice for food. I slept thru darkness & drank water & pissed mightily out the door in the brightness of haar then slept straight again & I did not rouse & now it is night once more.

My right hand has faded to an afterache, & scabbed over well.

My left hand still burns, & is hot & swollen to the touch, the wound wet & glistening.

I have found a lamp & lit it. No one else is here, & the girl is asleep. I have taken the foodstuffs from under her head & sucked half the ribs of the roast seal to the bone.

There is a stable out the back. The cracked sign says *Falca-* & I cannot find the other half. Inside, they still have two horses, hungry & their stables unmucked. The horses started as I entered, but their muzzles were warm & eager on my good hand. This in itself raises questions.

Who raids a station but leaves the horses?

The animals are healthy; I have restocked their hay.

Drank of their water, & if it was undignified, it was cold & fresh. I took a bucket & tried to clean the wound on my hand.

When I got back, the girl had taken the cot, & now she is snoring loudly.

My hand is red as meat.

I will try for sleep again, on this chair.

TUESDAY 29TH JUNE, 1847

Still the haar is upon us.

We have breakfasted on roast seal. It is dry & covered in crumbs & no longer appetising. I have found a bag of flour in a cupboard, & while there are two hearths here & plenty of lamps, I have not the heart nor a saucepan to merit lighting a fire. We finished the still water, & Bridget has refilled our bottles from the horse's trough.

I have found a pile of ledgers & more paperwork tipped in the grass out the back. According to a torn ledger, this is the Falcarragh Customs Outpost. Presumably they have a boathouse nearby. I can hear the sea, so we cannot have journeyed far inland.

Bridget tore a page from the ledger & handed it me.

BRIDGET: Draw mother. Draw Aisling O'Leary.
MYSELF: What, child?
BRIDGET: Draw Aisling O'Leary. Draw her.

A picture of her mother. She is clever enough, & I understand her purpose. A likeness, so we might inquire of her whereabouts, without use of the incriminating name. I managed a fair three-quarters portrait in pencil. Harder from memory, of course, & I did not draw the uniform, but rather with a fine silk-shouldered gown that Emily once wore, but Aisling O'Leary's strong chin, her well-built forehead & deep-set eyes. A little diamond choker resting on her throat, for luck.

The girl was much pleased, & has it now folded into our small sack of guns, meat, plumcakes & sketchbooks.

There is not much of anything else here. No lights, no humans, no voices. I have let out both horses. Smacked one of them off into the field. The stronger, a mare, I have girdled & saddled & brushed & watered & made sweet whisperings to.

Bridget is pulling me to go.

My left hand pulses. I have changed the dressing, using a piece of curtain, but I cannot bear to look on it. The wound is fresh & wet, the fingers swollen like a seal's flipper.

My body is foul.

I have taken the blanket from the cot for the girl.

No one has come here. By my reckoning, it has been almost two days. I cannot make sense of it. Why has no one come to re-man the station? To check on the horses?

Why have the locals or raiders not stolen the horses?

I do not think we will get help back to Tor Mor.

Our only hope is a return to civilisation. To Letterkenny, to secure funds from Hancock, or any other means. With enough resources–& barrels of water–I may return to the birds. More likely now, we will move on to Londonderry, & a ship back to England.

Against myself, I have started hoping for the latter.

The sooner we can leave this god-blasted island, the better.

There are eleven other people in this hovel, apart from the girl & I. At any given instant one of them is rattled with coughing.

There is the woman who led us here, & her failing infant, & I think three more of her children, & two other children I believe not her own, & five other wretches more aged: all of them gaunt, ill-dressed paupers. One wretched old woman is utterly wracked by phlegm, short for the world.

Our hostess might be called Cathleen, or Catleen, & has exceptionally thin hair.

None of the residents have addressed me since I came in. Only the children whisper to each other. There is a small hearth but no chimney. It was I lit the fire; there was plenty of timber outside, but none of the others stirred as I fired the kindling & now the smoke gathers in here, drawn fitfully out by the window & the door.

I sit by the door for clean air.

My left hand pulsates under its dressing.

I can see the horse from here, & but for the light to write by, I am tempted to move outside. The girl is out with him, nickering & whispering. A night in the cold may be preferable to breathing in here.

I thought the guano on the island & my outhouse would have prepared me for the worst of stenches. But in here it is worse. There is but one bed in a corner, taken up by the woman & her own four children. The rest sprawl on heaps of dirty straw.

The day was deplorable.

We left Falcarragh Customs House in the morning, I knew not where to: simply taking the road with the hope of finding a village. I had Bridget on the horse in front of me, holding her with my bad left hand, the reins with my right. The haar was so thick we could not tell one direction from another.

The child restarted her urgency as we left the Customs House.

BRIDGET: Come on, Ig. Find mother. Come.

I could not believe we would find her; indeed, we have not. But throughout the day Bridget's noise grew progressively quieter, perhaps coming to this realisation, as each fresh encounter left its mark on her. The more we travelled, the more we saw how the entire structure of civilisation has broken down.

First, we met nothing but haar. The horse hesitant, & me also, unwilling to go faster than a trot where we could not see the road. Most of the time we could make out the path just well enough to keep out of the ditch.

MYSELF: Is anybody there?
MYSELF: Halloo! Halloo!

But eventually we came to a village. So thick the haar, we could only see the houses on the side of the road the horse took. The buildings looked at first empty. No one was in the street & no one would answer my call.

I banged on the doors of four different houses.

MYSELF: Hello. We are lost.
MYSELF: I can hear you inside. Please help us.

At the fourth house I broke propriety, & I pushed back the door into a bare room. Six people sat in the dark.

MYSELF: Hello, we are lost. Can you help?
OLD MAN: (something possibly in Irish)
MYSELF: We need to get to Londonderry. I believe we have come from Falcarragh Customs House.
OLD MAN: (something in Irish)

Bridget came & discoursed with him. I walked outside. One of the occupants rose & urinated directly onto the street, splattering my boots as I uttered an oath & stepped back; he made no eye-contact, but shook himself off, & then went back to resume sitting on the floor.

I stood out by the horse.

When Bridget was done, she took my hand.

BRIDGET: Come on, Ig. Come.

She made me to understood we were travelling in the wrong direction & must head back the way we came.

The wind had risen, chilling the haar but also thinning it by degrees, so we could now behold both sides of the road at once. We passed the Customs House again & I could now make out the gable end & runway of the boathouse. At some point we stopped so I could adjust the dressing on my hands & I washed myself in a stream.

As I got off the horse, a dog started barking at me, from a hole in a stone wall.

MYSELF: (proffering my good hand) Here, boy. Here, boy.

He backed off, growling. I approached, crouching so as not to spook him. When I followed, I saw he had been digging under a pile of rocks. The rocks were a makeshift grave. I could smell the putrefaction & see the human clothes thru the stones.

I did not look closer, for want of my nerves.

The dog cowered at my approach, but growled, preparing to defend his prize.

MYSELF: Get away. Get away, boy. Get away.

BRIDGET: Come on, Ig. Come.

MYSELF: Go on, boy. Get home. Get.

I could not rout the dog, & we rode off without washing.

Later, we crossed a stone bridge. Here I clambered down to a stream below & drank & bathed & changed my dressing. At one end of the bridge, we found an abandoned suitcase, small enough for a child. Bridget's clothes are ramshackle now, her little bailiff's coat still holding together but the nightshift grown terribly ragged. I unlatched the suitcase & took out a fabulous pinafore. A pretty, frilled yellow thing.

MYSELF: Bridget. Look at this. Try it on.

I tried to coax her from the horse to put on the dress. She eyed me somewhat oddly.

BRIDGET: Come Ig. Come.
MYSELF: The dress, Bridget. Wear it.
BRIDGET: No.

She would not.

We rode on.

At some point we passed a crowd walking the same road. The haar had thinned so we could count their number; a band of twenty-three, with two handcarts. Most bore bags over their shoulders. I rode to the front of the crowd.

MYSELF: Listen to me. Hear this. We are looking for a woman. Here is her likeness. Do any of you recognise her?

MYSELF: It is a simple question. Please observe this picture. Please.

MYSELF: Damn you. Won't you at least confirm this is the road for Londonderry?

They barely raised their eyes, & not one of them took the likeness from my hands. Bridget turned to me ruefully & got off the horse.

They would talk to her, in their own tongue.

As she moved thru the crowd, one of them did meet my gaze. A young girl who sat on top of a handcart. She did not speak, nor, after locking eyes, would she look away. Each time I checked thereafter, her gaze was on me.

Bridget came back with no new information.

We rode on.

The fog cleared. Out of the whiteness, rocky & heathery hills sprung about us. Frequent chunks of granite in the middle of gorse bushes. An empty landscape of abrupt hills & rock formations, bare of livestock. It grew sunny, even warm. I had become cramped on the horse, & the girl fidgeted, shifting our small sack of belongings.

We found a sign for Letterkenny.

I was comforted somewhat that we were on the right track.

Soon after we saw a cart ahead of us, drawn by two horses. It bore what looked like sacks of grain in great abundance. It was guarded by three men in official brass-buttoned uniforms, on horses, & flew the Queen's colours. I thought we had found salvation.

MYSELF: Ahoy there! My good fellows! Hold up! Wait for me!

They did not stop initially. I kicked the mare into motion so they might hear me. But when they saw us, they spurred their own beasts in an attempt to outrun us. I thought it a mistake & knew we would be faster than a loaded cart.

MYSELF: Hold up! We are not rebels! We are English! We are English!

That their attempt to outrun us was misguided was quickly apparent. When they saw we were gaining, a young blond officer turned on his horse & pulled out his rifle & waited for us to approach with its barrel levied on us.

MYSELF: Do not shoot. We are English.
THE OFFICER: (with a Mancunian accent) Hold back. If you approach, I will shoot.
MYSELF: For humanity, man, I am English also. We have become lost, & we urgently require assistance.
THE OFFICER: (looking me up & down) Wait here.

I became aware for the first time of the shock of my appearance. I am long bearded, untrimmed, badly bruised, in my filthy woollen overalls, one hand a mass of bandages. A bareheaded wraith on my lap. We watched as he rode to the cart & conferred with the other men. Presently he rode back to us.

THE OFFICER: If you follow us, we will shoot. This is your final warning.
MYSELF: I am as English as you, man. English!

They rode off & we tarried, not knowing what to do.

We dismounted & let the beast graze & ate ragged strips of seal. Relieved ourselves in the bushes. I washed my face as well as I could in a ditch & drank from a stream. The water was sweet, at least: I rinsed my head & body, & reset my dressings.

We waited long after the horizon was clear, then rode on.

We have not come upon the grain convoy again.

Later, we passed an old man sat by a waystone. He was wearing nothing but a shirt held loosely closed with one button, & a pair of briefs, & no houses nearby. He spoke a good, clear English.

MYSELF: Hello, sir. I am wondering if you can help us.
OLD MAN: Hello hello hello.
MYSELF: Do you speak English?
OLD MAN: Do I speak English, he says. Do I speak English.

I got off the horse & sat down beside him.

MYSELF: This is the road to Letterkenny, is it not?
OLD MAN: This road will take you to Letterkenny. Every road will take you to Letterkenny.
MYSELF: Is it or is it not the road to Letterkenny?
OLD MAN: This is the road you want.

Bridget jumped down & dug out the likeness of her mother & handed it to him.

MYSELF: Tell me, friend. We are looking for this woman. Have you seen her?
OLD MAN: This woman?
MYSELF: Have you seen her?
OLD MAN: I have, of course.
MYSELF: Where did you see her?

OLD MAN: I see a lot of people going by here.

MYSELF: Yes, but we are looking for her. Maybe wearing a man's uniform. Dressed as a man. Have you seen her?

OLD MAN: I have. I know her well.

MYSELF: Where was she going?

OLD MAN: The road only goes two ways, son. To Letterkenny, & away from Letterkenny.

He found some humour in this. Bridget had dug thru our pack & took out a chunk of seal, & offered it to him, even as I shook my head. I could see his ribs clearly thru his shirt.

OLD MAN: Oh Jesus, no. I couldn't eat. But can I keep the picture, son?

MYSELF: What?

OLD MAN: Can I keep the picture?

MYSELF: No. I mean. No.

I had to pull the likeness gently from his grasp, peeling his thin dry fingers back so he didn't rip it.

OLD MAN: (finally relinquishing the paper) That's all right, son. I don't need it anyway.

We rode on.

The only sound was keening wind & the clopping of hooves.

We came upon a small crowd of children as the shadows grew longer. They were sat in a field by a house, & had lit a small fire, & had a pot on the boil. Bridget wanted to talk to them, & I let her dismount. They were boiling a jackdaw. This I knew from the feet protruding from the pot & the feathers all over the ground. They were taking turns with a spoon, eating the soup. Someone was shouting from a house behind them, but the children ignored the voice. Bridget showed them the likeness; then came back ashen-faced to the horse.

We rode on.

I thought to find a house for the night. We had passed so many empty abodes, some burnt hollow, some with the thatch still intact. So eventually we chose an intact house at random, with a blue door & unburnt, & I dismounted & knocked, & called out thrice, & on hearing no response, I tied the horse, & went in.

I saw what I thought was a woman's carcass against a wall, holding the body of an infant.

I told Bridget to wait outside, & went in to move the body.

When I put my hands on her, the woman jerked & clutched the baby & started screaming.

THE WOMAN: Aaaaah. Aaaah. Aaaah.
MYSELF: I am sorry. I am sorry.

She would not hear my apologies, but screamed & screamed in the dark. I stood back, quite terrified, trying to speak, but her noise did not abate.

BRIDGET: Come on, Ig. Come on.

Bridget had come in, put a hunk of seal on the table & pulled me back to the horse.

As night drew on, we got weary. The horse was weary & growing slow to obey, but I was wary of trying another cottage. In a field over a hill, we saw a commotion: there was a crowd, maybe one hundred people around a fire on benches & stools. In the centre was a huge pot from which soup was being ladled into bowls. So many people amassed

I could scarce believe it. A man stood near the pot, reading the scripture with a clear Glaswegian accent, as the horde milled & coughed about him.

I tried to get thru to him.

MYSELF: Excuse me. We are English. Excuse me.
MYSELF: I am sorry, I am trying to get thru here.

The crowd was unwilling to part. I got roughly shoved twice, once by a man, once by a woman who knocked my swollen hand & made me cry out, before I realised we would be better joining the queue.

We had the horse tied to a post outside the field.

Some children had gathered around it.

I worried for the horse, but wanted to talk to the pastor. When we were eight places from the front, I managed to interrupt his reading.

MYSELF: Good sir. Please hear me out. I am English. We are. This girl & I. We are trying to get to Londonderry. Good sir, I apologise, but please—
PREACHER: The scripture is for everyone sir. Let me read in peace. Let me read.

He would respond no further. When I tried to approach him again, I was shoved from behind.

We picked up bowls & shuffled to the benches.

The portions were very small & thin. Oatmeal with carrots & vague trace of stock, but at least it was warm. So much coughing was there, I covered my nose as I ate.

Bridget took the likeness from me after finishing her soup. I held the sack under my arm & tried to follow her movements with my eyes thru the torchlit crowd.

There were now three men standing by the horse.

When I finished my soup, I rose & put my hand on the bridle. The men sidled off. When Bridget found me, I could see she was upset. She jammed the likeness in the sack, untied the horse & tugged him onward.

BRIDGET: Come, Ig. Come.

She led me to the side of the field, where the woman in whose hovel I now sit was waiting with her children. No words passed between me & the woman, but she spoke in Irish to Bridget.

She led us to her hovel. Eleven people, me, & the child. The eldest boy came to me some moments ago.

THE BOY: Your horse. Watch your horse, sir.

That was all he said.

I will take our small blanket & sleep outside with the horse. The cold is in my bones though: I worry that my hand is making me feverish. I have considered tying the harness to my arm as I sleep, but that is madness; I would be dragged thru the marsh.

WEDNESDAY 30TH JUNE, 1847

I woke wet into a harrowing bright dawn.

The horse was fine. The Irish have not seized her. The ferns are so verdant in the absence of livestock, she is feeding well. As I write this, I am taking some warmth indoors, & now all the children of the hovel have gone out to stroke her. Bridget is coaxing them to bravery; at first they feared me—Fear More!—but now the eldest boy is sitting on the mare's back as Bridget leads them around by the reins.

She has taken out the last two plumcakes & shared them with the children. One she broke—pulling & twisting the hard rind for the moist cake inside—& passed out in muddy handfuls. The second she has given to the mother, who refused to eat it, & put it wrapped in a fine cloth on what passes for a mantle, likely for her children.

Her listlessness appalling, her self-abnegation profound.

All the sealmeat is gone from the bag.

Bridget is overgenerous with our food.

All of them—children & adults—barely respond to my attempts at communication. I have harangued the mother somewhat & with her broken English, she has confirmed that the road at the bottom of the hill will take us to Letterkenny in a matter of hours.

We must go.

My hand bothered me all night. A horror under the cloth. But the pain is in abeyance this morning.

Bridget is trying to offer them our small sack of flour now.

We have no means of rendering the flour edible on the road but I am aware of our lack of means until we get to Hancock's house. We shd get there before nightfall if my calculations are correct, & altho I can no longer have faith in the man, I have no doubt he will have funds sufficient to secure our passage back to Cockerham. But until we find Hancock, I fear we are as destitute as the Irish.

I have tried to make clear to Bridget she can gift the flour only if she takes back the second plumcake.

She was unhappy with this, & initially feigned obtuseness, but the scowl on her face gave the lie to her pretence. So now I will have to confront our hostess myself. No doubt her children will make mournful sounds, & Bridget will rankle.

I will thank her nevertheless for her hospitality.

It is time to go.

❂

We have found not Bridget's mother, but McGonigle.

The girl saw him first.

He has come to Hancock's small estate, where he has been holed up for the last two hours.

As I write, it is evening. We are hid in a hollow of the hill below them. I find myself at an utter loss to know what to do.

If there was any doubt, now there is none.

McGonigle & Hancock are clearly in cahoots.

I dare not approach lest they are armed. They might kill me yet to prevent news of their criminal misconduct getting back to Sir Phillip. But nor can I leave. Hancock is my only source of funds in a destitute land. Without fare for our passage to the mainland, we are no better off than the sea of miserable Irish on the road.

We made good time this morning toward Letterkenny. The horse was fresh, the air was clear. Passed maybe fifty diverse persons along the way. At the top of a hill, we found a little waterfall, where we emptied & filled our bottles & cleaned ourselves of the filthy air from the hovel. My wound bright, but somewhat less swollen to my eye. Bridget was keen to press on; every person we passed, she reached for the now tattered likeness of her mother.

But as the crowds grew thicker, a fellow rode downhill to join us on a plump white mare; a stern-faced, square-jawed fellow, an officer of the law. George Davies, a Dubliner, we found out, when he eventually answered my own questions. Initially, he believed us thieves & approached us in hostility. It took some explaining to stop him seizing our horse.

DAVIES: Robbed, you say?
MYSELF: Yes. By the men of Inishtrahull. I am here under the patronage of Sir Phillip of Barrow, of the Royal Society.
DAVIES: But you say the horse is not from Inishtrahull?
MYSELF: No. As I told you, we found it abandoned.
DAVIES: You can offer no paperwork for it?

This was the flavour of our conversation, or counter-interrogation; the lack of paperwork for both the horse & the girl became a sticking point for him. He had the idea the girl was a workhouse escapee. Bridget quite shrank from his presence, turning her face when he tried to look in her eyes.

DAVIES: She is not your daughter?
MYSELF: No. She was delivered into my care.
DAVIES: What do you mean, delivered?

I was increasingly uncomfortable with his presence. I had no papers, he was right, & despite my assurances that I could be vouched for by Hancock of Londonderry, his manner was such that I worried we might soon be walking with the Irish destitutes. The buildings began to grow denser, & as we passed into Letterkenny, he tried to convince me to accompany him to the workhouse. Gradually, I found my tone sharpening.

MYSELF: I have told you, I have every plan to deliver both horse & girl to their proper owners, but first I must meet with Hancock. Do you doubt my word?

DAVIES: Where does this Hancock live again?

MYSELF: Just east of Letterkenny, man, by a couple of miles.

We came to a subdued impasse as we rode into the growing bustle of the town, but he did not leave our side. The workhouse was on the outskirts, & the closer we got, the more obvious the bedlam. The building was a great grey edifice, & all around the outside crowded the horde of destitutes with their tattered belongings. Maybe six score people in a line surrounded the building, & beside it, a huge barn that stank of effluence.

When we got close, Bridget became suddenly animated.

BRIDGET: (hissing) Ig! Ig!

MYSELF: What?

Over the crowd, on horseback, was McGonigle.

At first, I did not recognise him. He had on some kind of broad-brimmed hat & a riding jacket, for a crude imitation of a gentleman. But then I saw two large sacks tied to the back of his saddle & recognised the hangdog hold of his shoulders.

MYSELF: McGonigle.

BRIDGET: (something in Irish)

George Davies—who at this stage I considered a particularly obnoxious thorn in our side—noted our discomfort,

& as we were pulling away, reached over to put his hands on my reins. I turned & met his eye.

MYSELF: What in the name of God are you doing, man?
DAVIES: The girl is perturbed.
MYSELF: Why are you holding my reins?
DAVIES: I have some more questions. It is a simple enough matter. Accompany me to the station & you can explain it all there.
MYSELF: (suddenly angered) Why? Why the devil should I? Are you arresting me? Are you? Arresting an Englishman? Setting your hands on a loyal & decorated subject, a widely feted ornithologist? Here at the behest of Sir Walpole Phillip of Barrow, under the employ of the Royal Society?
DAVIES: (hesitating) No. I am not.
MYSELF: Then relinquish your bloody hold, man!

I jerked from him & pushed on thru the crowd. Perhaps I was rash! I could have had the entire constabulary here with me now! As it was, it was all I could do to keep an eye on McGonigle, weaving thru the paupers down the hill into town.

I tried to hold back, to see where he was going, & keep at least forty yards between us. His horsemanship was atrocious. He fidgeted in the saddle, keeping one hand on his goods, yanking the reins to turn his white-brown mare, twice nearly toppling the shuffling paupers in his path.

I knew the contents of the sacks.

Desdemona. Lady Macbeth. Cleopatra. Othello. Lear. Canute.

When we crossed the bridge out of town, I let our distance grow. He seemed largely concerned with controlling the horse. For the first few miles I kept turning to see if George Davies pursued us, but he did not.

At a copse a few miles east of Letterkenny, McGonigle dismounted to defecate off the roadside.

We pushed into gorse & waited for him to remount.

Bridget was breathless & I let her nibble the hard rind of the plumcake.

McGonigle was, is yet, I suspect, after a sale of the birds. They will likely try to offload them in Londonderry for transport to London for a more propitious sale.

I still could not quite believe they were working together. But as he remounted & we left the smoke of Letterkenny, the road grew more familiar, & their collaboration dawned on me like a spreading weariness. My hand started to pulse again, as we came into a valley less than half a mile below Hancock's estate, the land marshy & poor, dotted with whin & marsh grass.

His estate sits at the top of a muddy path that splits from the main Londonderry Road some eight miles out of Letterkenny, heading northwest into the hills. He has a few hectares of pasture on either side, & lives in the small stone house with the attached stable at the brow of a hill—paltry by English standards but sturdy & bright compared to the squat Irish hovels—a two-storey house, respectable, hidden from the main road by yew trees, overlooking a large inlet from the Atlantic.

I am sitting at the bottom of the hill in the whin bushes now.

I have tied the horse to a sapling.

I do not know what to do.

If I leave, McGonigle will escape justice.

But if I go accost them together—criminals both—they are like to overpower me.

We have nowhere to go. I cannot trade on my elevation of station or my Englishness at the port.

I need funds to get us to England.

Hancock. Hancock & McGonigle.

If I wait until McGonigle leaves, I may yet convince Hancock to release me the money.

I have taken out the pistols & cleaned & refilled them. The girl understands more than her age would suggest, & has been suppressing her need to fidget or moan, sucking on the last of the plumcake, staring quietly up at the house.

It has been more than two hours now.

❊

Gunshots.

Just now. Two gunshots. From the house.

It is dark.

There is shouting.

❊

Hancock is dead.

We waited hours for McGonigle to leave the house, but he did not. The girl had fallen asleep, & only my own anxiety was keeping me awake. The moon had risen, massive & full, across the bay, when two gunshots rocked the dark.

The horse bucked, pulling against the sapling.

I panicked & put my hand on her, ready to flee.

Bridget stood & called out in Irish & looked up the hill.

MYSELF: Come, girl. This is too much. Let us go.

But it was too late.

Some insanity possessed her.

For reasons I still cannot fathom, she cried out repeatedly in Irish, & when I went to grab her, she ran for the house.

MYSELF: No, girl. Come back here. Come back here now!

In the silver light, ducking trees, she was already halfway ascended, coursing like a hare. I confess I did not want to follow. The blood had quite drained from my stomach & there was no vital force in my limbs, but the bloody girl would not heel.

I picked up the two pistols & made after her. But she was too nimble; she got there before me. I lost her up by the dry stone wall of Hancock's garden, like a shadow flitting, as I fumbled with the pistol in my swollen left paw. There were lights in the house; I tried to keep low; McGonigle's horse was tied to a post by the kitchen door.

I was panicking, short of breath.

The girl had to be either on the far side of the house, or within.

MYSELF: (hissing) Bridget! Bridget!

From inside, I could hear muttering, & movement. Then: raised voices, a crash, & another gunshot.

I crouched behind the wall & trained one pistol on the door.

MYSELF: Bridget?

There were footsteps within; I panicked, shaking; it was not Bridget, but rather McGonigle burst out with a gun in his hand; before I could register him, I fired; the shot went over his head, & he jumped face down into the dirt, & I ducked behind the wall again.

McGONIGLE: Mr Green—is it yourself?

When I peeked again, he had flung his body lengthwise over his horse. He had her untied but the beast was rearing, & him draped across, smacking her rear with the hand holding the pistol, & she started to gallop out the gate with him clung on, & she made it down thru the field.

MYSELF: Halt. Halt.
McGONIGLE: (something in Irish)

He did not look back.

My shouting was tactically obtuse; I had raised the alarum to my presence. For all I knew Hancock could have been coming out after him, ready to shoot me; I dared not loose another shot, lest I be accosted unarmed. I had been concocting scenarios in my head, of a score of brigands, & now I had announced my presence to anyone who could hear.

Gone was my need to keep silent, then.

MYSELF: Bridget! Bridget, are you there?
MYSELF: Hancock, if you have the girl, release her now!
MYSELF: I have three officers of the law out here with me!
MYSELF: Come out now, Hancock, or it will be worse for you!

No one answered. The air was still, but for the hoofbeats of McGonigle down the hill.

I peered thru the shutters into the kitchen. An oil-lamp, pewter; oatcakes. A jug of water had been smashed.

I crept in & lifted the lit kitchen lamp.

There was creaking upstairs; no audible footsteps.

In his study, I beheld the sacks of the Great Auks, & beside them, the dishevelled carcasses of Desdemona & Lady Macbeth.

I dared not examine them, but nor could I fully draw my eyes away, despite the putrid air. They were half plucked by rough use. I could not easily tell the difference between the two until I saw the scoring on Desdemona's beak. The mishandling of their bodies, their rot, had swollen them beyond recognition.

I stood there, arm over my mouth, nauseous at their stench.

MYSELF: Hancock? Hancock?

MYSELF: I warn you, I am armed. The constabulary are here! Show yourself!

Still no one called out. But there was a movement upstairs–a creaking, a growling.

I could find no further guns in the study.

MYSELF: I warn you, I will shoot on sight!

Silver moonlight lit the stairwell. From my angle, I could see nobody on the landing. I turned the lamp off so as not to make myself a target, let my eyes adjust & crept up, gun raised.

A lantern was lit in his bed chamber.

The door open, the back window also.

When I looked in, I did not know what I saw.

Hancock lay against one wall, below a full-size mirror. There was blood on the wall & blood on the mirror & a crack down the middle of the pane.

On top of him, in the moonlight, there was straddled a huge brown dog.

At first, I thought the dog was licking his wounds. But so unbelievably big was it, so long of the leg & seemingly articulated at the neck, so rugged & angular the rough pale plumage of its ruff, I would have easily supposed it a malformed wolf or some theatrically adorned circus-beast, had I seen it in India. I know these Irish have outsized breeds—their wolfhound, etc—& I can only assume, now in the lamplight, that this was some half-starved mongrel Hancock had recently taken in, or perhaps that had made its way to his house on its own. For surely this is the only viable explanation. McGonigle & Hancock must have come to some violent disagreement over the garefowl, perhaps due to the putrefaction of the specimens, & in the altercation Hancock ended up shot through the head: at which point the hound, be it stray or recent adoptee, starved like every other creature in this land, seized its opportunity to sate its hunger, & ate of his face.

That is what I surmise now.

I did not think so clearly then.

Feverish with the pain of my hand, as I saw the dog's chops & mane matted with blood, & a string of Hancock's skin hung from its teeth, I had to stifle my screams. For one moment, I nearly believed the dog's eyes to be the eyes of Aisling O'Leary.

MYSELF: No. No. Get out. No. Get out of here. Get out.

I raised the gun, but I only had one shot. The dog did not move. Merely beheld me with its large brown eyes. I picked up the bedpan & started banging it.

MYSELF: Get out. Get out. Leave us. Leave me be. Get out!

With a sudden jerk of the head, the beast dashed towards me; I shot; I missed; it sailed over me to the landing & leapt from the second story window into the courtyard.

I sat where I had fallen, breathless. Hancock lay on the floor before me, his jaw snapped off & half his throat missing. My stomach could not cope with the tumult, & I spewed water onto the floorboards.

Then I heard Bridget screaming outside & stumbled over to the widow.

MYSELF: Bridget? Girl?

My nausea rendered me unable to focus; I rubbed my eyes to make them work; cresting on the far hill, I eventually made out McGonigle now sitting upright in the saddle, working the horse at a gallop, across the valley. So bright the moon, I could see the great hound too, already approaching the yew trees. But there, pelting downhill after them, screaming in Irish, Bridget was running too.

MYSELF: Bridget? Bridget? What are you doing?

She was leaping small bushes, hurling herself over rocks. The hill rough tussocked, but she flung her legs as if she had no fear of falling. The moonlight had her shadow elongated to grotesque proportions & I do not believe, even at my height, I could have matched her for speed.

But she is just a child.

What hope had she of catching a horse or a hound?

I stumbled back out of the house, losing my footing on the bottom flight of stairs, following in the direction of her shouting. But by the time I reached her at the foot of the hill, she had fallen to her knees, gone silent, rasping heavily & harshly for breath beside a stream. Her face was sunken, & wet, & utterly haggard.

She had stopped shouting.

Her face registered my presence not at all.

When I touched her shoulder, she barely moved.

MYSELF: Bridget? Are you mad, girl? What is wrong?
MYSELF: Bridget. Rouse, girl. Look at me. Are you hurt?
MYSELF: Bridget.

She would not answer.

Since that moment, she has neither responded to my gestures or words. She stared glassily, & I had to lift her back to the house. Not with her voice nor her facial expressions has she registered my presence, even as I laid her flaccid by the kitchen door, where I stood, utterly bewildered, trying to get my bearings.

I wanted to take the girl & run.

But we had no money.

No food.

I called out, at the door.

MYSELF: Is anyone in there?
MYSELF: I am armed.

No call returned.

I went back in.

I did not take the auks. I could not bear to touch them. Their juices had soaked through the sacks & were seeping onto the table. The smell of the untreated carcasses had rendered them obscene. Even Canute, when I tugged him half out of the sack on the counter, has been rubbed threadbare & made slick with their rancid juices.

It filled me with desolation.

Nor did I return to Hancock.

I cannot mourn him. I was quite certain he was beyond all help. Though I do not know the extent of his dealings with McGonigle, from all evidence, he is far from innocent. But having one's face gnawed by a starved dog is a sight I will not cleanse easily from my memory.

Yet, like a vagrant in a house of the dead, I went back to raid his house for the money that is my due. I held my nose & rummaged in chests & through the desk in his office, trying not to look at the auks.

His papers were in disarray. Likely McGonigle had already been through his materials; & it was my arrival that routed him. I am a more thorough thief than McGonigle. In the back of his writing desk, behind the drawer, where a girl might keep letters from her paramour, I found a small leather purse of coin, like as not, meant to pay McGonigle for the auks.

It is mine now.

I will need the money to secure our passage from this forsaken land.

☼

The girl hung wordlessly in my arms as we rode on towards Londonderry. But the horse was exhausted from two days hard riding, had grown sluggish & clumsy, & the girl kept flopping forward against the horse's neck, soon passing out entirely, so I needed to cling her against me with my bad arm & risked killing us both if my own eyes closed. So when we came to a small house on a hillock looking out on a long beach, I dismounted, & tied the horse to a tree.

MYSELF: Hello?
MYSELF: Hello. Do not be alarmed. I am English.
MYSELF: We are travellers in need of aid.

There was a man with a low-brim hat wrapped up in blankets outside the house, seated with eyes closed on a small wooden bench. He had a rifle held sideways on his knee in the moonlight, his left hand resting on it. I approached, girl on my shoulder, my bad hand held palm out, as a sign of peace.

MYSELF: Sir?
MYSELF: We are desperate. We need a place to sleep.

The house behind him in good repair. A painted wall around a little vegetable garden. Glass in the windows. A pretty abode & as well maintained as any small Welsh cottage.

MYSELF: We bear no ill will. We need but some water, a place to rest.
MYSELF: Please. I beg you. Please. We will be gone in the morning.

On the wall behind him, a muddy spade.

On the grass before him, two graves, freshly dug, in the middle of his vegetable garden. One filled in. One still empty.

The man himself was dead.

Of course he was.

Why would he not be?

He appears to have died on this bench in a pause between burials before he could throw himself in the second hole.

At first, I found this incredible, & then suspicious, then hilarious, & started laughing as I sat on the bench beside him, but after a while my laughter had lost any sense of surprise, & I was just making noises, something between a sob & a sort of growling, guttural howl.

The girl kicked & started bucking at my noises in her sleep.

MYSELF: It's all right, child. It's all right. He is dead.

I rose & carried her inside.

This is the house I am sitting in now.

It is by all means a well-to-do cottage. Not as grand as Hancock's, but beautifully maintained. There is thatch in the roof & a little brick chimney. A kitchen, a stove, & an oil lantern in every room. Matches on the stove. Matches! There is crockery arranged on shelves, a cupboard, a gun-rack & a larder. The larder has three sacks of grain, a sack of flour & a small bunch of carrots, & two rabbits were hung from a hook.

Such a wealth of food, I wondered what has done for the man?

Fever?

The rabbits had turned, & were covered with flies, & I cast them in his empty grave outside.

There is a sitting room with a chaise longue.

There is a bedroom. It smelled indeed of a fever ward as I came in. Like someone had died in it. There is a bedpan & stained sheets but the windows had not been opened & the air was sour. But there is a linen cupboard, with fresh linen in it.

I left Bridget on the chaise longue, & refreshed the linen from a cupboard, then put her to sleep in the empty bed. Since then I have been sitting at a table in the kitchen, smoking bona fide clay pipes from a box under a counter, bearing witness here in my journal by lanternlight.

I have found raisins in the larder. Raisins. I have been picking at them.

The sky is brightening. I must sleep but striking matches is fascinating.

THURSDAY 1ST JULY, 1847

They have stolen our bloody horse!

I woke on the bench outside the cottage, beside the dead fellow. The proprietor. I had meant to sleep inside—somehow I ended up out here—blinking into the bright sky, & our mare was being untied, & by the time I realised what was happening some bloody lank destitute with a brown hat was thundering off on her back down onto the road.

I struggled to my feet, neglecting to seize the damned rifle in my bleariness, rather tripping up on it as I ran after him, shouting.

What hope had I of stopping him without a gun?

The travellers on the road raised their heads at my approach.

MYSELF: You there. You. Stop him. Stop.
MYSELF: That's our horse! Give me back our horse!
MYSELF: Stop him! Stop him!

I ran all the way down to the road, where a fresh group of maybe a dozen destitutes stopped & turned to face me as I panted & shouted after them, but the bloody thief was already eight score yards ahead.

Not one of them interceded to stop the man.

Had I remembered the rifle, they would have moved!

Rather, they looked on in something close to bemusement.

Toothless, filthy people. Ragged. At least one of them snickered at me.

MYSELF: What the hell are you looking at?
MYSELF: You should have bloody stopped him.

The thief had made it down as far as the end of the road, & had turned to look at us, now only a silhouette of a man on horseback in the bright slant light of the morning. I had to give up the chase to catch my breath. Some woman on the road put her hand on my arm, & spoke to me her island gibberish, smiling.

MYSELF: What the hell are you looking at? Couldn't you have stopped him?

She was too close. I shoved her away, at which she grimaced & shoved back, touching my bad hand as she did so, & I yelped & fell.

MYSELF: What are you bloody looking at? You're all imbeciles! Toothless bloody stupid imbeciles!

I said more. I roared at them. Grew loquacious in my anger. Told them what I hoped for their land. Their hygiene. Their filthy bodies, their ugly women. I was intemperate. They backed in a circle to watch me, & I found myself raising in volume as they did so. When the horse thief on the hill lost interest & rode off toward Londonderry, my energy renewed, & I picked up stones to throw as the crowd moved away.

MYSELF: You think they will take you in Liverpool? In Boston? You think you will give up your indolence? How will you understand them if you can't even understand me? Lapping at the pap of the state! You can't even feed your children! Etc.

I am not sure how long I ranted thus.

I do know that Bridget appeared at my side with what looked like a walking stick, which she smacked off my bandaged hand.

MYSELF: Aow. Bridget. What the hell?
MYSELF: Bridget! What are you doing?
MYSELF: Aow. Stop hitting me!

She hit me a number of times on my bad arm, short hard knocks, so I dropped the stones & lost my vehemence. Bridget's face was a mess of grime. There were tear stains & blood on her forehead, but it could not dull the fury of her expression.

MYSELF: They stole the horse, Bridget. They stole the horse.

Her demeanour did not brighten. Rather she grabbed & half dragged me by my bad arm back up through the marram tussocks, stumbling to the cottage, into the kitchen, where there was a pan, a cloche of butter, flour, & a small bag of raisins.

She had made a dough in a bowl. For flatbreads. Raisins, flour, water.

MYSELF: I am sorry. You see. They stole our horse.

BRIDGET: (cutting me off) Eat this, Ig. Eat this.

She is right. We are, both of us, much weakened, & out of sorts & we will not see the horse again.

The girl glowered at me as I lit the stove & formed & fried the flatbreads. Her face utterly harrowed, unashamedly stealing raisin after raisin from the bag.

The flatbreads were excellent.

The girl has just recovered from a fresh bout of weeping.

The cause: she broke the butter cloche, giving herself a two-inch gash on her hand.

MYSELF: Stop that! Stop it now!

MYSELF: I cannot stand that noise. Stop it.

Nothing would pacify her. She had collapsed bawling on the floor among the fragments Eventually, I dropped the coldness of tone I have been harbouring since our altercation & lifted her into the chaise longue & tried the holding. I whispered stupid half-truths. Told her that her mother knew where we were going & was sure to find us. Told her of Connie's dwelling in Bowland, where you could run in the forest all night & no one would hear you. That her mother would come there & take her out for ices & sherbet. But she rose to a fury, mother this, mother that, a guttural flood of Gaelic I had not the words to quench.

MYSELF: (at a loss) Everything is sad. It is sad. I know.
MYSELF: What do you want me to do?

We have not the luxury of convalescence! There is work to be done. More work, now we have no horse. There was nothing for it in the end but to let her get on with it. I left her on the chaise longue with a drink of water beside her & rose to attend to the dishes.

My hand is grotesque, a coiled mushy thing, but I washed it out as best I could. Then I put my head in a butt of water & drank my fill, my beard slopping down my filthy overalls: I beheld my reflection & tried to clean the blood off my face & arms. There is soap in the kitchen, but I could only get so far with my bathing without stripping off.

Eventually, when I checked in, the girl had given up on crying & had gone exploring the bedrooms.

Just now, she came in, waving a short slip at me, presumably from a woman's wardrobe.

BRIDGET: Ig? Ig?
MYSELF: You want it? Go on. It's yours. Happy birthday.

How readily we become inured to theft.

❋

I have been rooting through the house here & have not come away emptyhanded. The contents of Hancock's hidden purse: a total of twenty-four half sovereigns. Buried among the clay pipes in the kitchen, I have found a further small cloth parcel, in which there are wrapped fourteen silver crowns & nine half-crowns. A smattering of pennies.

All in all, £16–5s–7d.

325 shillings. Just over 15 guineas in all.

If not a princely sum, a small fortune in Ireland.

Consider it blood money. For the auks.

It will get us to Liverpool easily.

My mind races. We have lost the horse. It cannot be more than a day's walk to Londonderry now. What if we are stopped? What if the man Davies rides out & questions us? Looks for the missing horse? We have no papers. We have nothing.

I look at the crowds passing on the road below us.

Starved, exhausted, determined.

Children in their arms.

My own clothes are no cleaner than the worst of them.

We have ample funds for the passage.

We will blend in wholly, if I can but keep my mouth shut.

We should go. Used the soap & the slightest daub of lime on my hand to clean the wound. Cut my hair with scissors; found shaving soap & a bowl. I was apprehensive on shaving, unsure of what lay beneath.

I look old & gaunt & bruised.

I have done what I can.

I have been thru the old man's shirts in the cupboard, & none of them are quite long enough. His trousers stop halfway up my calves, but even short trousers are better than my woollen overalls.

My body is foul.

The girl has run down to the beach. The waves are much calmer than on Tor Mor: there is no fear of slipping off a ledge on this long stretch of sand.

No. I lied. The girl has found rocks at the end of the beach & is diving off them. Hurling herself from a height into the water. Idiot child. Safe sand lies all around, & yet she finds the one spot on the beach where she could break a leg.

We must go.

It is a warm day.

We will go, presently.

First, I will join her for a swim.

from

Punch, or The London Chiarivari

VOLUME 12

SATURDAY 3RD OF JULY

A SWIFT PROPOSAL

Dear Sirs—It would not be for me to advise Parliament on any supposed legal or Christian duty to the recent flotsam of twenty-five thousand Hibernian migrants cluttering the hovels of Liverpool, when the country is already full to the brim, nor raise concerns about their dental hygiene or readiness to work, and the threat they pose to the livelihoods of labourers from Glasgow or Bristol! Nor would I dream of suggesting their use in the production of fine leathers for ladies' gloves! But as I stroll through the docks of Liverpool this evening, surveying these noble Celts, lounging in their various states of national dress, undress and distress, I cannot help think how even the good Rev. Swift might have baulked at their guttural speech, and remember how, when the Lilliputians arrived on our shore, clamouring for succour, we had at least the foresight to demand that they learn to speak Brobdingnagian correctly, to prevent their awful sibilant tittering from maddening us so.

Yours, an appalled Brobdingnagian.

Acknowledgments

I have consulted a great many scholarly texts in the writing of this book; of particular note Cormac Ó'Gráda's work on famine and famine cannibalism has been particularly brilliant. Prof Colin Beale, for his help on seabirds and auks, was invaluable. Special thanks are due to Leslie Gardner, Warren Mortimer, Ruth Weiner, Cathal Gallagher and Peter McAnena, for their feedback on the manuscript. The staff of the Seaview Tavern in Malin Head are due thanks, for their music and the best chowder in Donegal.

Most of all, thanks are due to Neasa, Roisín, Katja and Leonie, for their warmth and craic. I love you all.